MU01075624

His

PERFECT
BRIDE

BRIDE SHIPS ⚓ NEW VOYAGES

His
PERFECT
BRIDE

BRIDE SHIPS ⚓ NEW VOYAGES

JODY HEDLUND

sunrise
PUBLISHING

His Perfect Bride
Bride Ships: New Voyages, Book 3
Published by Sunrise Media Group LLC
Copyright © 2025 Jody Hedlund

Print ISBN: 978-1-963372-40-3

Scripture quotations are taken from the King James Version of the Bible.

This is a work of historical reconstruction; the appearances of certain historical figures are accordingly inevitable. All other characters are products of the author's imagination. Any resemblance to actual events or locales or persons, living or dead, is entirely coincidental.

For more information about the author, please access her website at www.jodyhedlund.com.

Published in the United States of America.
Cover Design by Hannah Linder
Cover images from Shutterstock

Bride Ships: New Voyages

My grace is sufficient for thee:
for my strength is made perfect in weakness.
Most gladly therefore will I rather glory in my infirmities,
that the power of Christ may rest upon me.

2 Corinthians 12:9

One

Manchester, England
May 1863

S HE HAD TO FIND A WAY TO HELP HER
family.
Sage Rhodes stepped carefully through the muddy street
in front of the Manchester City Mission and glanced at the square
of tattered paper in her hand. The short list of charities was growing even shorter.

"Two left out of the five," she whispered. "Only one after the
City Mission."

She was running out of options.

The familiar clench of desperation wrapped around her empty
stomach.

She stuffed the paper back into her skirt pocket and pulled in
a breath of air to fortify herself for the humiliating task of asking
for help.

The May morning air was damp with the spring rains that were
nearly constant. Dark clouds sagged with moisture, and sooty coal

smoke poured from towering chimneys rising into the skyline for as far as the eye could see . . . Hundreds of plumes of black smoke from hundreds of chimneys from the hundreds of factories.

If only those hundreds of factories were filled with the usual workers. Last year, as a result of the war in the United States, the cotton imports from Southern states had come to a standstill, and most textile mills in Manchester had closed.

Some were beginning to hire back employees. But too many people—especially women and children—remained jobless, including her. Even though her dad had been among those rehired, his hours as a mule spinner were sparse and sporadic. He only made enough to keep the family from being evicted from their one-room flat. They were constantly hungry and cold. Their garments were turning into rags. And they were restless with so little to occupy their time.

To make matters worse, Dad's health was rapidly declining. Ever since he'd resumed his position, his white lung disease had returned with a vengeance. His barking cough wracked his body, keeping him awake at night so that he was exhausted all the time.

As Sage made her way up the front stoop of City Mission, she stuffed her list of charities deeper into her pocket. She tapped the mud off her clogs then straightened her shoulders. She'd never thought she'd resort to begging, but she would do whatever she had to for her family.

The three-story building was tucked between a bathhouse and a women's boardinghouse. Even though the red bricks were darkened from coal dust, the place was well-kept, and the area was safe and mostly clean, absent of the squalor of the crowded slums where she lived with her dad and three younger sisters.

She opened the door and stepped into a large front room that was busy with women—probably volunteers. One group seemed to be organizing clothing donations. A couple of others were studying a map and list of names, likely making plans for how to spread charity and the gospel to as many poor and hopeless people as possible.

At Sage's appearance, every person paused in their conversations and swiveled to look at her—with kind eyes, to be sure. Each of the charities she'd visited so far had been staffed by sympathetic people who'd offered her suggestions. But none had been able to give her what she really needed—passage for her and her family to Vancouver Island.

She smoothed a gloved hand down her dark gray wool cloak before untying the headscarf knot underneath her chin. She slipped off the threadbare covering, hoping that without it she appeared older and more capable than her nineteen years.

She'd taken the time to coil her reddish-blond hair into an elegant chignon, and she'd worn her Sunday best—a simple blue skirt and a white blouse. Both were frayed and thin. But she'd disguised the worn hems with lace she'd taken from the curtains.

She knew she was considered pretty with her fair hair, unblemished skin, and blue eyes. Her heart-shaped face, dainty chin, and high cheekbones were all family traits and added to her beauty. Today, she had to use every single asset to her advantage, even her looks.

"May we help you, dear?" A middle-aged matron stepped away from the map. Her milky white hair framed a pleasantly plump face. With spectacles perched upon her nose, her eyes were as round as bobbins. She was attired in a modest gown that set her apart from the working class but wasn't so elaborate as to put her in the aristocracy.

Sage lifted her lips into a practiced smile—one she'd tried to perfect that showed her to be an upright and respected woman. After all, most charities made a distinction between the worthy and unworthy poor—those who'd fallen into hard times versus the shiftless, lazy, and drunkards.

She was praying she would get a better reception and more assistance if she proved beyond a doubt that she was the former—a woman of stellar repute who'd simply experienced the hardships of the recent economy.

"Thank you, ma'am." Sage spoke as calmly and as politely as possible, trying to sound cultured and not like a poor mill worker. "I was hoping someone here might have information on any emigration opportunities."

"Emigration?" The hesitancy in the woman's question told Sage that she wouldn't have any more success here at the Manchester City Mission than she'd had at the other agencies she'd already visited.

Still, she had to try. "Yes, my sister was one of the women recruited last autumn by Miss Rye to travel to Vancouver Island."

Sage hadn't received any letters from her older sister since she'd left in September on the *Robert Lowe*. With every passing day without word from Willow, Sage was growing more and more convinced that she had to take matters into her own hands, which was what she'd finally done yesterday when she'd made the list of local charities to visit about the possibility of emigrating.

The woman nodded. "Ah, yes. Miss Rye and her Female Middle Class Emigration Society."

Sage didn't know anything about a Female Middle Class Emigration Society. All she knew was that Miss Rye had overseen two emigration opportunities to the Pacific Northwest last year for single women. The ships had been called bride ships because the women were expected to go and find husbands in the English colony where there was an overpopulation of unmarried men in need of wives.

Sage wasn't interested in finding a husband, not when she was still reeling from the broken engagement with David just a few months ago. Even so, she was more than willing to endure sailing on a bride ship with her sisters if it took them to Vancouver Island and to Willow.

She kept her practiced smile in place. "Do you know if Miss Rye is planning to recruit more women for another bride ship?"

The middle-aged matron glanced at her companion who was taller than most women by a hand's span. She had thick dark brown hair that was smoothed back into a tight knot, causing her sharply pointed features to look severe. Her gown, while fashionable and a pretty rose color, did nothing to flatter her, making her look flat-chested and overly thin. The woman wasn't youthful, but she also didn't have any signs of age. Perhaps she was in her thirties.

"Miss Lennox is visiting from London," the matron said with a nod to the tall woman. "She may be familiar with Miss Rye's current plans."

"Certainly." Miss Lennox set her map down. "I am indeed in several organizations with Miss Rye."

At last. Sage released an inward sigh at discovering someone who knew about Miss Rye. Surely now she would make more progress in learning when the next group of women would be leaving.

Hopefully by the time the ship set sail, her family would have the first letter from Willow with some money that would allow Dad to accompany them as a paying passenger in steerage. If not when they left, then a letter would arrive soon after their departure, and he could follow them to the new world.

Sage gave a small curtsy to Miss Lennox. "Could you please tell me when Miss Rye plans to send another bride ship?"

Miss Lennox swept her gaze over Sage, as if she were personally assessing Sage's worthiness of joining the endeavor. "I regret that I do not have such information."

Sage curbed her disappointment. "I see."

"However, I can tell you Miss Rye is currently accompanying a ship of women bound for New Zealand."

That news was even worse. Miss Rye would be unavailable for months. "Is someone taking her place in organizing other voyages?"

"The committee is weighing the cost of the ventures and has found them particularly taxing. I would not be surprised if they decide against any future trips."

Sage's heart sank. She'd tried to warn herself that another ship may have already sailed, or that Miss Rye would seek out candidates from a different area to give other women a chance at emigration. But she hadn't expected that the efforts to send women to the colony would end altogether.

"I'm sorry to hear such news." Regardless, Sage had to persist with her efforts at finding help with emigration, with or without Miss Rye's bride ships. "Would the City Mission be willing to sponsor a few women who would like to emigrate?"

This time the matronly woman with the spectacles answered. "I'm afraid that's outside our scope of what we're capable of doing here at the mission."

"I understand." Sage wasn't surprised by the rejection. She'd heard the same thing from the three other charities. "Do you know of any other organizations who might be sending women?"

Everyone was quiet, so much so that Sage could hear the patter of a fresh rain shower on the two front windows. The others in the room had resumed their work but were casting curious looks toward Sage, obviously still listening to the conversation.

The matronly woman's eyes behind her spectacles remained wide and kind, but it was clear from her expression that she had no suggestions for Sage.

Miss Lennox, however, blinked several times before nodding. "Another organization in London is considering sending women to Australia. If you'd like me to pass along your name—"

"I couldn't go to Australia."

"Of all the places I've traveled, Australia is one of the loveliest."

"I beg your pardon, ma'am. It's a kind suggestion. However, my sister already lives on Vancouver Island, and I would like to be near her in Victoria."

"Vancouver Island? Victoria?" Miss Lennox cocked her head with a glimmer of interest.

"Yes, ma'am."

Miss Lennox leaned in and whispered something to the matronly woman. The two conversed in low tones for a moment before Miss Lennox narrowed her gaze upon Sage. "Do you have any experience as a maidservant?"

For a fraction of a second Sage considered fibbing. But no, she couldn't. She would strive as always to do what was right. "I've only worked in the mills, ma'am. But I am a fast learner. I would have no trouble learning the duties of a maid."

Domestic servants were needed in the colony. At least that was what Miss Rye had told the bride-ship women leaving on the *Robert Lowe*. No doubt Willow had found a position as a maid in a wealthy home in Victoria, and Sage would gladly do the same.

"Your sewing skills, Miss—?"

"Rhodes. Sage Rhodes."

"How proficient are you at mending and altering, Miss Rhodes?"

"Quite good. I have a steady hand and perfect stitches."

For several minutes, Miss Lennox asked more questions about Sage's skills, education, family, daily habits, and even religious beliefs. Sage guessed Willow had probably been asked such questions too, before being accepted by Miss Rye as one of the bride-ship candidates.

Finally, after Miss Lennox reached the end of her inquisition, she pressed her thin lips together, the tightness making her look even more severe. "My brother lives in Victoria and is getting married in October. I am leaving next week for Vancouver Island to attend the wedding."

"That sounds wonderful. I wish you safe travels." If only she had the means to travel wherever she wanted in the same manner.

Miss Lennox straightened her thin shoulders, looking almost

regal. "My father and mother have always insisted I take a lady's maid on my travels."

The rushing of Sage's thoughts sputtered to a halt. Was this woman insinuating that she go along?

Miss Lennox nodded as though answering Sage's unasked question. "I have thus far insisted on going alone for this particular trip, since I am uncertain if I shall return or stay in the colony." She paused and looked pointedly at Sage, as though expecting a comment.

Sage scrambled to find a polite answer. "I'm sure you find yourself in a dilemma, ma'am."

"Indeed I am, as I love my parents dearly and have no wish to disappoint them. I also do not desire to inconvenience my lady's maid with my indecisiveness."

"Of course not."

"Then it appears we are in agreement."

They were? "Ma'am?"

"I shall hire you as my lady's maid for this voyage and for the duration of my stay in Victoria. When—if—I decide to return to London or continue my journey elsewhere, then I shall give you the freedom to remain in the colony and find other employment."

Sage's mind whirled. The offer to be a lady's maid was a really good one, especially for an unskilled and inexperienced woman like her. Such a position often required specialized training, apprenticeships, and working in other household positions first. Surely there were qualified women who would be thrilled to become Miss Lennox's lady's maid, even if she was indecisive about her destination.

Furthermore, Sage couldn't possibly leave her sisters or dad. They needed her, didn't they?

"Of course I shall give you a fair monthly wage." Miss Lennox paused and glanced at the ceiling as though calculating numbers in her head. "Shall we say three pounds a month? Thirty-six pounds for the first year."

Sage bit back a gasp. It was as much, if not more, than her dad made, especially now with the reduced wages, and it was unheard of for a woman like her who had no training or experience.

"Does that sound agreeable?" Miss Lennox was watching her carefully, likely gauging her reaction.

"It is more than agreeable, ma'am." Sage couldn't deny she was interested. But she forced herself to remain calm and to think logically about the possibility.

The fact was, ever since Mum's death last winter, Sage's carefully crafted world had begun to unravel. No matter what she did or how hard she tried, she couldn't weave her neat and tidy life back together. It just kept unwinding so that she was left with a tangled heap.

She was more than ready to leave the messes behind and start over some place new.

"But . . . ?" Miss Lennox asked.

"But I do have my three younger sisters and was hoping to bring them with me." Truthfully, they were old enough to take care of themselves. Briar was almost eighteen, Fern sixteen, and Clover fourteen. Even if Fern had started mingling with the wrong man and the wrong crowd recently, Briar was responsible enough to manage both Fern and Clover.

Miss Lennox's brow creased. "I regret that I cannot offer each of them passage as well, Miss Rhodes. But it's simply not feasible at the present."

"I understand—"

"Why not take some time to think on my offer. I shall finish with my charity work here tomorrow and leave by rail for London the day after. If you decide to accept the position, please let me know."

"I will. Thank you."

Miss Lennox nodded then picked up the discarded map and the list and began studying both again.

Sage didn't have to be told she was being dismissed. She could see that easily enough. With a final curtsy, she exited the mission and wrapped her scarf back over her head. The rain was still falling, forcing her to also don the hood of her cloak as she huddled deeper into the woolen garment.

She fingered the square of paper in her pocket. She had one final charity to visit. But what hope did she have that the place would have any emigration opportunities when no one else did? The trip would be futile, and there was no sense wasting time with the visit. Her best option was to consider Miss Lennox's proposition.

She hastened through the narrow lanes until she turned onto Market Street, where the stench of the livestock greeted her as did the calls of the merchants bargaining with customers. She fingered a second list in her pocket, the one with the few meager food items she needed to purchase. She didn't really need to write out the list—not when she bought the same bread, cheese, and fish with nearly every trip.

But she liked writing lists. It was one small way to keep order in her world when everything else was falling apart and when she'd already lost so much—her employment, Willow, Mum, and David.

David.

Her heart pinched with the need for him—a need she no longer had a right to feel, not when he belonged to Bessy and was getting married soon. In fact, he was getting married on Ascension Day.

That was just a few short days away.

The pain inside swelled forcefully, bringing Sage to a halt in the flow of shoppers in the storefront markets.

What had she done wrong to lose him?

Even after analyzing their relationship for weeks, she still hadn't been able to figure out her shortcomings that had driven him into the arms of another woman. She'd loved him and had tried to be the perfect fiancée. She'd been supportive and respectful and agreeable, had even delayed their wedding day because he'd said he wasn't ready.

As hard as the truth was, she couldn't deny it. After two years of courtship, he just hadn't been ready for *her*—not when he'd been willing to get married to Bessy so quickly after he broke off the engagement.

Sage glanced around, praying she wouldn't see Bessy anywhere. Since they lived in the same neighborhood and went to the same church and had the same friends, Sage often saw the pretty woman. If that wasn't bad enough, it was even worse when she saw Bessy with David. She could only imagine how much more difficult seeing the two would be after they were married.

"No." The whisper came out harshly.

She couldn't live that way, constantly being reminded that the man and the life that should have been hers belonged to someone else.

The desperation from earlier rose to choke her. She had to get away from Manchester. She couldn't stay another week, couldn't bear to be here another day.

She spun around and began to stride back the way she'd just trekked. The muddy street squelched beneath her clogs, splattering her skirt in her haste. For once she didn't care. All she could think about was the need to start a life someplace new—someplace far from David.

She was practically running by the time she reached the front door of Manchester City Mission. Without a moment of hesitation, she opened the door and stepped inside.

"I'll do it." She locked in on Miss Lennox. "I'll take the position as your lady's maid."

Two

AS SAGE STEPPED OFF THE STEAMBOAT landing stage onto the wharf, relief and gratitude mingled within her chest and brought a sting of tears to her eyes. She wanted to fall to her knees and kiss the ground, but she held herself stiffly and properly behind Miss Lennox.

After one hundred twenty days of voyaging halfway around the world, they'd finally arrived in Victoria. Their ship had actually dropped anchor in nearby Esquimalt Harbor on Vancouver Island the previous day, but they'd been detained along with all the other passengers until a steamboat was available to transport them into the shallower waters of James Bay.

With the morning sunshine warming her back, Sage took shaky steps down the wharf.

"Come along now, Sage." Miss Lennox was already two steps ahead with her long stride, her sights fixed upon the sprawling town of Victoria on the gently sloping embankment. "There's much to be done today."

"Yes. I've got the list." First thing that morning, Sage had compiled the usual list outlining their day.

"I do love your organization."

"Thank you, ma'am." At least in that one area, Sage had excelled in her new lady's maid job.

The voyage across the Atlantic Ocean had been difficult with tumultuous seas and storms, particularly around the Falkland Islands near the tip of South America. Sage had tried not to be seasick, but against her best efforts, she'd become violently ill during the rough weather, as had most of the other passengers.

As an experienced world traveler, Miss Lennox hadn't been bothered by the ship's swaying or the sea's swelling. She had instead proven herself to be a compassionate and charitable woman, tending to not only Sage but also to many other passengers.

Thankfully the journey through the Pacific Ocean north had been calmer. When they'd reached San Francisco, Sage had been feeling almost normal again—normal enough to go ashore with Miss Lennox and spend a few days touring the bustling American city.

Even though the experience in San Francisco—truthfully, the entire journey—had been unlike anything Sage had ever known, the first sights of Vancouver Island had surpassed everything else she'd yet encountered.

The miles and miles of pine forests had been the most startling of all. It seemed that everywhere she looked, every inch of land was covered in thick woodland, so rugged, so wild, so open, and so different from Manchester that it was almost as if she'd arrived in another world altogether.

The mountains, too, were awe-inspiring. To the south of Vancouver Island, the distant peaks of the Olympic Mountains rose in all their glory. To the west on the mainland of British Columbia were more mountains that led to the Fraser River Valley where apparently miners had flocked for a recent gold rush.

Sage wanted to pause on the wharf, spin in a circle, and take in the full view of the grandeur—the blue-green waves, the rocky coastline, the lushness of the land, and the sea gulls circling overhead. But she'd learned Miss Lennox, a woman of purpose and mission, rarely stopped to dawdle. Sage had also learned over the past four months of working for Miss Lennox that a lady's maid didn't dawdle either—or gape or do anything else that could be construed as ill-mannered.

From the start, Miss Lennox had instructed her on everything she needed to know about her position. While exacting and even demanding at times, the woman had proven to be a kind and considerate employer. And extremely generous.

Sage's wardrobe was testament to how generous. Miss Lennox had given Sage cast-off garments that didn't fit or were no longer the latest fashion. Sage had needed to shorten the skirts and let out the seams in the bust of most bodices. But once done, the gowns were more beautiful than anything Sage had ever imagined owning, along with the shoes, stockings, hats, gloves, and other items from Miss Lennox.

What would Willow say about the fancy clothing and the fashionable bonnet? Would her sister recognize her?

Sage scanned the waterfront and the smattering of fishing boats and canoes that remained in the bay while the majority were gone for the day. The shore was crowded with piers, wharfs, and warehouses, where longshoremen were loading and unloading barrels and crates of goods.

She hoped for a glimpse of Willow but knew she was being too wishful to think that she'd be able to see her sister the moment of her arrival. But maybe she'd see Caleb, Willow's friend, who'd also traveled to the colony. It was possible he'd taken a job along the waterfront.

As she stepped off the wharf onto the grassy embankment, Miss Lennox halted and perched her hands on her hips. She pursed her lips and peered at a nearby barn-like building that had the word *Livery* painted above a door that was wide enough for a wagon to enter.

A set of stately brick buildings stood off to one side—the government buildings, according to one of the other steamboat passengers. The rest of the town was made up mostly of white wooden-framed buildings that lined wide streets. Although the streets were unpaved and had lots of ruts filled with puddles, the town had a tidiness about it that was refreshing and different than overcrowded and dirty Manchester.

"I hope Jackson will be home this morning." Miss Lennox strode forth again, this time making a line directly toward the livery. "What if he's away? Perhaps even out of town working on one of his projects?"

Sage scurried to keep up. "If so, he will need to return soon for the wedding."

Miss Lennox had explained during the long days of the voyage that her brother, Jackson, who was twenty-nine and two years younger than her, had been living in the British colonies of Vancouver Island and British Columbia for the past four years working as an engineer, building roads and bridges. Before that he'd resided for five years in Manitoba, designing roads and bridges for the Hudson's Bay Company. Miss Lennox had only seen him once in the nine years he'd been gone.

With as much as Miss Lennox—Augusta—had spoken of her brother, mother, and father, Sage felt as if she knew them all well, almost as if she'd met them already. Augusta's mother was Lady Catherine Lennox, the daughter of an earl, and her father was Jackson Thomas Lennox, who had made his fortune during the early days of the Hudson's Bay Company when fur-trading had been a lucrative business. He'd also been an explorer and had located important trade routes in North America and the Arctic, for which he'd been knighted.

Lady Catherine had been ill over the past year, and Augusta had returned home from India to be with her. Upon news of the illness, Sir Jackson Thomas had decided to finally give up his traveling in order to be with his wife because her brush with death had opened his eyes to the fragility of life, or so Augusta claimed.

Now that Lady Catherine had recovered and had her husband there to dote on her, Augusta had been eager to resume her traveling. She'd wanted to visit the Pacific Northwest and had expedited her plans when the family received a letter from Jackson in Victoria indicating he was engaged to be married and was building a fine home named Fairview for his bride-to-be.

The wedding was scheduled for early October, and Augusta had been worried that if the ship had any delays, she might miss the special occasion. As it turned out, they'd arrived with a couple of weeks to spare, and Augusta had been animated during the past few days as she'd prepared for seeing Jackson again and meeting her future sister-in-law.

Animated might not be quite the term to describe the intense woman with her boundless energy and unending drive. Sometimes being with Augusta exhausted Sage. But she'd certainly learned to appreciate and even enjoy the woman's company.

Augusta halted outside the livery door. "I shall make arrangements for a carriage to transport us and our luggage to Fairview. You watch for the stevedores with our trunks and wave them over here."

Winded from the quick walk, Sage drew in a steadying breath that was filled with the now-familiar scent of sea and salt. "Yes, ma'am."

Augusta was already several steps inside the dark interior of the establishment, as fearless as always.

Sage turned her attention back toward the sidewheeler where

other passengers were still disembarking and deckhands were unloading cargo from the main deck. The morning sunlight glinted on the bay and on the distant peaks, once again stunning her with the beauty of this remote colony of the Queen's empire.

Homesickness still plagued Sage from time to time, usually more keenly at night when she was left alone with her thoughts. However, the ache was mostly dull now, not as fresh and painful as it had been during the early days of the voyage when she'd missed her sisters and dad terribly.

Even the ache of missing David had faded. Only once in a while, when she saw happy couples together, would the ache throb harder and remind her of all she'd lost—a future with a hard-working and handsome man, a home of her own, and a house full of children.

"No more," she whispered as she steeled her shoulders. "Never again."

She'd made up her mind to become a spinster like Augusta, devoting herself to her work as a lady's maid.

Throughout the whole journey, Sage had studied the woman, watched her interactions, and admired her strength. Augusta had shown great contentment in being unmarried and untethered from the usual duties required of women. She lived fully and never let anything hold her back, giving much of her free time to charities and helping others.

If Augusta could make a satisfying life for herself outside of being married, then Sage could too.

Maybe she'd never become an adventurous, world traveler. Maybe she'd never be as determined and driven. And maybe she'd never become as independent and self-sufficient. But she'd realized she didn't need a man in her life to make her happy any more than Augusta did.

After all, men and relationships seemed to bring nothing but heartache and trials and disappointments.

Yes, spinsterhood was the best course for her future. Besides, a lady's maid's life was not her own. Sage had learned that from the start of her employment. She was on duty from the moment she arose in the morning until after Augusta went to bed, with only sporadic breaks throughout the day.

Once her sisters and dad immigrated, she would stay busy with them too. And with Willow.

Another thrill tingled through her. She would get to see Willow soon.

"Then you believe he's home?" Augusta stepped out of the livery, speaking with a young man who followed her outside, leading a team of horses and a conveyance.

"Oh aye." The young man was more of a boy, probably not older than twelve, and was lean and going through a growth spurt so that his trousers were well above his ankles. "Everyone 'round here knows about Mr. Lennox's bridge that collapsed."

Augusta stopped short. "Bridge collapsed?"

The boy halted the team just outside the livery. "Back in the spring. A whole bunch of workers got killed when it happened."

Augusta's expression turned serious. "Is that so?"

"'Tis so. And he's not been seen since." The boy left them outside to go find a driver.

Augusta nodded absently and peered toward the distant mainland. Her usual no-nonsense expression was gone, and she seemed to be a thousand miles away.

Sage hesitated, not wanting to intrude but needing to show Augusta she cared. "I'm sorry the news about your brother isn't so good."

Augusta sighed. "If the news is true, then the tragedy couldn't have been easy on him."

"I imagine it must have been very difficult."

"For him especially. He's a sensitive soul."

"Then all the more reason he'll be glad of your visit. I'm sure he'll be thrilled to see you."

"Yes, of course. And your sister will be thrilled to see you."

Augusta had already said that once they were settled, she would give Sage leave to search for Willow. Hopefully, in the small settlement with so few women, Willow would be easy to locate.

After so many months of being in the colony, would Willow now be married? Perhaps even expecting a child? Sage just hoped Willow hadn't let her friendship with Caleb hold her back. As much as Sage liked Caleb and thought of him as an older brother, she had never approved of how reliant Willow had been on him.

"One thing is certain." Sage opened her parasol and held it over Augusta to shield her from the morning sunshine. "Willow will not expect to see me here." Not when Sage had been so happily planning to marry David. Willow had always joked that she'd been given Sage's leftovers and that Sage had gotten everything good, had the perfect life.

At one time, maybe she would have agreed, back when she'd been arrogant and self-assured and overly confident in herself and her abilities and looks.

Time and God had a way of humbling a person. Now she knew she most certainly wasn't perfect. She was far from it. And she owed Willow an apology for ever making her think she wasn't as good.

Yes, an apology was long overdue. She just hoped she would be able to find Willow and give it to her soon.

Three

WITH A ROAR, JACKSON LENNOX shoved at the model of the bridge that spanned one end of the dining room table to the other. Hundreds of tiny pieces of wood along with cables toppled onto the glossy mahogany surface.

"Rubbish!" Helpless rage roiled inside him. "All rubbish!"

Crying out again, he swept the wreckage off the table, letting it topple to the floor with a crash. One of the anchorages stood at the far end, illuminated by the brightly lit chandelier. It seemed undeterred by his outburst, mocking him with its grace and poise.

It was rubbish too.

He trampled over the wooden pieces now scattered across the oak floor, not caring that he was snapping and crushing the specialized model wood beyond repair. It didn't matter that he'd spent countless hours over the past week gluing and hammering everything together with meticulous precision. It didn't matter that it was his best design yet. It didn't matter that he'd almost figured out the problem—or so he believed.

No, none of it mattered. Not when his suspension bridge was still unsafe. Not when so many had suffered and died because of his failure. Not when more people would suffer and die if he didn't get the design right this time.

He reached the remaining anchorage, swiped it up, and threw it against the wall.

It hit with a reverberating crash that sent shards of wood flying throughout the dining room. A sliver hit him in the face, but the overgrowth of his facial hair kept it from cutting his skin. Even if it had cut him, he deserved the pain and the punishment. It was the least he should endure when others had endured far worse.

A few final bolts rolled to a halt on the floor, and then silence settled over the destruction—utter silence except for the angry huffs of his labored breathing. Not even his servant Elliot, somewhere in the mansion, made a sound.

During outbursts like this, the fellow stayed well away from Jackson, giving him the space he needed. It wasn't the first model bridge Jackson had destroyed, and it likely wouldn't be the last. Because that's what he was good at—making messes and mistakes.

At a firm knocking against the front door down the hallway from the dining room, Jackson scowled. Who was attempting to visit him so late at night?

He glanced to the thick draperies that were drawn to find bright light creeping through the slit between them. At some point, the night had passed and turned into morning. He'd obviously lost track of time and worked through the night again.

Not only had he lost track of time, but he couldn't remember what day it was. His eyes stung from focusing for so long on the intricate details of the bridge, and his stomach gnawed inside him. When was the last time he'd slept or eaten?

He tried to make his brain recall the details of the past week, but it was a blur. In fact, the past four months since the accident were fuzzy. He'd done little else except to study his architecture and engineering books, draw elaborate diagrams, and build complicated models.

He peered around the dining room at the empty decanters, half-full glasses, and plates with stale food. Elliot had clearly tried to feed him.

The knocking on the front door resounded again, this time louder.

Jackson stepped into the dining room doorway and glanced in the direction of the stairway that led to the lower level and kitchen. He wanted to believe Elliot was gone to the market. But he was probably in his cups and foxed.

Jackson tentatively moved into the hallway. The barren floors were covered with dust and dried mud. The papered walls were without any pictures. The only thing on the wall was a gilded oval mirror.

As Jackson caught his reflection, he recoiled at the stranger that stared back at him. His dark hair was overlong and unkempt and needed not only combing but washing. The face was hidden behind a bushy beard, long sideburns, and a mustache. Gray-blue eyes were outlined by dark circles and the forehead was creased with lines.

He was coatless and vestless, with several buttons of his dress shirt undone. His trousers were wrinkled, and like everything else, needed laundering.

There was a wildness to his expression, one that reflected the turmoil of the monster that had taken up residence inside him. Yes, he was nothing more than a monster. Not only did he look like one, but he acted like one too.

"Hello?" came a woman's voice from outside the front door.

A woman? Had Meredith come to pay him a visit?

His heart gave a rapid beat. He couldn't let Meredith see him like this. He scanned himself in the mirror again, fresh disgust filling him. He was a filthy, bedraggled mess.

Hastily, Jackson ran his fingers through his hair, but the strands only stood up all the more. He fumbled for a button on his shirt, but he couldn't find one and glanced down to see that only threads dangled there.

"Jackson?" the woman called.

Jackson halted his attempt at grooming. The voice was too firm and practical to belong to Meredith.

Besides, there was no reason for her to call on him. After the collapse of Queen's Bridge back in May, he'd done what he should have much earlier—he'd cancelled their engagement and set her free.

Initially, she'd been upset about his decision, but that hadn't lasted long.

His mind swirled with her last visit over two months ago when she'd come to tell him that she'd found someone new and was engaged again. He'd told her he was happy for her, and maybe part of him really was happy that she'd found a decent fellow to care about her after having to endure a bird-witted man like him who was consumed with his work.

The truth was, Meredith had deserved a husband who would be devoted to her—a man who could appreciate her and give her the time and attention she needed. He'd never been that kind of man, had never made her truly happy.

Regardless, she was married now—at least he assumed so. That meant she wouldn't come visiting. Not anymore.

So, if not Meredith, who was the woman at the door?

"Jackson Lennox?" The female on the portico was persistent and pounded the door again, long and loud.

Jackson glanced again toward the servants' entrance, hoping to see or hear Elliot coming, but there was still no sight of him. "Blast you, Elliot."

Jackson growled in frustration at his incompetent servant. What use did he have for the fellow? For that matter, what use did he have for the enormous house he'd built for Meredith? He didn't need twenty rooms, not for just himself. While Meredith had already started to decorate and fill some of the rooms, half were sitting empty.

"Jackson, are you home?" the woman called.

With another growl, he jammed his fingers into his hair. Then he stalked into the hallway and approached the door. "Who is it? And what do you want?"

His manners were as appalling as his appearance. If his dear mother could hear him or see him, she would not be at all pleased with the man he'd become. How had he turned into this angry, bitter person?

"Jackson?" The voice on the other side of the door radiated surprise. "Is that you?"

He had the distinct impression that he wouldn't be able to get rid of this visitor unless he opened the door and scared her away. So without any further hesitation, he threw open the door and planted himself with both feet wide, his arms crossed, and his fiercest scowl.

The woman on the front stoop didn't take a step back, didn't even flinch. Instead, her eyes rounded—familiar, kind eyes set in a familiar thin face that belonged to his sister.

"Augusta?" In the many years he'd been gone from England, he'd only seen her once five or six years ago, and yet hardly anything about her had changed. She was still thin and bony, her narrow face hadn't aged, and her dark brown hair was styled in a tight bun without a single hair out of place.

She was taking him in too, her eyes widening as she scanned him from his untidy hair down to his scruffy shoes. With the morning sunshine bathing him in full light, no doubt she was seeing every stain and blemish and just how bedraggled he'd become.

Before he could say anything, primarily apologize for his rude welcome, she stepped forward and wrapped him into a hug. Although she was tall for a woman, he was still several inches taller than her, both of them having inherited their height from their father.

"It's so good to see you, Jackson," she murmured as she squeezed him tightly.

He hugged her in return, his thoughts churning with this new twist of fate. His sister was here at his house in Victoria. While he wasn't in a pleasant frame of mind to have company, he was glad to see her. They'd never been particularly close since he'd been away at school for so much of his childhood and she'd spent so many years traveling. However, he had always cherished her, and he'd also always admired her for her strength of character.

She gave him a final squeeze before pulling back and assessing him again, holding on to both of his arms as if she were afraid that if she let him go, he'd run away and hide. Unfortunately, if that's what she was thinking, she wasn't half wrong.

Her brow puckered with more lines than had been there the last time he'd seen her. "How are you?"

He'd never been more terrible. But he couldn't very well say that, so he shrugged. "I apologize for looking a fright. I've been working nonstop."

She was tactful enough not to comment on his appearance. Instead, she offered him a warm smile. "The work here in the colony must be very demanding."

He could never explain to her all that had happened with the new bridge in the Fraser River Valley or his role in its collapse. At least not at the moment. "And you, my dear sister? How are you?"

"I'm delighted to finally be here."

"And mother? How does she fare?" After getting recent letters that Mother suffered from influenza, he'd been unnerved.

"Doing much better. I believe she shall make a full recovery, or at least I was confident of that especially because she seemed so happy to finally have Father all to herself."

Jackson wasn't sure he could respond without saying something bitter about their father, so he kept silent.

Augusta was well aware of the conflict he'd always had with their father, and thankfully instead of talking more about the man, she changed the subject. "It was quite a rough voyage here, wasn't it, Miss Rhodes?" She turned toward a woman standing several paces away on the flagstone pathway. A hired hackney was parked on the street beyond, and the driver was already unloading the luggage from the back platform.

"It was very rough." The woman was decidedly younger than Augusta by at least ten years if not more. She had a quiet, deferring air about her that told him she was a servant, likely a lady's maid, which would account for why she wore a fashionable gown and not the black uniform and white apron of a regular maid.

Even though he had sworn off women after breaking his engagement to Meredith, he wasn't blind and could see easily enough that Miss Rhodes was attractive with high cheekbones, a delicate nose, and dainty chin. Her hair was an unusual reddish blond that highlighted the creaminess of her skin and made her light blue eyes vibrant, like the color of the sea in the summer. She also had a womanly figure that her gown displayed to perfection, leaving no room for speculating just how stunning she was.

In this remote colony where men outnumbered women, she would have numerous marriage proposals within the next month. In fact, the young men would be fighting amongst themselves to win her, and she would have her pick of a husband. Then Augusta would be without a lady's maid. His sister probably hadn't thought about that when she'd made her plans.

Ah, well. It would be for the best. He wasn't in the right frame of mind to entertain Augusta, much less have a young maid like Miss Rhodes residing in his home for the duration of his sister's visit.

Augusta stood back and surveyed the front of his home. He'd drawn up the plans himself and had helped oversee the construction when he hadn't been on the Fraser River overseeing the building of the bridge.

"You have a lovely home, Jackson." Augusta's keen gaze filled with appreciation.

The steeply gabled roof and the three stories with castle-like turrets on the sides each contained round windows that overlooked the distant mountain peaks. He'd designed arched windows on the second floor and large bay windows on the first. The entire structure was painted in blue with detailed trim work around the windows, doors, and eaves that gave the home an elegant appeal, as did the wrought iron along the portico.

He'd had requests from other prominent families in Victoria who were interested in having him design their houses. However, as much as he had relished the project, architecture was only a hobby. He was an engineer at heart, his mind constantly at work concocting complex feats that no one else could accomplish, apparently not even him—like the suspension bridge that was supposed to span the Fraser River and make the traveling easier to and from the gold fields and all the new settlements that were springing up.

He held in an exasperated breath, one aimed at himself for his failures and mistakes. For now, he had to be gracious to his sister. She likely wouldn't visit long. She never did when she was traveling, since she claimed she grew restless when she was in one place for too long.

"Please, do come in." He stepped aside and waved a hand at the front hallway, but then he stopped short at the sight of the mess. Not only wasn't he in the right condition for hosting visitors, neither was his home. He spun and blocked the doorway. "On second thought, I wonder if you'd be more comfortable at one of the nice, new hotels. My home isn't suitable for company."

"I'm sure it will be just fine." Augusta waved a dismissive hand.

"After staying for four months in a cramped berth on the ship, your home will feel like a luxurious palace."

Jackson tried to remember if he even had furniture in his guest room. If not, he could give up his bedroom to Augusta. He didn't sleep much anyway.

"Besides," Augusta said as she motioned toward the hackney driver, who was carrying a trunk, "we shan't stay long. Only until the wedding."

His heartbeat stuttered to a stop. He'd written home last autumn about his plans to marry Meredith this coming October after a year-long engagement. But he hadn't corresponded to let his family know he'd ended the relationship. Even if he had, the letter wouldn't have reached Augusta before she'd set sail on her voyage to Victoria.

"I'm so looking forward to meeting Miss Hodges." Augusta pushed past him into the house.

He wanted to grab her arm and stop her, wanted to warn her, needed to tell her the truth about Meredith and the wedding. But he could only stand back as she stalked into the entryway.

She only took four long steps inside before halting abruptly. She scanned the entryway, likely cataloging his discarded, dirty clothing draped over the stairway railing, socks balled up on the floor, shoes tossed in every direction, and hats sitting atop stacks of unopened mail and newspapers.

She was at the right angle to also peer into his front parlor. Although he hadn't been in the room in days, he guessed it was in the same state of disarray as the rest of the house.

The hackney driver halted just inside the door too, and had grown wide-eyed as he took in the disorder. Only the lady's maid remained outside.

Augusta was silent for several long heartbeats before pivoting with a frown. "Jackson Lennox, you have some explaining to do."

Four

ON THE FRONT STOOP, SAGE HELD herself as motionless as possible, wishing she could disappear. All along she'd wanted to give Augusta privacy for her reunion with her brother and had offered to wait in the hired carriage. But Augusta had insisted on including Sage in everything like always.

The moment Jackson Lennox had thrown open the front door and greeted them with a scowl, Sage had retreated several steps. He was fiercer and wilder than any man she'd ever met, certainly not the *sensitive soul* Augusta had claimed that he was. With his tall and imposing build, he wasn't overly muscular, but neither was he as lanky as Sage had pictured for an educated, aristocratic man. In fact, with his midnight hair sticking on end and his thick dark brows and bushy beard, he was what she imagined a dangerous pirate looked like.

He was just missing the bandanna and eye patch. And the sword.

With the surprise and consternation on Augusta's face, clearly she'd been taken aback by the state of her brother's home and appearance. Did his unkemptness have to do with the bridge accident they'd heard about at the livery?

"Well?" Augusta persisted. "What is going on here?"

Jackson's shoulders slumped, and he hung his head as though defeated, sadness rolling off him in waves. For several long heartbeats, he didn't reply. Then he straightened his shoulders and faced Augusta, a hint of belligerence returning to his demeanor. "I called off the wedding."

Sage wasn't entirely surprised by the news. She couldn't imagine too many women who would find a man like Jackson appealing—not with how disheveled he was. And intimidating. Not only that, but he had an air about him that was off-putting, as if he had no desire to interact with anyone.

Of course, he did seem genuinely glad to see Augusta. But already, just minutes after being reunited, he'd encouraged them to stay at a hotel.

"What do you mean you called off the wedding?" Augusta's tone was controlled and calm, and Sage had learned that nothing ever ruffled the woman, that her inner strength was as stiff and strong as a ship's main mast.

"I broke my engagement with Meredith—Miss Hodges." Jackson's back remained rigid. He had that in common with his sister. "Now she's married to someone else."

According to Augusta, Meredith Hodges was the daughter of Vancouver Island's Surveyor General, a titled Englishman who'd brought his family to Victoria about the same time Jackson had moved there.

Had Meredith secretly been seeing someone else the same way David had with her? Was that what was causing the sadness that emanated from Jackson?

Augusta cast a glance at Sage, her eyes filled with tenderness. Sage hadn't intended to bare her heart to Augusta about all that had happened with David, but the long days and weeks together during the ship's voyage had provided too much time, and eventually Augusta had been able to pry the sad tale from her.

"I'm sorry, Jackson." Augusta spoke gently. "That must have been difficult."

"Not at all. I was not suited for her and am relieved she's found someone else."

"Oh." One of Augusta's narrow brows rose.

"She deserved someone better than me."

Augusta didn't immediately respond. She was probably trying to understand the disparaging comment and was also probably wondering if it also had to do with the bridge accident. Although Augusta was refreshingly direct at times, she was still polite and wouldn't push for more information right away. She would bide her time and learn more details soon enough.

"Either way, I'm sure recent months have not been easy on you." Augusta surveyed the disorderly entryway as if making her point. "Now that I'm here, I shall assist you with putting things in order."

"I do thank you for the offer." Jackson's voice took on an edge. "But that is not necessary. I'm managing just fine."

"Miss Rhodes and I would like to help, wouldn't we, Miss Rhodes?" Augusta picked up a discarded hat and placed it on the coat-tree.

"Yes, of course. I'll do anything that is needed." Sage would be relieved to make herself more useful and to feel as though she were actually earning her money, since her duties with Augusta had been so light and infrequent thus far.

"I shan't *need* anything." Jackson tossed Sage a glare, one that gave her full view of his eyes, which were a chilly gunmetal blue, fitting for an ill-tempered man.

"Come now, Jackson." Augusta retrieved another hat and hung it. "We've arrived just in time, for it is quite clear you could use the help as well as some cheering up."

The scowl furrowing Jackson's forehead only deepened.

Sage had the feeling he wanted to grouse at Augusta too, the same way he had at her. But he clearly loved his sister enough that he seemed to swallow his retort. "I meant what I said. You really should stay at a hotel."

"Nonsense." Augusta motioned at the carriage driver who had placed one of the trunks on the floor. "We're staying with you, Jackson. That's all the arguing about it I want to hear." With that, she picked up her full skirt and started up the steps, calling to the driver. "Come along."

The carriage driver hoisted the trunk and began to tromp up the stairway.

Sage guessed she ought to follow after Augusta to situate them into their new accommodations. But to do so she would have to pass by Jackson, who still took up half the doorway.

He jammed his fingers into his overlong hair, narrowing his gaze on Augusta as she ascended.

It was becoming more obvious with every passing moment that he really didn't want them here. It was also becoming all too obvious to Sage that she didn't want to be here either, not in a home where the master was like a caged feral animal who might strike out at any moment.

"Make haste, Sage." Augusta was nearly to the top of the stairway. "We have a great deal to do today and cannot dawdle."

Sage scurried forward, not wanting Augusta to think she was incompetent or lazy or even scared. She'd done her best to prove herself so that Augusta wouldn't have regrets about bringing her, and she didn't want to fail the dear lady now that they'd reached their destination.

As she sidled past Jackson in the doorway, she murmured, "Excuse me, sir."

He didn't budge except to stiffen.

She made it two steps past him into the front hallway before his low voice stopped her. "Don't get comfortable. You will be gone before too long."

Sage faced the stairway only a few feet away. Augusta was already heading down a second-floor hallway, and the carriage driver was on her heels.

Was Jackson threatening to have her dismissed from her position?

If so, he didn't know who he was dealing with. She wasn't easily pushed aside or intimidated. After all, he wasn't her employer and wasn't in charge of her.

Augusta was the only one she had to listen to, the only one she needed to please. She didn't have to impress Jackson or to try to win his admiration. In fact, he could end up disliking her for all she cared.

Slowly she turned and lifted her chin. She might not be anything more than a poor woman from a poor family from a poor Manchester neighborhood. But she wouldn't let this overgrown grizzly bear make her feel worthless.

"I'm employed by Miss Lennox." She spoke with a firmness she'd always used on her sisters when they were misbehaving. "If you have any complaints, please address your concerns to her."

With that, she finished crossing to the stairs. As she ascended, she could feel him watching her, probably scowling at her. She waited for him to demand that she stop and leave. But other than a huff of clear irritation, he didn't say another word.

Sage worked tirelessly for hours, and the labor felt good. Even when Augusta took a break from their cleaning and organizing to visit with Jackson, Sage kept on with a new list of tasks she'd made with Augusta's input.

The list was long, filling two sheets of paper. The first page contained the most pressing needs like getting the guest rooms ready, airing out the mattresses, washing sheets and covers, beating the rugs, dusting the furniture, and wiping away the cobwebs that seemed to fill every corner.

While Sage washed the sheets, she also laundered the basic necessities out of her and Augusta's clothing. Sage had washed their clothing as best she could for the duration of the voyage to Victoria, and now their garments were past ready for a full and thorough laundering.

Although Sage had suggested sleeping on a pallet on the floor until a dormer room could be made ready, Augusta had insisted that Sage take the guest room directly connected to hers, both rooms already having a sparse amount of furniture, including beds.

The bed in Sage's room was bigger than any she'd ever seen, and she was too embarrassed to admit to Augusta that she'd never slept on a real bed before. Even the tiny bunks in their ship's cabin had been an improvement from her usual pallet on the floor in her family's flat.

The rest of the week became a blur of work. Every inch of the enormous house was in need of cleaning, especially the kitchen, which had to be scrubbed and rescrubbed from top to bottom. Augusta promptly fired Jackson's servant because it became clear that the fellow hadn't done anything but cook for Jackson, and even that task had been poorly done.

While Augusta assisted with some of the chores, she spent most of her time organizing her brother's affairs—especially looking for hired help. Her efforts to find suitable staff were difficult, and Augusta lamented the lack of qualified personnel, which was the opposite of Manchester where so many people needed work.

Augusta not only took charge of Jackson's affairs, but she also seemed to make it her mission to finish furnishing and decorating the rooms of his house. Sometimes she brought Sage along to help with the shopping at the few stores in Victoria that supplied household goods.

On those occasions, Sage inquired about Willow and Caleb. But no one recognized the names, and no one could give her information about her sister. Although the bride-ship women had stayed at the Marine Barracks when they'd first arrived, now, all these months later, the women had either married or been employed.

Even though Sage had no luck in finding Willow, she knew it was still early and that she would eventually track her down. After all, Victoria wasn't nearly as big as Manchester, and once she was no longer so busy, she would take more time to investigate Willow's whereabouts.

While she admired Augusta for her willingness to bring order to her brother's life and to help him establish his household, Sage didn't quite know what to make of Jackson or why he was so helpless to take care of himself.

She saw little of him, except in passing. He spent most of his days closed in the dining room, creating a model suspension bridge. If not there, then he was in his study. It was evident from the hallway that both rooms were messy and would need cleaning eventually.

Nevertheless, she made good progress with the rest of the house so that by the end of the first week, the rooms were organized and spotless. Augusta finally found a cook who had been working in one of the restaurants in town but who was more than willing to take the private job with better pay.

With the cook now established and the kitchen stocked with most of the supplies that were necessary for a household such as the Lennoxes', Augusta made it known that she was determined to have meals together, even if they had to eat them in the smaller and cozier breakfast room because Jackson's model took up the dining room.

So Sage hadn't protested Augusta's request to join her and Jackson for the evening meal.

With as busy as she and Augusta had both been during their first week in Victoria, they hadn't been able to enjoy each other's company the way they had during the voyage.

For the meals on the ship, Augusta had asked Sage to accompany her as a companion and friend rather than merely a servant. At first, Sage had felt out of place whenever she took the role of Augusta's companion. But she'd quickly learned the social requirements, and thankfully, Augusta was kind and never put on airs.

With the waft of their first proper evening meal in the air, Sage helped Augusta dress in a fine gown and styled her hair. Then Sage donned one of Augusta's tailored castoffs, a lovely pale peach silk with small bows on the skirt and matching bows on the off-the-shoulder collar. She adored the gown more than any others for how it complemented her hair.

When Sage finished, Augusta was waiting in the parlor, and they ambled into the hallway like two friends rather than a lady and her servant.

"I'm told the furniture will come from San Francisco in a matter of weeks," Augusta said as they approached the breakfast room. "A console, candlestand tables, a waterfall bookcase, and armchairs for the formal parlor."

As they stepped into the room, Sage halted at the sight of Jackson already sitting at the oval rosewood table. Although he was still shaggy-looking with his overlong hair and unshaven face, at least he'd taken the time to put on a freshly laundered and ironed light-blue dress shirt and matching cravat that complimented his tan suit.

He started to rise from his chair as men did in the presence of a lady. But as his gaze landed on her, he halted halfway up. His eyes widened, revealing the gray-blue more distinctly.

Obviously he hadn't been expecting her to come to dinner with

Augusta, perhaps believed the extra place had been set for a guest. And obviously Augusta hadn't informed him that guest was her lady's maid. Why? Because the dear woman knew she was crossing social boundaries by including Sage and guessed Jackson might oppose it?

Sage's stomach dropped with a sudden thud. She was an imposter, and Jackson would have no qualms in telling her so in spite of Augusta's kindness.

Augusta didn't release her grip on Sage's arm. Instead, she smiled at Jackson, who finished standing. "Thank you for taking time away from your work to join us. Even if we are in the far-flung outpost of civilization, we cannot neglect behaving as civilized people and having civilized meals together."

Jackson's gaze hadn't budged from Sage. He was scanning her simple chignon that she'd hastily fashioned after putting on the peach gown, and then his gaze swept over her face before drifting lower.

She'd drawn the attention of men before. That was nothing new. Even on the ship voyage, men had stared at her and paid her compliments.

But this was Jackson, Augusta's brother, and she didn't quite know what to make of his silence, his intensity, and the full focus of his steely eyes. Beside her, Augusta had grown quiet, her brow furrowing as she watched Jackson.

What was Augusta worried about? Jackson showing an interest in her?

Not that he was interested. Such a prospect was laughable. Of course, he might be noticing her appearance tonight. The gown was truly flattering, and she knew she looked especially pretty in it.

But beyond a mere acknowledgement of her beauty, a man of Jackson's class and wealth would never seriously consider someone like her of an inferior status. It was one thing for Augusta to befriend her, but it was another thing altogether for a gentleman like him to form a relationship.

Unless the relationship was illicit.

Embarrassed heat rushed through Sage at even the prospect. Was Jackson the sort of man who might consider it though?

He hadn't struck her as such. Then again, she hadn't spoken more than a few dozen words to him since arriving. He'd been a recluse, and the sadness from the first day she'd met him hovered about him all the time.

Even so, this awkward moment was a glaring reminder that she didn't belong in the fancy gown, didn't belong at a formal dinner, and most definitely didn't belong in either Augusta's or Jackson's life.

She was from another world entirely, and she couldn't forget it.

She took a rapid step back, breaking free from Augusta. "I'm sorry. I shouldn't be here. I'll leave the two of you to dine together."

Five

J ACKSON KNEW HE WAS BEHAVING LIKE a buffoon by ogling Sage so openly and boldly, but her presence had taken him by such surprise that he hadn't been able to stop himself.

Or maybe he'd been without a woman for too long that he'd forgotten how to behave. More likely, after the weeks and months of shutting himself off from the world, he'd become a savage.

It could also be because Sage was a very lovely woman, much lovelier than he'd anticipated. Yes, there was even something about her that made his blood heat a degree or two.

Meredith hadn't had that effect upon him. For all the many months he'd courted her and then been engaged, he'd never been tempted to ogle her, and the temperature of his blood had never heated.

Of course, when they'd shared kisses once in a while, he'd felt a pull toward her. He was a man with needs, after all. But he'd never had the urge to just stand and stare at her as he was doing at the moment with Sage. And he'd never had the urge to keep staring, very nearly as if he couldn't get enough of this woman before him and needed to keep drinking her in.

"But of course you must stay, Miss Rhodes," Augusta was saying while narrowing censuring eyes upon him. "Forgive my brother for his rudeness."

"I can't join you." Sage took another step back, her blue eyes wide and filled with such uncertainty that they somehow tugged at him. Was *tugged* even the right word? Moved him? Stirred something inside him?

He didn't know how to explain it, but at the prospect of her running off and hiding away the rest of the evening, he had to say something. He waved at the two empty places at the table across from his. "Please. The table is already set." The words came out gruff, almost a demand.

Sage shook her head. "I don't want to impose."

Augusta reached for Sage's hand and tucked it back into the crook of her elbow. "She's not imposing, is she, Jackson?"

Technically, he'd never eaten with a servant. Not even lady's maids sat down to dinner with the family—not here or when he'd lived in Rupert's Land, which had been even wilder and more uncivilized than Victoria.

But Augusta never had put as much stock in class differences, and clearly still didn't. So how should he answer his sister so that she didn't throttle him?

Sage was watching his face, and at his delayed answer, a slight blush moved into her cheeks.

His hesitation was only making matters worse. The problem was, he hadn't really wanted to have dinner with Augusta in the first place and had only done so to pacify her. Now having Sage present, too, would only make him feel more awkward because it was clear she didn't like him and had gone out of her way to avoid him all week.

"You're always so kind to me." Sage squeezed Augusta's arm.

"But now that we're here in Victoria, I do think I would be remiss to act as though I am a fine lady or a part of your family when I am only hired help."

"You're more than hired help to me."

This time Sage broke away completely from Augusta. "I'm sure you'd love some time to reconnect with your brother without the bother of my presence."

"Your presence is delightful."

"Thank you, ma'am." Sage gave a slight curtsy and then hurriedly retreated into the hallway.

As soon as Sage's footsteps faded, Augusta leveled a glare upon him.

A needle of guilt pierced him. Yes, he was at fault for driving Sage away. He could admit it. She'd clearly intended to join them for dinner, but she'd sensed his reluctance and his unfriendly attitude.

"Well, that was uncalled for." Augusta stood rigidly in her formal gown. The low lighting cast a shadow over her narrow face and made her look tired and older.

The guilt inside him only pricked harder. His sister had come all this way to visit him. The long voyage hadn't been easy or without trials. In addition, he hadn't been welcoming, and his home had been in shambles.

Regardless of the circumstances, she'd made the best of the situation. She'd taken charge just as she usually did. Without any complaint, she'd set to work, helping him pick up the pieces of his shattered life—whether he'd wanted to pick them up or not.

Although he hadn't particularly liked the commotion or the intrusion on his privacy, he'd understood on some level that it was past time for him to stop living the way he had been and to start making some changes.

But what changes?

The helplessness and despair that had been plaguing him for months still gnawed at him.

With a shake of his head, he expelled a sigh. "Please, sit down, Augusta. We may as well have the dinner your new cook has prepared." They were here now, and he had to stop focusing so much on himself and his own problems and show Augusta he still cared about her.

Besides, the scents coming from the kitchen had been taunting him for the past hour—roasted duck, wild herbs and vegetables, and even the sweetness of a berry tart.

Augusta stood stiffly a moment longer before approaching her place at the table. Before he could reach her chair and pull it out for her, she was already sitting down. He helped to push her in before he sat across the table from her.

She unfolded her linen napkin and laid it in her lap, then she straightened the oyster fork and soup spoon, although both were perfectly placed above the plate.

He hadn't known he had linen napkins or formal silverware. Either Augusta had purchased both this past week or Meredith had done more to prepare their home than he'd realized.

He sat unmoving and forced himself to speak first. "Forgive me for being a brute. It seems that I am acting out what I have become."

Her eyes softened, and all the love she had for him was shining there.

His throat closed up. He couldn't remember the last time anyone had looked at him like that—probably not since he'd last seen her or his mother. Certainly his father had never given him such love, had only ever doled out criticism.

"You're not a brute, Jackson." Her voice held tenderness. "You've just become lost and need to find solid footing again."

Was she right? He did, indeed, feel lost, as if he was stuck in the wilderness of the great Fraser River Valley and unable to find his way through the thick forests and rugged mountains to the place where he wanted to be.

Where was that place? What was his destination?

"Once in a while, we need someone to come alongside us," she continued. "I hope you'll allow me to be that someone to support you."

He had pushed away everyone else—his friends, business associates, and even the woman he'd intended to marry. They'd all wanted to support him, but he hadn't been ready four months ago to interact with anyone, had been too consumed with guilt. Could he accept the support now?

He swallowed the protest that easily surfaced—the protest at having anyone else involved in his life, at least not until he figured out what had gone wrong with his bridge and how he could fix things.

But what if he never was able to get it right? What if the ruins remained in the canyon, a testament to his failure and the destruction and deaths that had come about as a result?

"Are you thinking about the bridge?" she asked as if sensing the direction of his thoughts.

He stared down at his empty plate.

"I heard what happened." Augusta spoke quietly, but the force of her words barreled into him anyway.

He sat back against his chair, the angst inside swelling hard and fast. Of course she would have heard. Everyone knew about it. The suspension bridge had been touted as one of the greatest feats of the modern world. He'd been lauded as a genius for developing it. Governor Douglas, the Hudson's Bay Company, and every industry in Vancouver Island and British Columbia had been counting on the bridge.

After starting work last summer and then resuming again this spring after the winter thaw, the construction crew had been nearing completion. The accolades had been rolling in for his achievement. Requests for his expertise from around the world had begun to pile up. He'd been on the cusp of fame and fortune that was his own making and not a result of his famous explorer father. He'd even received a letter from his father with a rare compliment for his work on the bridge.

Then one day in early May, during a downpour that had turned into sleet, the freezing moisture had expanded in one of the columns with a new hollow structural section that he'd developed. In all his initial calculations of the dimensions of the steel structure, including the nominal width, depth, and diameter along with the wall thickness, he hadn't calculated the permissible variations for freezing action.

The ice had split the column and weakened the rods, and he hadn't realized the damage that had been done until it was too late. The full crew had been at work when the column had collapsed, bringing down the west abutments and timber towers along with all the men who had been working on that end of the nearly completed bridge.

His mind had replayed the moment of the bridge crumbling more times than he could count. He'd been on the east bank overseeing the cables being installed when it had happened. He'd watched in horrified silence as the section had broken away from the bedrock and fifteen men had plunged ninety feet to their deaths below.

"It wasn't your fault, Jackson." Augusta spoke in her no-nonsense tone. "Accidents happen to everyone—"

"It was my fault, and that's all I want to say about it!" The words came out a half growl, half roar. His pulse was spurting forward, sending frustration to every part of his body, tightening his muscles, and pounding through his head.

He had the sudden desperate need to flee from the room and from Augusta, barricade himself in his study, and pore over the equations that he'd worked and reworked to test the effect of freezing on a hollow structural section. He could escape in the equations and in the numbers, even if only for a little while.

Augusta pursed her lips. Although he could sense she wanted to talk more about it, she only eyed him warily.

The truth of the matter was that he was entirely to blame for the bridge's failure and for the deaths. If he'd been more thorough, if he'd anticipated the freezing, if he hadn't let the pressure of deadlines rush him—then maybe he could have prevented the tragedy.

He grabbed onto the edges of his chair to keep himself from standing and stalking away. He couldn't behave in such an uncouth manner, not after all Augusta had done for him over the past week, not when she had arranged for such a fine meal that evening, and not when she didn't know the whole story.

He sucked in a deep breath, closed his eyes, and tried to calm his erratic pulse.

At the tread of footsteps and the clinking of dishes, he opened his eyes to find the new cook entering the room carrying a tray laden with soup bowls, the first course of their meal.

The cook was a rotund fellow with a fleshy face, orange-red hair, and a long curling mustache, and he looked as if he enjoyed eating his food as much as he enjoyed cooking it. He went by the French name of Gustave and added a few French words into his otherwise Scottish dialect.

Jackson took another deep breath and scrambled for a way to change the subject. But he'd never been socially adept, had always been awkward in conversing with people, had never known what to discuss when it wasn't related to his building or engineering projects.

Fortunately for him, Augusta had no trouble with talking. "I am keenly anticipating all of the courses you've planned, Gustave."

"Oui, Mademoiselle." He butchered the French words so much so, that when Jackson caught Augusta's gaze, he could see the humor there.

Both he and Augusta spoke fluent French. In her world traveling, Augusta had also learned several other languages. He'd lost count of which ones and how many. But she was like their father in her abilities.

Gustave was wearing a long white apron over a tight black suit. His expression was somber, and he was concentrating on the tray, as though he feared spilling the soup.

"I am contemplating hosting a small dinner sometime soon." Augusta unfolded her linen napkin. "Would you be able to provide cuisine for . . . say, ten to fifteen guests?"

Jackson had barely started to calm his racing pulse, and now at Augusta's proposition, his heartbeat tapped irregularly again. He was hardly ready for a dinner with just his sister, much less ten to fifteen people.

"Oui." Gustave placed a bowl of soup in front of Augusta, either beef bouillon or French onion, if the dark liquid was an indication. "I should be delighted to do so." The lilt of Gustave's Scottish accent was undeniable.

Jackson opened his mouth to protest the dinner plans, but Augusta spoke before he could. "Just a few neighbors, Jackson. You wouldn't deny me the opportunity to get to know them, would you?"

She picked up her soup spoon and poised it above her bowl. Then she cocked her head and waited for his answer.

How could he deny her anything? He couldn't. And she knew it.

Regardless, he couldn't stomach the prospect of one of the guests bringing up the bridge, asking him about the accident, or inquiring into his plans for the repairs. And invariably someone would.

He'd halfway lost his temper with Augusta when she'd mentioned it. How could he remain collected and in control of himself if other people were barraging him with questions about it?

No, having a dinner party was a bad idea.

He started to shake his head.

"You'll stay right by my side all evening." She dipped her spoon into the soup. "And I'll be the perfect hostess."

She was implying that she would take care of all the awkward moments and be sure to direct the conversation away from difficult topics. Essentially, she was giving him another push to start living again, and deep inside he knew he needed to let her push. Why, then, was the next step so daunting?

"Then it's settled." Augusta rattled off the names of several of the neighbors and clearly knew more about them already than he did. "We'll host the dinner on the Friday evening of next week."

He quickly calculated the days. Ten. Maybe in that time he'd find a way to get out of attending.

Six

S AGE ADMIRED THE DRAWING ON THE piece of paper she'd found behind one of Jackson's bookshelves. After the past few hours of cleaning and organizing his study, one thing had become clear. Jackson was a very talented man. His diagrams of various items were meticulous. His sketches of bridges were extremely detailed. And his mathematical equations were elaborate and took up whole pages.

When Augusta had boasted about how intelligent Jackson was, Sage had assumed the doting older sister was exaggerating. However, if anything, Augusta had under-represented Jackson's abilities.

Another thing that had become very clear after living in Jackson's home for over two weeks was that the man was utterly and hopelessly disorganized. He left clutter in his wake everywhere he went and was always so buried in his papers and books and models that he never seemed to notice anything else.

With the dinner party taking place over the coming weekend, Jackson's messiness was interfering with Augusta's desire to have the house in complete order. Not only was she planning the menu and seating and entertainment for that evening, but she had also continued her steady purchase of items to decorate and fill the mansion. The choices were limited in what was available, but Augusta had brought home framed pictures, potted plants, mantel clocks, candlestick holders, vases, and more.

Although Sage accompanied Augusta from time to time, Augusta had taken to running errands by herself most days. Sometimes she was gone for such long hours that Sage had begun to worry, especially because when Augusta returned, she seemed frustrated or worried or perhaps both.

Sage had been tempted to ask if something was wrong, but she hadn't felt the same freedom to cross social classes that she had during their ship voyage.

Part of it had to do with the way Jackson had put her in her place a week ago at the evening meal. Augusta had later apologized for her brother's rudeness and had invited her to supper again the next night, but Sage had made excuses to stay away and had instead eaten with Gustave in the kitchen.

Whatever the case, Sage had continued to do the daily work of cleaning and tidying the home as well as laundering, ironing, lighting the fires, emptying the ashes, bringing in more fuel, and any other task that needed doing... like cleaning Jackson's study.

Sage had been reluctant to even enter the room. But Augusta had insisted it needed to be scoured before the dinner party and had pleaded with Sage to make sure the job was completed.

Even though Sage had suggested closing the study door so none of the guests would witness the mess, Augusta claimed that doing so would only cause everyone to be curious and speculate about what they were hiding behind the closed door.

So this afternoon, with Augusta having gone on another errand, Sage had forced herself into the study. At first, she'd intended to just collect the discarded clothing as well as the unwashed plates and cups. But once she'd started gathering the items, she'd been unable to stop tidying everything else.

She'd put books back on the shelves and alphabetized them. She'd placed all Jackson's correspondences in the mail slots of his desk by the order in which he'd received them. She'd returned his pens and other utensils in the holders next to the mail slots.

The sheets of papers containing all his work had still been scattered over his desk, on chairs, and even in heaps on the floor. While she'd initially hesitated in touching them, she'd finally begun the laborious process of organizing those too.

If there was one thing she excelled at, it was in organizing. She soon had every single paper in the room sorted into three piles on top of his desk—close-up diagrams, sketches of bridges, and the mathematical equations. Then she cataloged each pile, putting papers into chronological order. Although some of the diagrams and equations didn't have dates, thankfully most did.

Finally, she'd polished every piece of wood, beat the dust from the rugs, and washed the floor. Now with the window freshly washed and the draperies drawn to let in the sunshine, she finished examining the diagram she'd just discovered behind the bookshelf—one that showed a cross section of an interior part of the bridge.

She didn't understand what it represented, but the lines and measurements and equations around it fascinated her, nonetheless. Not because she was interested in engineering but because it gave her more insight into Jackson.

They still only saw each other in passing, and they only spoke to each other to relay Augusta's requests. Even so, Sage had learned that not only did he excel at his work, but he was a devoted and kind brother, sitting with Augusta for meals, conversing politely, and inquiring into her life. He hadn't seemed happy about the dinner party request, but he'd allowed Augusta to proceed with her plans anyway. He spoke fondly of his mother, and he seemed to genuinely care about his family, although Sage sensed that he wasn't as close to his father.

Sage had also learned he wasn't concerned about material possessions. He didn't care what his sister purchased or how she decorated the house. He probably didn't notice the changes unless Augusta specifically pointed them out to him. Even then, he complimented her efforts rather than being offended that she'd taken charge of his home.

Yes, Jackson Lennox was a complicated man, but underneath the beast, Sage had witnessed a softer side that she liked. Once in a while, when she looked past his overgrown hair, she even glimpsed a handsome man.

Augusta seemed to think that Jackson had taken the bridge accident personally and had cancelled his wedding because of his guilt over the tragedy. She also believed that God had brought them to Jackson to be part of his healing journey.

Maybe that was true for Augusta. But Sage wasn't here for Jackson. Her first priority was to Augusta as a lady's maid and saving her earnings for her family's passage to the colony.

Sage placed the last, lone diagram in the right place within the stack, then picked up her duster.

"What do you think you're doing?" The sharp question came from the doorway.

She spun to find Jackson stepping into the room. His appearance was as rumpled as always—his shirt untucked, his sleeves rolled up, his vest hanging open, and his cravat undone. His dark hair was sticking on end, and his mouth was set into a grim line amidst the scruffy facial hair.

He was glancing around the room, his forehead furrowing. "What have you done?"

"Augusta asked me to clean the study—"

"This is my private workplace!" With each word, his voice rose a decibel. "I don't need it to be cleaned!"

"I was following Augusta's orders. She wanted it cleaned by the dinner party."

"I didn't approve of anyone touching anything." His agitation was growing more tangible with each passing moment, and he began stalking to first one bookshelf then the next.

"Believe me," she said more forcefully, "I didn't do this for your sake. I did it for Augusta's."

"You've been meddling since the moment you got here."

"Meddling? Is that what you call cleaning?" She knew she needed to bite her tongue and stay quiet. But there was something about his ranting that irked her, especially because she'd tried to be polite thus far, had exceeded her duties to help him, and had kept a cheerful and uncomplaining attitude like Augusta's.

"I put up with your meddling elsewhere, but you shouldn't have come in here!" This time he roared the words, his face turning a ruddy shade and his gaze bouncing from one piece of furniture to the next. "Now you've destroyed everything."

"I've picked things up." That was simplifying the situation. And his accusation that she'd *destroyed everything* was ludicrous since it was obvious she'd worked a miracle in his study and cleaned it beyond anything he could dream of.

"I didn't want it picked up!" His breathing was rapid and his expression almost panicked. "I wanted it left alone."

While she didn't think he'd lash out at her physically, she was glad to have the large desk standing between them. She'd never been afraid to speak the truth to her sisters and tell them what they needed to hear in difficult situations. She'd always done so calmly, priding herself for her ability to keep her emotions and temper under tight control.

But at the moment, a strange pressure was building inside her— frustration at this man's rudeness and ingratitude.

He scowled at the open draperies and the sunshine pouring in. "This is inexcusable! Unacceptable!"

"Do you know what is inexcusable and unacceptable?" She began to round the desk, her voice rising with uncharacteristic anger. "Your behavior. You're acting like a child having a temper tantrum."

He didn't miss a beat in his ranting, almost as if he hadn't heard her. "You shouldn't have moved my stuff! I knew where everything was, and now I'll never be able to find anything."

She couldn't keep back a laugh of disbelief. "Never find anything?"

"I had a system that worked for me!"

"Did it really work?" Now that she'd let her frustration loose, she couldn't seem to force it back down. "From what I've observed, the only system you have is that you lose or misplace everything."

If Jackson was surprised by her impertinent statement, he gave no indication. Instead, he merely roared back. "I left stuff out so that I'd know where to look when I came back to it."

"Oh, please. You know that's not true." She was practically shouting now too. "You know what the truth is? The truth is that you're a selfish, shaggy beast, and you don't think of anyone else but yourself."

As soon as she finished, she cupped a hand over her mouth, suddenly mortified.

His steel-blue eyes met hers—hard, unyielding, and angry.

For a moment neither of them said anything, their angry words still lingering in the air.

What kind of person was she becoming to lose control of her emotions and her words so easily? Fresh frustration swelled inside her, this time not at him, but at herself. A wave of remorse rolled over her along with mortification. This wasn't like her, and she needed to apologize, but she couldn't get the words out.

He pivoted and faced one of the tall bookshelves, his back rigid, his shoulders straight.

This would be a good time for her to make her escape from the room before he yelled at her again and before she said more that she would regret.

She started forward, lengthening her stride.

Before she made it to the door, his question snagged her. "You alphabetized the books?"

"Yes. And now I regret that I did." She tossed her answer over her shoulder, not willing to pause and subject herself to another rebuke.

She hurriedly stepped into the hallway, her firm tread echoing in the silence of the home. She hastened into the parlor and didn't stop until she crossed to the front bay window.

Dragging in a deep breath, she peered outside, her heart racing and her mind careening with everything that had just happened.

What had she been thinking to argue with a man like Jackson Lennox and speak to him so disrespectfully? If he went to Augusta and told her about the incident, Augusta was sure to be disappointed in her, and Sage couldn't bear the thought of disappointing the sweet woman.

Even so, Jackson's anger and belligerence raked across her nerves, setting her on edge once again. Surely she was justified in telling him how selfish he was. Someone needed to deliver the news.

She was surprised Augusta hadn't been more forthright with Jackson yet, because normally Augusta was a forthright person. Maybe, however, she wasn't sure how to approach her brother, not after so many years apart and not after what had happened with the bridge. She was likely trying to be patient and win him over steadfastly.

A sigh slipped from Sage. She should have done the same, exhibited patience and steadfastness instead of railing against him.

Blinking away her regrets, she took in the view out the window. On the clear afternoon without a cloud in the perfectly blue sky, she could see across the Strait of Juan de Fuca. The imposing but majestic sight of the Olympic Mountains greeted her and reminded her of the beauty of this new land, especially with the colorful changing trees in the lower elevations.

Maybe this new world and new life wouldn't always be easy, but she couldn't forget that it came with fresh opportunities and possibilities and life that she'd never been able to experience back in Manchester.

She and Willow would put their resources together and try to make a way for the rest of their family to come.

If ever she found Willow...

Sage hadn't had any luck, and finally Augusta had started asking around after the bride-ship women who had come on the *Robert Lowe*. But since the colony had experienced two boatloads of women arriving so closely together, they hadn't met anyone yet who had definitive news about Willow.

Sage wasn't sure how long she stood looking out the bay window before a clearing throat startled her. She spun to find Jackson just inside the parlor door, a stack of papers in his hand, the one with his diagrams.

He was riffling through them. "You organized my work by the dates?" His voice was level, the edge from before gone.

"Yes." She kept her voice level now too. "I made three separate files and categorized each by the dates. I thought it would be helpful if you could see the progression with each new diagram."

He flipped through them one by one. The furrows in his forehead lessened, and one of his brows quirked up.

Her muscles tightened again as she waited for the monster from moments ago to rear his head and yell at her. Instead, he released a *harumph*, paged through the sheets again, then turned and left just as suddenly as he'd entered.

Perhaps she had taken the cleaning and organizing too far. It was just that she was used to taking charge of her family, of keeping everyone and everything in order. She was by nature a perfectionist . . . although she'd clearly failed in being perfect enough, especially for David.

A sting pricked her heart—the sting of his rejection. It wasn't as strong as it used to be, but sometimes it still hurt and was the reminder that she was inadequate and was better off remaining a spinster.

Seven

"It's a surprise." Augusta's voice rang out cheerfully in the balmy afternoon as she dragged Sage through the overgrown gardens behind Fairview.

Sage tripped over a loose stone in the path but held on tightly to Augusta's hand. Sage wasn't familiar with how formal gardens were typically arranged, but on the few occasions she'd been in the spacious yard, she'd liked the natural feel to it, as if she were stepping into the wilderness of the island instead of a neat and artfully arranged yard like the Firths' next door.

Earlier in the day, Augusta had paid a visit to Mrs. Firth and her daughters. Although Mr. and Mrs. Firth were invited to the dinner party which was now only three days away, Augusta had naturally accepted the invitation to have tea and get to know the ladies of the Firth family before the event.

When Augusta had arrived home, Sage had been helping Gustave in the kitchen prepare tiny cakes to serve for dessert. She'd anticipated accompanying Augusta to the last dress fitting for her party gown and hadn't expected to be led out into the backyard.

After spending all of yesterday afternoon organizing Jackson's study, Sage still had several lists of all the things needing to be done before the dinner. But she couldn't deny Augusta a *surprise*, especially when she seemed so excited about it.

Besides, Sage wouldn't complain about taking a break from the constant attempt to avoid seeing Jackson. Since the incident in his study, she'd felt as if he'd been watching her more carefully.

Maybe she was being overly suspicious, but on two different occasions, he'd seemed to seek her out. The first time had been last evening after dinner when she'd been polishing the goblets for Gustave and putting them away. Jackson had paused in the entryway of the butler's pantry, opened his mouth as if to say something, then had moved on. This morning, she'd been ironing several of his shirts in the laundry room when he'd again passed by.

Both appearances had been unusual since Jackson rarely ventured away from his work, much less into the menial areas of the house.

Whatever the case, she'd felt him watching her more in one day than she had during the previous days of her visit combined. Maybe after their argument yesterday, she'd upset him more than she'd realized. Maybe now he was scrutinizing her and looking for her to fail in her duties in order to bring the complaints to his sister.

Thankfully, Augusta wasn't swayed by Jackson's moodiness. In fact, she rarely seemed bothered by anything her brother did. Attired in a lavender gown with a skirt that swayed like a bell, Augusta's dark hair was combed back as severely as usual beneath her matching lavender bonnet. Although Augusta wasn't fair and youthful, Sage had grown to appreciate the subtle beauty the woman displayed, especially in the lovely arched angles of her face.

Sage ducked under a branch and squeezed past a hedge of shrubs that were aflame with the changing leaves of autumn now that September had passed. With October well underway, the foliage had become more vibrant, bathing the landscape with an array of crimson and gold and burnt orange.

She breathed in the chilly air filled with a freshness she would never grow tired of—a smoky pine scent that was clean and wild and so opposite anything she'd ever experienced in Manchester.

As Augusta led her through the overgrown gardens, they found themselves at the back end of the property of both houses. While Fairview's yard wasn't yet enclosed, the Firths' home was much tidier with a tall wrought iron fence with fleur-de-lis points that ran the length of the boundary.

A young woman stood just inside an arched gate in the shadows of a low-hanging maple, and at their approach, she turned toward them. For a half a second, Sage's heart stopped beating. Was this Willow?

As the young woman ducked out from underneath the tree and then opened the gate, a slant of sunlight highlighted pale blond hair that was plaited in a long braid, not the reddish blond that Willow and Sage shared.

Considering the black maid's uniform, white apron, and lacy cap, Sage guessed this pretty young woman worked for the Firths. As she exited the Firths' yard and rounded the fence into the overgrown grass and shrubs of Fairview, her eyes gleamed with excitement.

But why?

"Sage?" the woman asked as she swept her gaze over Sage.

Who was this woman? Sage turned toward Augusta for the answer.

Within the shadows of her lavender bonnet, Augusta was beaming now too. "This is Juliet Dash, one of the Firths' maids."

Before Sage could curtsy or offer a handshake or even say hello, the newcomer was flinging herself upon Sage, wrapping her into a hug, and squeezing her. "Holy Moses, I can't believe it's you."

Sage wasn't sure whether to return the embrace or push the

woman away. Instead, she patted Juliet's back, then tugged herself free. "I'm sorry. Do I know you?"

Juliet laughed, her eyes crinkling with mischief. "Of course not. But I know so much about you, I'd almost count you a sister if I'd had one."

Sage's mind began to spin with the implications of what Juliet was saying, and anticipation now bubbled inside her. "You know Willow."

Juliet nodded. "We shared a cabin on the *Robert Lowe* during the voyage here to the colony and became fast friends."

Augusta must have discovered Juliet's connection with Willow during the tea a short while ago and made arrangements with Juliet—probably secretly—to meet at the back gate.

Juliet was still smiling and taking in Sage, as if she couldn't quite believe what she was seeing. "You'll never guess, not in a hundred thousand years, what happened to Willow."

Was that a note of sarcasm in Juliet's tone? Or was she being serious?

"She got married," Juliet continued.

"That's wonderful." Willow had come on a bride ship, so it was only natural she would have found a husband after being in the area for nine months. Sage knew she ought to be happy for her sister. Why then did the news only make her feel the pain of losing David all over again?

"I'm sure you'll also never guess who the lucky fellow is."

"I'm sure I won't."

Juliet's smile turned into a smirk.

Was Juliet referring to Caleb, Willow's long-time best friend, the man she'd sworn she would never marry because they were ever and only friends? Caleb had also been adamant that he would never get married. "It has to be Caleb."

Juliet nodded.

Oh dear. What had changed Willow's mind about marrying Caleb? And his about her?

The last night that Sage had spent with Willow on their pallets in the chilled dampness of their flat, Sage had encouraged her sister to use the opportunity to break free of Caleb and learn to be independent.

That obviously hadn't happened. In fact, it would appear the complete opposite had occurred.

"She and Caleb got married back in the spring." Juliet seemed to sense the questions that Sage hadn't yet voiced. "Never saw anyone as much in love as the two of them."

"That's lovely to hear." The words sounded forced, certainly not congratulatory or excited that Willow had finally found love, even if it was with Caleb.

"Theirs is a long story." At a call from somewhere in the Firths' yard, Juliet glanced toward the upper stories of the house which rose above the gardens. She was probably being summoned back to her work. "I'll have to let them tell you their tale when you see them."

Did that mean Willow wasn't working in service as a domestic after all? "Where are they living?"

At another distant call, this one more demanding, Juliet backed up a step and began to make her way to the gate. "They have a farm on Salt Spring Island."

A farm? On an island? "So she's not in Victoria?"

"No, the island is north of Victoria and north of Saanich Peninsula. Not too far if you go by steamboat."

"Lovely," Augusta interjected. "Sage and I shall go together and make a day of it, sightseeing along the way. Perhaps on Saturday once the dinner party is behind us."

"Of course." Sage tried to feel grateful to Augusta for her generosity, but she didn't want to wait to see Willow, and she certainly didn't want just infrequent visits by steamboat. But after more than a year of being apart from Willow, what were a few more days?

Juliet entered back through the gate, latched it, and then began to stride away with a wave. "When you see her, tell her hello from me. And let her know I'm still happily working for the Firths."

"I will."

After Juliet disappeared through the Firths' elaborate garden, Sage followed Augusta back inside. She was grateful to the dear woman for finally locating someone who could give her information about Willow. Even so, Sage found herself feeling more homesick than ever for her family, knowing Willow was so close and yet still so far away.

When Augusta insisted on going to her dress fitting alone, Sage didn't protest. Instead, she'd assured Augusta she would be busy with her lists of chores, which included tidying the dining room.

Thankfully, Augusta had already convinced Jackson to relocate his current bridge model to his study. Now that the study was organized, they'd discovered there was room for a table, especially after they'd moved out two wingback chairs.

After transferring the model, Jackson had left behind a mess of fragments and glue and nails and other items that Sage couldn't name. As usual, though, she organized everything, sorting the pieces by size and kind into small bowls.

When she finished, she hesitated outside the closed door of his study with the tray of bowls. Should she just place it on the hallway floor?

Maybe she ought to knock and take the opportunity to apologize. After all, she had overstepped the boundaries yesterday, and she understood his frustration at her for walking into his private sanctuary and having it completely overhauled by a stranger.

Not only had she rearranged everything, but she'd also riffled through his personal possessions as if they were common items that had no meaning. She'd taken the liberty of moving and categorizing without any of his input. And she'd acted as if she knew better than he did how to do his work.

Yes, she needed to ask for his forgiveness. But their interactions had already been strained from the start, and now the strain would be even worse. If she brought it up, would she only make things more awkward?

Regardless, she would feel better if she made peace with him. She didn't know if peace was truly possible with a man like Jackson, but she had to at least try.

Without giving herself a chance to back away, she knocked on his door.

No one answered.

She stood motionless and could hear him moving around, muttering to himself.

She knocked again.

Long seconds ticked past, and he still didn't respond.

Was he ignoring her? If so, she wasn't surprised.

She expelled an exasperated breath then lowered the tray to the floor. It was probably for the best. She'd already been incorrigible once and didn't want to put herself in another situation where she might react poorly.

She began to move away. As she did so, the door swung open, and Jackson's imposing presence filled the doorway, his tall frame and unruly hair nearly touching the top of the doorframe.

With furrowed brows, his gaze snagged on her. "Wait."

She halted.

He was even more disheveled than usual, wearing the same garments from the previous day, his face more haggard, and the dark circles under his eyes more prominent. His eyes had a tortured wildness, as if he were running from demons he couldn't escape.

The frustration she'd felt yesterday was gone, and remorse rushed in at full force. What had she been thinking to scold this man when he was already suffering and didn't need her censure?

"I'm sorry—" She offered the words at the same time that he spoke the exact same thing.

They both stopped abruptly and stood silently.

He reached up a hand and rubbed at the back of his neck, his shoulders slumping as he did so. "I'm the one who should be apologizing, not you."

"No," she hurried, needing to apologize before he cut her off. "I shouldn't have taken so many liberties with your things—"

"It's amazing." The words came out earnestly, and the steel in his eyes softened.

What did this mean? That he wasn't angry with her anymore?

"Your organizational skills . . . the room . . . the order . . ." He fumbled over his words and then blew out a breath. "Thank you. I didn't realize how helpful it would be."

She exhaled too. "Really?"

He nodded eagerly toward his desk, which was a clutter of papers again. "Yes, seeing everything in order made me realize several steps that I needed to add, and I spent all of last night drawing up those missing pieces."

"I'm relieved. Even so, I apologize for barging in and taking charge the way I did. I should have asked you—"

"I would have said no, and then I wouldn't have known what I was missing." His voice was quiet . . . and normal, giving her a glimpse of the kindly gentleman Augusta had originally described to her.

He seemed to be studying her face, almost as though he were seeing her for the first time—truly seeing her as a person and not just as Augusta's maidservant.

She pushed forward with the rest of what she knew she needed to say. "I also apologize for being rude to you. I said things I shouldn't have."

"You only said what was true and what I needed to hear."

"No. I was unkind and could have spoken much more graciously—"

"I'm completely to blame for everything. I was the one who was unkind and should have been much more gracious."

She wouldn't argue with him on that score. He should have been nicer. "That doesn't excuse my behavior."

"You were—are—a saint compared to me."

That was the trouble. As hard as she'd always tried to be a saint, she had failed to be one.

He took a step backward and cocked his head toward his desk. "I have no right to ask you this, not after the way I've treated you, but I would be greatly obliged if you would show me how I might organize the new drawings."

She hesitated. She'd said what she needed to and ought to go on her way.

"I promise I will keep the *beast* caged." His emphasis on the word *beast* didn't seem to contain any anger or vengeance. Instead, his eyes held a warm plea, one that seemed to be asking her for a second chance.

"I'm sorry. I shouldn't have called you that."

"It's true. I have been beastly and deserve the censure." He ran his fingers through his unruly hair. "So what do you say? Will you lend me your keen insights again?"

How could she refuse him? Not when his expression was filled with hope and sincerity.

"I don't know what more I can do. But I can at least take a look at what's on your desk."

He stepped back even farther and waved her ahead of him into the study. "Thank you, Miss Rhodes."

As she made her way to his desk, a tiny thrill whispered through her. He liked her organizational skills, asked for her help, thought she had something valuable to add to his work. Nothing like that had ever happened to her before.

She positioned herself in front of the diagrams once again strewn about in disorder. "I will likely be able to help you better if I know what I'm looking at. Will you explain everything to me?"

He moved to stand beside her. "Really?" His voice held surprise.

"Yes. Really."

He hesitated only a moment before telling her about the various parts of the bridge, and even though most of the details were beyond her comprehension, she grasped enough to have a basic understanding of what he was doing.

When they finished organizing the diagrams again, he pulled out another stack of papers from one of his drawers—a stack she hadn't seen yesterday—and they started going through those next.

This time he didn't need any prodding to explain the original designs for the suspension bridge, his first drafts. Together they put them into a progression from the first until the last, stopping along the way to discuss the differences and changes.

"What are you two doing?" The question from the doorway interrupted Sage's thoughts as she shifted the papers on Jackson's desk.

She paused to find Augusta entering the study, her eyes wide as she took in Sage sitting in Jackson's chair while Jackson stood beside her.

Sage looked down in surprise. When had she ended up in his chair?

She glanced to the window to find that the afternoon had passed into evening. How long had she been in Jackson's study?

It felt like it had only been minutes. But maybe it had turned into hours.

Augusta's gaze shifted between her and Jackson several times. She didn't appear angry that Sage had neglected her duties. Instead, her eyes held only curiosity. "Gustave said that the two of you were shouting at each other yesterday. So I didn't expect to find you working together today."

Sage quickly pushed back from the desk and stood. "I was helping Mr. Lennox organize his study."

"I asked for her help," Jackson cut in.

"Not to worry, ma'am." Sage sidled past Jackson and started toward Augusta. "I finished the dining room."

"I'm not worried." Augusta was still studying the two of them as though trying to make sense of finding them together. Sage didn't understand it either. What had come over her to linger so long?

She smoothed her hands down her skirt self-consciously. "I shall work later tonight if necessary—"

"If Miss Rhodes is behind in her duties," Jackson said gruffly, "then I'm to blame. You'll not punish her on my account."

"I'm not upset." Augusta's tone was as polite as always. But was she upset? "There's no one to blame. All is well."

Sage bustled past her into the hallway. "I'll help you get dressed for the evening meal, ma'am."

Augusta didn't move. When she finally pivoted, she took Sage in again, this time from the top of her head down to her toes. "Sage is a beautiful woman, would not you agree, Jackson?"

Eight

AUGUSTA WAS SHREWD. SHE HADN'T asked him about Sage's beauty without having an ulterior motive.

As Augusta's question stretched out unanswered, Sage lowered her head, but not before Jackson caught sight of the mortification in her expression.

He muttered a rebuke to himself under his breath. He was making the situation awkward by not answering, likely making her believe that he didn't think she was beautiful, which wasn't the truth. But the truth wasn't any of Augusta's business.

He spoke the next best thing that came to mind. "Sage is a very capable and sturdy woman." Once the words were out, he realized he sounded like he was lauding the capabilities of a new mare. "What I mean is that Sage—Miss Rhodes—is intelligent and very organized and has been a great help to me this afternoon."

One of Augusta's narrow brows rose into a look upon him that said he'd never get away with hiding anything from her.

"Would you like me to draw a bath, Miss Lennox?" Sage asked quietly. "At the very least, I can lay out your evening gown."

"That would be fine." Augusta didn't take her gaze from Jackson. "Thank you, Miss Rhodes. I shall be up shortly."

Sage hurried away through the hallway and up the stairs. As soon as her footsteps faded, Augusta faced him with a frown. "Please do not toy with Sage."

Toy with Sage? A rumble of anger formed low in Jackson's gut. "You think so little of me that you believe I'm capable of toying with your lady's maid?"

"I have seen the way you look at her." Augusta spoke as frankly as always. "The way you were looking at her just now."

"I'll not deny that she is fine-looking." She was more than fine. Every time he saw her, either in passing or even from a distance, he noticed her beauty. It was difficult not to, not when everything about her was so stunning—the unique reddish-blond shade of her hair, the wide blue of her eyes, the full shape of her lips, the slender length of her neck, the lushness of her curves.

"She's exquisite, and you know it." Augusta spoke in a low, warning tone. "And I shan't have you taking advantage of her, Jackson."

The anger thundered more loudly inside him. "I have never taken advantage of a woman, and I do not plan to start with Miss Rhodes."

Augusta's lips pinched together severely for a moment. "You do like her."

"She was helpful today. That's all."

"According to Gustave, she yelled back at you yesterday. What other woman has ever done that?"

None. Not even Augusta, even though he'd probably deserved her yelling at him plenty of times. "And what's your point exactly?"

"She has the backbone to stand up to you, and you like it."

Maybe he did like it. He certainly had warranted Sage's wrath because he had behaved like a child throwing a tantrum—one of her allegations. And he'd also behaved like a shaggy beast—another of her very true accusations.

"Not only do you like her backbone, but you like *her*." Augusta was clearly determined to make him admit to liking Sage. "The more you get to know her and see all her wonderful characteristics the way I do, the harder it will be for you to resist her."

"I'm not interested in women right now." He was focused on fixing the bridge. That's why he'd called off his engagement to Meredith—or at least one of the reasons. "So please, let us drop the matter."

"Not before you give me your word that you will not do anything untoward and will treat Miss Rhodes with the utmost of respect at all times, even when I'm gone."

Gone? Augusta made it sound as though she was going on a trip and leaving Sage behind. Or maybe she was merely referring to times like today when she was absent and the two of them were alone together at the house.

"Vow to me, Jackson."

"Vow what?"

"Vow to me that you will never take advantage of her."

"I'll never take advantage of her." He might not have gotten along well with his father, but he did respect his father's faithfulness and loyalty to his marriage vows and the way he'd always set a good example in treating women respectfully, even the serving staff.

"Thank you." Augusta's gaze softened. "I like Sage a great deal. She's incredibly smart and sensitive and caring and giving. I just don't want her to get hurt."

"I won't hurt her."

"I shall hold you to that, brother." This time she gave him a tender smile.

"You have nothing to worry about."

"Thank you."

After Augusta headed upstairs, Jackson pivoted and faced his desk, now immaculate and organized. Immediately his thoughts filled with the vision of Sage as she'd looked sitting there bent over his drawings, listening to him with rapt attention as he'd rambled on and on.

She'd been genuinely interested in what he was saying and had asked him astute questions in return. Augusta was right in saying she was incredibly smart—smarter and more interesting than any woman he'd ever talked to before. Most women didn't care about his engineering or his work. Admittedly, it was technical and complicated and probably dull to most people. But Sage had seemed to want to understand it.

In addition, she'd been humble enough to come to him today and apologize even though he'd been the one who needed to apologize to her. He'd been working up the courage to talk to her all day, had tried on a couple of occasions, had known he needed to tell her he was sorry for being such an oaf. Because it had taken him all of five minutes after she'd stormed out of his study yesterday for him to realize how proficient and organized she truly was and what a benefit that would be.

Even though he'd apologized to her today, his words had been weak and insufficient. He'd have to try again, and this time make sure he was clearer. If he could find a way to show her he was sorry, that would be even better.

The next morning, Jackson's stomach pinched nervously as he squinted through the darkness of his bedchamber at his outline in the dresser mirror and attempted to straighten his cravat.

The heavy draperies were closed to block out the sunshine, just the way he preferred so that he didn't have to view himself. First of all, he didn't want to waste time worrying about his appearance. Secondly, he loathed seeing the man he'd become.

Why, then, this morning was he straining so hard to take in his image through the darkness? Because he wanted to appear his best when he located Sage and apologized to her again?

He snorted and backed away from the mirror. That was ridiculous. He didn't give a dash how he looked around Sage. Not in the least. She'd already made it clear that she saw him as a shaggy beast.

He combed his fingers through his hair, the strands wiry and wild and in much need of a haircut. Then he brushed his fingers over his beard, the hair coarse and long and requiring a trim, or even a shave altogether. In the past, he'd always kept his face cleanly shaven the way most gentlemen of his rank did. Maybe it was time to return to his daily shaving and grooming.

With one of the draperies in reach, he yanked it open, letting light spill into his chamber. Then he faced the mirror again and forced himself to stare at his reflection.

An overgrown moose peered back. He looked worse than he'd realized. Today it wouldn't matter how well he tied his cravat or what color suit he wore. None of that would diminish the fact that he resembled a wild creature who belonged more in the mountains than in an elegant home like his.

He scowled at his reflection. Then he spun away, stalked across his room, and threw open his chamber door.

Passing through the hallway, Augusta paused with Sage halting directly behind her. Both of them startled, as if they hadn't expected to see him in the doorway. He supposed that was only natural since he hadn't spent much time in his chamber in the weeks they'd been visiting Fairview.

"Good morning, Jackson." Augusta recovered quickly and smiled at him tersely. She reached for his arm, tucked her hand into the crook of his elbow, then guided him down the hallway toward the stairs. "Will you join me for breakfast?"

The two women were attired in lovely day gowns, their hair perfectly fashioned, ready for the morning ahead. Somehow today, at the sight of them together, he felt even more like a moose, or perhaps a buffalo.

He could hear Sage's quiet footsteps behind them, and he wanted to stop and greet her and allow himself a longer view than the brief one he'd taken in passing. But after Augusta's warning yesterday about treating Sage with respect and not taking advantage of her, he didn't want to give his sister any reason to call into question his motives.

As he took his place at the table in the breakfast room, he couldn't keep from hoping Sage would stay. But she disappeared before he could manage even a nod, leaving him alone with Augusta to eat the simple fare of poached eggs, fruit, and oatcakes.

After they finished, he retired to his study. For a reason he couldn't explain, he left his door open, so that when she passed by later with his sister, he halted in sketching his newest diagram and listened to their conversation about how Augusta would be fine on her errands without a companion. Augusta was rattling off a list of things that yet needed to be done before the upcoming dinner party the following evening.

"Are you sure you don't want me to accompany you?" Sage's voice held a note of concern. "I can assist you this morning and work on the list for the party this afternoon."

"No, no." Augusta spoke as firmly as always. "I shall be just fine on my own. My errands will only bore you."

Augusta had hired a driver to take her around town but was looking for a permanent coachman. She'd mentioned the previous evening that she was also still attempting to hire another maidservant.

Maybe he ought to get involved and locate a Native woman. He'd built relationships amongst the Songhee who had been helpful to him during his explorations of the colony during his first years here. Of course the smallpox epidemic of the past year had brought death to many Natives, and he didn't know if his acquaintances had survived. If so, he suspected at least one of the wives or daughters would appreciate an opportunity to work in his house.

As it was, Sage shouldn't have to do so much. In fact, as Augusta's lady's maid, she wasn't supposed to be carrying the bulk of the housework and should be free to focus solely on Augusta.

With consternation rising inside, Jackson pushed back from his desk.

"Don't worry about me," Augusta insisted from near the front door. "The men aren't interested in me the way they are in you."

"That's not true," Sage chided softly, probably assisting Augusta into her coat and bonnet.

Men interested in Sage? Of course all the fellows in town were ogling her just the way he'd predicted. Who wouldn't notice her? Even *he* was interested in her, although he had no plans to act upon that interest and not just because he'd vowed to Augusta that he wouldn't.

Moreover, Sage wasn't the type of woman he would consider, at least for a serious marriage relationship. Men of his social standing didn't marry the hired help. They might have dalliances with maidservants, but that's as far as such relationships ever went.

Jackson wasn't the dallying type. Even if he were, he'd vowed to his sister he wouldn't have a dalliance with Sage. Maybe he hadn't said so in those exact words. But he knew as well as Augusta that's what they'd been talking about.

"You're a fine catch." Sage spoke earnestly. "And the men would call on you if you spared them a moment of your time."

Augusta huffed. "I don't have time to spare."

"You have to make the time."

He hadn't thought to ask Augusta about her relationship history, and she hadn't spoken of any man in particular. But surely a woman like her from a prestigious family and with an extremely large dowry would have attracted many men. So at thirty-one why wasn't she yet wed?

Yes, Augusta had been away from London for long months at a time with her traveling. But that wouldn't stop Mother and Father from finding a suitable man for her to settle down with. Most likely, they had tried, but Augusta had refused their efforts for one reason or another.

"Let's not focus on me," Augusta said. "Let's focus on you instead."

"I already told you. I've decided to become a spinster."

A spinster? Jackson couldn't hold back a scoffing sound.

The two women grew suddenly silent.

He knew he should feel remorseful for eavesdropping, but he felt only irritation at himself for getting caught.

"Nonsense." Augusta spoke again. "You'll never be a spinster. You're much too young and pretty and kind. You'll make a lucky man a wonderful wife, and you'll be a wonderful mother."

"No, I've already decided I won't get married." Sage's tone was kind, but her voice contained a note of determination that was oddly jarring.

"Not every man is like David." Augusta's voice dropped to a whisper.

If she thought by whispering he wouldn't be able to hear, then she was wrong. And if she thought he'd ceased eavesdropping, she was wrong about that too. This conversation about Sage was much too important to ignore.

Who was David, and what had he done? Sage had obviously conversed with Augusta about her past. Did he dare ask Augusta about it the next time they shared a meal together, or would it be impolite of him to pry into Sage's private life?

"Thank you, Augusta," Sage whispered back. "But I'm happy as your lady's maid, and I have no wish to do anything else."

"You will eventually when the right man comes along."

The front door opened, and moments later, Augusta stepped outside, and the door closed behind her. Sage seemed to linger by the door before her footsteps padded quietly down the hallway, drawing closer.

Jackson bolted up from his chair and frantically eyed his study. Should he sit back down and pretend to be busy? He certainly couldn't stand frozen in place. If she glanced inside, she would find him gaping like an idiot and doing nothing.

Before he could make up his mind over what to do, she was passing by. She didn't spare a glance his way but continued down the hallway as if she didn't realize he was there.

A strange desperation seized him. He couldn't let her go past without talking to her. He had to at least use the opportunity to apologize again for his bad behavior from the previous day.

"Miss Rhodes?" he called out.

Her footsteps came to a halt.

He hastened to the doorway of his study and found that she'd paused near the servants' hallway that led to the rooms at the back of the house.

"Yes, Mr. Lennox?" She had one hand on the door handle, obviously in a hurry to get to work. Or maybe she was in a hurry to get away from him.

Now that he'd initiated contact with her, what should he say?

Awkward silence settled between them. He tugged at his cravat which suddenly felt like it was strangling him. Without any windows, the back area of the hallway was shadowed, and he couldn't see her expression. But if he'd been able to, he expected that he'd find aversion. After all, he'd been disgusted seeing himself.

"Is there something I can help you with, Mr. Lennox?" She spoke hesitantly, as if she was afraid he might lash out at her for saying the wrong thing.

"Yes, I do need help." As soon as he spoke the words, he wanted to slap a hand to his forehead. What was he doing? Making up a reason to be near her?

She released her hold on the door handle and took a step back his way. "After how much I imposed upon you already?"

"You did not impose. Quite the opposite."

"I'm relieved you see it that way."

His mind scrambled to come up with any help he might need. But what? After she'd already organized everything, what was left? As oblivious as he was most of the time, he probably wouldn't be able to spot a need even if it walked up to him and slapped him in the face.

With an exasperated breath, he scrubbed a hand down his shaggy beard. What could he possibly have her do?

Why did he need her to do anything? He could just ask for her forgiveness and let her be on her way. That would be the logical and sound thing to do. On the other hand, the desire to spend time with her was beginning to overshadow the need to do anything else today.

"I would be happy to help again, Mr. Lennox." Thankfully her tone was genuine.

He slid his hands into his overgrown hair and tried to make himself think of something. But with her pretty blue eyes upon him waiting so expectantly, he couldn't formulate any ideas.

Not only wasn't he proficient in carrying on conversations with most people, but he'd been especially inept in talking with the fairer sex.

He jabbed his fingers deeper into his hair. "My hair."

One of her eyebrows quirked. "Your hair?"

"Do you know how to cut hair?" The moment the question was out, he knew he needed to retract it. "No, no. I shouldn't have asked. Forgive me. It's ludicrous—"

"Yes, actually. I can cut hair."

He shook his head. What had he been thinking to ask her to

do such a task? That was the trouble—he hadn't been thinking. Even though he could solve the world's most difficult mathematical equations, sometimes he felt like his brain couldn't function well with normal, everyday things.

"I always cut my dad's hair, and my sisters.'"

"I cannot subject you to mine. It is in a terrible state—"

"I don't mind." She took a hesitant step toward him.

"Please forget I even mentioned it."

She was silent a beat. "You would make Augusta very happy if you shaved and got a haircut before the dinner party tomorrow evening."

"I would?" Augusta had suggested it on a couple of occasions, but he hadn't known his doing so would actually make her happy.

"She truly cares about you the way you are," Sage said quickly as though to reassure him. "But she has mentioned how much a haircut and shave would please her."

He didn't need reassurance of Augusta's love. He knew his older sister loved him and always would, no matter how he looked or behaved. Yet, if he could do this one little thing to please her, then maybe he ought to do it.

"Very well," he said before he could find an excuse. "Let us proceed with a haircut."

Nine

S HE WAS DOING THIS FOR AUGUSTA.
Sage repeated the words silently as she followed Jackson outside into the overgrown backyard. She had scissors and a comb along with his shaving kit while he carried a chair from the breakfast room and a basin of warm water.

Long, dry grass crunched beneath her feet, and the morning sunshine bathed her head. She drew in the fresh air that she was growing to love and tried to calm her racing pulse.

Jackson paused only a dozen steps from the back porch. "Where would you like me to place the chair?"

"How about under the shade of the maple?" She nodded at the closest tree at the center of the yard. Some of the golden leaves had already fallen, but most were rustling gently in the breeze.

Jackson placed the basin in the grass, situated the chair, then stood back from it, as if he were to touch it again, he might get bit.

For as nervous as she was, the same sense of urgency as before prodded her. She needed to give him the haircut right away before he changed his mind, ran off, and barricaded himself in his study.

From the hesitancy he'd had all along, she suspected his decision had been rash, and that he'd regretted it from the second he'd uttered it.

Regardless of how either of them felt, she was determined to see the deed done. For Augusta's sake.

"Go ahead and sit." She placed her items on the grass behind the chair.

He stared at the chair without a sign that he'd heard her.

She rounded the chair toward him, grasped his arm, and gently guided him to the chair. Then she pressed against his shoulder until he lowered himself. When he was finally seated, he remained stiff and unmoving.

"I promise this won't take long." She draped a towel around his shoulders to protect his clothing from the hair.

He remained silent.

Maybe she needed to distract him, get him conversing about something he loved. Since he'd been talkative when he'd discussed constructing bridges, perhaps he'd enjoy sharing about his designing and building of his house.

The back side of the fairy-castle-like house was every bit as elaborate and beautiful as the front with large windows, elaborate trim, and tasteful shades of blue. "You have a lovely home. Augusta mentioned that you came up with the design yourself."

"I did."

"What made you choose this particular style? Is it similar to your childhood home?"

"Oh no. This is completely different."

"How so?"

Thankfully, her questions seemed to put him at ease, and he began to share all the details that had gone into designing the house. As he talked, she set to work cutting his hair into the most fashionable style that she'd seen during the ship voyage as well as her time so far in Victoria—a side part with the hair combed back from the face.

Long dark locks fell into the grass, until at last she had his hair short enough to shape neatly and trim evenly. All the while she worked, he talked and seemed oblivious to what she was doing. When she finished and came around to the front with the bowl of lathered soap and the razor blade, he finally halted.

She cocked her head and studied him. He no longer looked quite so overgrown, but the dark facial hair was overbearing and needed to go.

Without waiting for his permission, she dipped her fingers into the soap mixture and touched it to his jaw.

He flinched.

"You were telling me about the turrets." She gave a nod to the closest one. "What purpose do they serve? The rooms at the top seem too small to be bedrooms or even sitting rooms."

"I see what you're doing here." He'd stiffened again, his back straight and his shoulders rigid against the chair.

"You did want a shave too, didn't you?" She smoothed more of the soap mixture over his face.

"Do I have a choice?"

She shifted the razor blade to his skin and made the first long rake, removing the hair and leaving stubble in its place. "Not really." She'd all but made it impossible for him to leave now, not unless he wanted a stripe in his beard.

He was silent as she scraped again, the soothing sound reminding her of her dad and the many years she'd watched him shave in the small mirror that he perched on the high window ledge of their flat.

"I know what you're doing," he repeated. "You got me talking so that I wouldn't notice you cutting my hair."

"It worked, didn't it?"

He reached up a hand and tentatively touched his head. "Yes, it most certainly did work."

"Tell me more about the turrets," she persisted. "What do you envision for them? Why did you create them?"

He didn't respond this time. Instead, his gray-blue eyes shifted to her face. "I've been rattling all about myself. Tell me more about you."

"What would you like to know?"

"Who is David?"

Her heart thudded a painful beat at the mention of his name, the same way it had when Augusta had spoken his name earlier. "You may ask me anything else besides that."

"So he's the reason you came to the colony?" He continued as if he hadn't heard her. "Because you wanted to leave him behind?"

She hesitated. Should she answer? She could surely do so without having to talk about David. "I came because I hope to earn enough to send for Dad and my sisters, so that they can come live here too." Although the ache for them had dulled just a little, she still thought of them and prayed for them every day and hoped they were surviving without her there to oversee them.

"Not your mother?" His question was hesitant.

Sage swallowed the heartache that came whenever she thought about her mum passing. "No, she died last winter."

"I'm sorry."

"She would be happy I made it."

For a short while, Jackson surprised her by asking more about her family, her sisters, her parents, and what her life had been like in Manchester. As she shaved, she told him about her years working in the mill, how she'd toiled long hours to help support her family, and that when the mills had closed, Willow had been the first of her family to immigrate to Vancouver Island.

"So you hope the rest of your family will be able to come soon?"

"Yes, I hope it won't be too long."

His gaze had been riveted to her face for most of the shave, and now as she allowed herself to meet his gaze.

The compassion in his eyes was unexpected.

A lump formed in her throat, and she rapidly shifted her attention back to the blade. His face was narrower without all the hair, a distinguished slender shape. His jaw was more angular than she'd realized, and his chin was strongly chiseled too.

She'd had to lather him twice and was now finishing the final drags to clear away the dark stubble that had remained. Each pull of the razor revealed fine, smooth skin. His lips were now visible, perfectly proportioned and firm, and she imagined he probably had a nice smile, if he ever smiled.

"I'm sorry you had to leave them behind." He spoke softly. "I can tell you miss them and are worried about them."

The sadness within her swelled again. "Once I see Willow, we can work together to make it happen." She only had to wait until Saturday, and she'd finally be reunited with her sister—at least she hoped so.

He stared off into the distance, turning suddenly quiet.

With a final scrape, she removed the last section of stubble. She set the razor blade in the basin of murky water then lifted the towel from his shoulders, shook the hair from it, and used the edge to wipe away the remaining suds on his face.

He sat forward abruptly. "I shall loan you the money for their passage."

A loan? She grew motionless, not sure how to respond.

"Yes, that's what we shall do." His posture radiated sudden determination. "I shall have my solicitor in London purchase their tickets and deliver them to Manchester."

"Thank you. That's a generous offer." She brushed at the remaining hairs on his neck. "But I could never accept the money, not when I don't know when or if I could pay it back."

"You could take as long as you need to do so." His tone held sincerity, as if he really did care about her family's welfare.

She swiped at the fine hairs that littered his shirt collar. "You're kind, Mr. Lennox. But it just wouldn't be right—"

"After all you've done for Augusta . . . and for me since your arrival . . . it's the least I can do."

She paused in her wiping. Should she consider his offer? It would be so wonderful to know that her dad and sisters were on their way, that they would all be together again, and that they could start a new life here.

"Please think about it?"

She stared down at the grass and twisted the tip of her boot. She could at least ponder the option, couldn't she?

"Consider it part of my payment for your willingness to give the shaggy beast a much-needed haircut and shave."

Remorse cut through her, and she lifted her gaze to his again. "Mr. Lennox, please. I called you that out of frustration but did not mean it."

Sadness rimmed his eyes. "I regret I have been so focused on my own problems that I've neglected to think about anyone else."

For the first time since she'd started cutting his hair, she stood back and took in the full effect of her work. As she swept her gaze over him, she drew in a sharp breath. The transformation was incredible.

"What's wrong?" He lifted a hand to his head as though maybe he'd find a bald spot.

"Nothing's wrong."

He had a very nice-looking face—suave, clean-cut, and refined. But taken as a whole, from his neatly trimmed hair, chiseled features, and long, lean body, he was incredibly handsome, especially with such unique gray-blue eyes.

He was the kind of fashionable gentleman who would draw everyone's attention as he strolled down a main thoroughfare. In fact, he was so debonair that she could picture him as a prince walking out of Buckingham Palace to the fanfare of ladies waving and smiling and vying for his attention.

"You don't like how I look now?" A note of worry edged his voice.

"Oh, I do." She tried to dampen her enthusiasm. She didn't want him to know she'd just been thinking about how handsome he was. That would be much too embarrassing. "You cleaned up very nicely, and Augusta will be delighted."

He peered at her as intensely as he always did, as though trying to see more deeply into her mind. But somehow this time, without all the scruff to hide his forceful personality and his attractive face, she felt a little bit like she had at the equator during her voyage there, the sun shining directly upon her, more concentrated and powerful, the heat of the rays making her suddenly too warm, and even weak.

He rubbed a hand over his bare chin. "I suppose I look like a different person entirely."

"Very different, yes." She needed to look away from him, but she was too fascinated by his face now that it was visible.

"My face does feel rather strange and bare."

"And cold?"

His lips twitched. Was that the beginning of a smile? What could she say that would bring the smile out completely?

She wasn't naturally witty or humorous. She couldn't banter for the life of her. She was actually too serious most of the time. Why at the moment did she care about any of that? This was Jackson, not a potential suitor.

She needed to clean up the supplies she'd brought out and then start on the list of tasks that still needed to be done before the dinner party.

"Something must be odd," he remarked quietly, "since you're still staring at me."

"No." She tore her gaze from him and stooped to pick up several items from the grass. "I apologize for staring. It was rude of me."

"It's not rude. I like it." The moment he spoke the words, he pushed up from the chair and ducked out from underneath the tree.

He liked that she was staring at him? That was an odd thing for him to say. Regardless, the words put her at ease, and she let her shoulders relax. The least she could do was put him at ease too. "You look grand, dapper even."

The stiffness in his posture fell away, and he seemed almost peaceful. With his back facing her, he tilted his face up and let the sun bathe his skin.

He stood that way for a moment, and even from behind, she couldn't keep from admiring him. He did, indeed, look like another man altogether with the short-clipped hair and clean-shaven face.

Stuffing his hands into his trouser pockets, he shifted around and faced her again. This time, he took her in from her neat chignon to her simple but fashionable blouse and skirt—another outfit that Augusta had given to her.

He'd been able to view her for who she really was all along. He'd even gotten a glimpse of her not-so-perfect side, and he wasn't mad at her. But he'd been hidden and was now just beginning to show who he really was. In some ways it felt as if they were meeting for the first time—at least from her perspective.

As his gaze slid back up her body, the intense heat in his eyes once again warmed her and even sent a strange tremor through her stomach.

He tilted his head to one side as if he were still analyzing her and calculating something about her. "Thank you. You were kind to be willing to aid me so graciously and with something that falls outside your duties."

Her duties. He was right. She was only a lady's maid. How could she forget about that even for a second?

"That's what I'm here for. To help." She curtsied and then resumed picking up the rest of the items she'd brought out. Somehow she needed to put their relationship back into the proper order and do away with the familiarity.

"Yes, I guess that's true." He hesitated then glanced at the house, as if expecting someone to be peering out at them from one of the windows, watching them.

No one was in sight.

Regardless, she hastened to dump the water from the basin, tossed the supplies in it, and then crossed to the servants' entrance that led to the kitchen in the lower level. All the while, she could feel Jackson watching her. And all the while, her body tingled with the realization he was watching her.

When she stepped inside and closed the door behind her, she leaned back against it, pressed a hand to her chest and to her heartbeat that was racing faster than normal. Then she lifted her hand to her cheek which felt hotter than usual.

What was wrong with her? Was she letting Jackson fluster her?

With a firm shake of her head, she started down the dark hallway toward the kitchen. "No," she whispered harshly. Just because he was surprisingly attractive didn't mean she would let him turn her head. Nothing good would come of allowing that to happen.

She didn't want to lose herself over another man. She was content working for Augusta and had already resigned herself to being a spinster.

Besides, as kind and progressive as Augusta was, she wouldn't approve of Sage spending time with Jackson. Even the smallest hint of inappropriate behavior would be grounds for dismissal, and at this point, Sage needed the job too much to do anything that might jeopardize it.

Just because she'd cut Jackson's hair didn't mean anything would change in their relationship. It would go on as it always had, and that's all she had to say on the matter.

Ten

I STILL DON'T KNOW HOW YOU CONVINCED Jackson to get a haircut and shave." Augusta sat stiffly on the stool in front of the dressing table.

Behind her, Sage pressed a sponge with bandoline over Augusta's finished coiffure to hold the elaborate style in place as she prepared for the dinner party. The clear, gummy mixture was scented with orange flower and worked wonders at preventing Augusta's hair from becoming frizzy, as well as holding in the florets woven throughout the arrangement.

The bedchamber was alight with sconces and lanterns, illuminating the gilded mirror and Augusta's reflection. In her new gown of the loveliest pale gold, Augusta shimmered like gold herself.

Sage had never seen the woman so radiant or so happy, so much that her cheeks were flushed and her eyes shining.

"Tell me your secret in getting Jackson to do whatever you want him to." Augusta held up a pearl earring to her ear and then waited for Sage's input.

"I have no secret." Sage shook her head at Augusta's choice and then pointed to the delicate gold flower earrings which were more elegant and matched the gown better.

Augusta placed the pearl back on the fluted crystal dish on the dressing table among an array of additional jewelry she'd brought with her from England. "You most certainly have cast a spell over him."

"There's no spell either, ma'am." Sage could feel that strange warmth starting to flutter low in her stomach—the one that had been creeping out from time to time since the haircut yesterday, especially whenever she saw Jackson, even from a distance.

The warm flutters had turned into steadily crashing waves the few times he'd sought her out and talked to her during the past twenty-four hours. Just this morning, he'd asked her again for some advice in organizing another group of diagrams that he'd unearthed from a closet.

Although she'd been busy ironing linen napkins for the dinner party, she'd wanted to help him and had taken much more time than she should have in his study, talking about the old designs he'd once made.

Throughout it all, she'd tried not to pay attention to how he looked. In fact, she'd even attempted to visualize him as a shaggy beast again so that she wouldn't think about how sharply attractive he was. But invariably, every time she was around him, she couldn't keep from admiring him and everything about his appearance.

Now, as the dinner hour ticked closer, Sage was wavering between dread and desire in seeing him again. But she'd never, ever admit to Augusta that Jackson was the one with the secret in getting her to do whatever he wanted and that Jackson was the one casting a spell over her.

"Well," Augusta said as she picked up the gold earring and began to fasten it. "You've worked a miracle for which I'm grateful."

"You're the one who worked the miracle by coming here and giving him the gentle push he needed to start living again."

Augusta didn't respond as she reached for the second earring. At a soft knock on the door, Augusta paused. "Come in."

The door opened, and Jackson stepped inside, wearing a black formal suit with tailcoat, along with a ruffled white shirt and black tie. With his hair slicked back with pomade and his face still cleanly shaven, he was the picture of the perfect gentleman. No doubt he was the handsomest man in the colony now. The young women in attendance tonight would vie for his attention.

With a stiff, polite posture, he paused in the center of the room where the light seemed to shine directly on him, giving Sage an even better view of his features—the hard lines of his jaw, the angled cheekbones, the smooth chin.

"Good evening, Augusta." He spoke to his sister, but his gaze fell upon Sage. It fell with a magnetism that tugged at her and tore down her resistance—if she had any left. He was studying her face like he'd taken to doing, as if he were exploring uncharted territory.

The attention was growing more intense with every interaction, and Sage didn't quite know what to make of it. What would Augusta say if she realized Jackson was looking at her so often?

Regardless of what Augusta might or might not notice, Sage couldn't keep the warm waves in her stomach from tossing back and forth.

"You look fabulous, Jackson," Augusta said as she peered at her reflection and straightened her earrings.

"Thank you." He darted a glance at Augusta before returning his gaze to Sage. "You do too."

Augusta reached for a crystal perfume bottle, lifted the top, and then dabbed the stopper onto her wrist. "You're all ready for this evening, then?"

"Yes." He stood awkwardly, as if he wanted to say something to Sage, but then he glanced at Augusta. "I have this for you." He held out his hand to reveal a gold bangle. Inlaid with several colorful jade stones, it looked as though it was made of real gold. Maybe it was.

Seeing the gift in the mirror, Augusta drew in a surprised breath and pivoted on her bench. "It's lovely, Jackson."

He crossed to his sister and tenderly slipped the bangle on her outstretched arm. "It's not as lovely as you. But I wanted you to have it as a token of my thanks for all you've done for me these past weeks."

Jackson only stayed a few minutes longer, making small talk to Augusta about the guests who would be coming that evening. Only after he left the chamber did Sage start breathing evenly again.

"Is there something going on between you and Jackson?" Augusta's question was as forthright as always, and even though she spoke it quietly, it seemed to echo in the room.

Sage paused in hanging Augusta's dressing robe back in the wardrobe, and her gaze shot to the chamber door. She prayed Jackson wasn't out in the hallway where he could hear Augusta's bold question.

"You may as well tell me the truth." Augusta was peering at her in the mirror.

"No, there's nothing." The emotion drained from Sage, leaving her blood cold. "I assure you that I would never encourage his affection."

Augusta held her gaze for several moments before nodding. "He vowed to me that he wouldn't toy with you . . . "

"He's not, ma'am." When had Augusta had a conversation with Jackson like that? Why would the two of them discuss her? "He looks at me once in a while. That's all."

"And you look at him."

Sage started to shake her head then stopped. "I'm trying not to."

"Then you're attracted to him?"

"As I said, I am not encouraging anything—"

"Do you like Jackson?"

"As an employer and as your brother." At least that's what she hoped was true. She didn't like him as more, did she?

"You've been good for him." Augusta continued to twirl the new bangle. "His moodiness doesn't frighten you. Neither does his intelligence nor his messiness nor his temper."

"I regret I was presumptuous in my rebuking him."

"No, no, no. You're fine." Augusta waved a dismissive hand then stood. "He needs someone who isn't afraid to confront him and be honest with him."

Sage's racing thoughts came to a halt. That someone could never be her, could it? "You can't really think anything would happen with . . . " She couldn't even associate herself with Jackson. The prospect of being with him was simply too preposterous to consider for even an instant.

"I hope you know me well enough by now to understand that I would never let class stand in the way of love."

Sage opened her mouth to respond but then closed it. What could she possibly say to that? Augusta had shown herself to be fair-minded, always trying to make her feel like a friend and less like a servant.

But the fact was, Sage was a lady's maid. There was no changing the fact.

"I won't tolerate a dalliance," Augusta said firmly. "But a real relationship . . . ?"

No matter how fair Augusta was and no matter what she might be insinuating, Sage had already made up her mind about marriage. "I'm not interested in having a relationship with any fellow."

Not with the shopkeepers who flirted with her whenever she went out with Augusta. Not with any of the miners who swarmed the town and tried to talk to her. Not with fishermen or stevedores or other locals who stared at her when she passed by. Most certainly not with an aristocrat who was from a different world and way of life altogether.

"As I told you, you're not meant to be a spinster." Augusta started toward the door. "So put the idea from your mind."

"You like being a spinster—"

Augusta halted so abruptly that Sage didn't finish her thought, especially because Augusta turned with one of her most severe gazes. "Let me be clear about one thing. I have made peace with being a spinster, but I would gladly give up my independence and traveling to be with a man who loves me."

Was there more to Augusta's story than she'd told Sage? Maybe Augusta had once been in a passionate and loving relationship that hadn't worked out. Maybe she was filled with regrets. Or maybe she'd lost the love of her life and never found anyone else who could compare.

A glint formed in Augusta's eyes. "Perhaps you need to be put into a situation where you can give love a chance to grow."

"What does that mean?" Sage didn't like the glint. It meant Augusta was planning something.

Augusta shrugged, then with a small smile, she turned to go.

"Please, Augusta. Please don't meddle in my love life."

Augusta swung open the door. "What love life?"

Now who was toying with whom? Augusta knew what Sage meant, but clearly she had to spell it out. "I'm not interested in Jackson in that way." Even as Sage said the words, they rang hollow. She couldn't deny the strange reactions she'd been having to him that were now growing in strength. But even if she couldn't deny the reactions, she could put a stop to them, or at least make sure they didn't develop into more.

Augusta stepped into the hallway and began to close the door. She paused with the door only a few inches wide. "Someday you'll thank me."

Before Sage could respond, Augusta closed the door.

Sage stared at the door for at least a full minute, unsure what to think or feel. With her thoughts in a jumble, she finished tidying Augusta's chamber. Then she went down the servants' back stairway to the kitchen to be of assistance to Gustave. Augusta had hired two more men for the evening to help serve the meal. But Gustave still had a great deal to do on his own and Sage offered to help him.

Several hours later, when the meal was over, the dishes washed, and the kitchen in order, Sage retrieved her shawl then made her way to the backyard.

The house was brightly lit, every window aglow, providing enough light for Sage to meander through the trees and shrubs with the cup of coffee and pastry Gustave had given her to show his appreciation.

Lovely strains of piano music filtered through one of the open side windows. The dinner party was still ongoing with drinks and desserts being served, which meant Augusta wouldn't need her for a while longer, not until after the guests left.

For now, Sage could take a rare break. With all that Augusta had spoken earlier, Sage needed a quiet moment to try to make sense of all her thoughts.

She wandered back until she found the smooth-topped boulder where she'd sat at other times over the past few weeks. Sipping the coffee and nibbling on the delicate Danish, she peered up at the clear sky filled with countless stars. Every time she viewed the stars, both awe and sadness filled her—awe that she was able to witness the beauty of the endless array of twinkling lights, but sadness that her sisters and Dad were stuck in Manchester with its dirty, polluted sky.

Tomorrow, though, she'd finally get to see Willow, and together they'd work out a plan for bringing their family to Vancouver Island just as soon as possible. Thankfully, Augusta hadn't forgotten about the plans to travel with Sage to Salt Spring Island the day after the party and had offered to help find a private transport, perhaps a fisherman, to row them there.

Sage smiled. Willow would be surprised to see her. No doubt her sister would shriek, rush at her, and squeeze her until she couldn't breathe. The reunion would be wonderful, even if it would be a little humiliating to share the details of David's rejection.

Sage shivered and took another sip of her coffee. At a clinking somewhere nearby, she halted. A soft grunt was followed by the clank of metal, and it was coming from the Firths' yard just beyond the shrubs.

Was someone in trouble?

She slid off her perch on the stone and tiptoed through the grass until she reached a spot in the shrubs where she could view the neighbors' yard. The darkness kept her from seeing much at first. But after a moment as her eyes adjusted, she glimpsed a young woman in a maid's uniform with a small garden trowel digging in the earth.

Was it Juliet?

As the woman tossed down the trowel, a shaft of moonlight revealed unruly red hair underneath a lacy maid's cap instead of Juliet's blond hair. This woman was also much slighter and waiflike compared to Juliet.

The maid knelt and tugged something out of the earth. She rested the item on her lap, then glanced around the yard, as though making sure no one else was there.

Sage held her breath as the maid's gaze passed over the brush that concealed her. Did she sense Sage's presence?

After peering around one more time, the woman dug into her apron pocket and removed something. In the darkness, Sage couldn't distinguish what it was, but with as furtive as the woman was being, Sage had the sinking feeling that the Firths' maid was up to no good. What if she was stealing from the family? It would be entirely possible, since they were at the dinner party and wouldn't be home to witness one of their maids taking valuables.

The woman opened the box on her lap, deposited something inside, then closed it. She tucked the box back into the earth and began to scoop the dirt over it. She worked quickly, and when finished, she stood and stomped on the spot with her boots to pack the earth down. Then she scattered dried leaves and other brush across the dirt to conceal it. Finally, she stowed the trowel in a corner of a nearby raised flower bed before she hastened away.

Sage stared in the direction the woman had disappeared. She couldn't jump to the worst conclusion and assume the maid was stealing. There was likely some logical explanation for what the woman was doing out in the garden late in the evening when her employers were away. What if she'd merely decided to store her earnings in the corner of the gardens? Or what if she had purchased something in town that she wanted to keep safe?

Yes, Sage needed to return to the house and do the mending. One of Augusta's hems needed shortening. A button on a blouse had come loose. And a silk stocking had a hole in one of the toes.

Expelling a breath, she backed up several steps. The best thing would be to pretend she'd never seen anything. After all, if she hadn't been in the backyard taking a break, she wouldn't have noticed the maid and the questionable activities.

Sage took another step backward, then halted. The problem was, she had seen it all. If she walked away and ignored what she'd just witnessed—a possible theft—then wouldn't she be guilty too?

Perhaps she ought to at least investigate what was inside the box. From what she'd been able to tell, the maid hadn't taken the time to lock it, so Sage could easily dig it up and take a peek at the contents. If there was nothing of any consequence, then she could go on her way with a clean conscience.

She stood silently for a few more moments before creeping along the line of shrubs until she reached the back corner and found the gate that Juliet had used when they'd had their meeting. It was unlocked and squeaked only a little as Sage let herself through.

She located the trowel and within minutes uncovered the box. From the feel of the fine wood, she guessed it was a cedar cigar box like the one that sat in Jackson's chamber. She lifted the lid and squinted to see inside.

There were only a few small items.

She bent closer and touched the largest one. It appeared to be a brooch with a raised cameo and a smooth jeweled edge. The second item was thin and seemed to be a hairpin with a cluster of pearls on one end. The third felt like a perfume button bracelet, similar to one Augusta wore from time to time.

The redheaded maid had definitely stolen the items. There was no other plausible explanation for the stash of jewels. The woman hadn't earned them or bought them. Sage didn't have to even see them clearly to know they were likely valuable heirlooms, except perhaps the perfume button bracelet.

Should she attempt to confront the maid and demand that she return them to the Firths? Even if Sage did that, what would stop the maid from stealing again and hiding more jewels in another place that Sage wouldn't know about?

Maybe she ought to interrupt the party, take the jewels directly to the Firths and let them know how she'd discovered the valuables. They could then confront the redheaded maid and bring about retribution.

Or perhaps she ought to wait until the party was over and then call on the Firths at their house privately in the morning before she left to visit Willow. After all of the planning for the gathering tonight, Augusta deserved to have everything be perfect without news of a theft to dampen the festivities.

Besides, there was no rush. The Firths' maid likely wouldn't return to the spot of her buried treasure tonight. If she did, Sage would make it appear as though no one had been there.

Quickly, she scooped up the three pieces of jewelry and stuffed them into her apron pocket. She put several small rocks inside the cigar box. Then she replaced the container where she'd found it, burying and concealing it just the way the maid had. She even put the trowel back in the corner of the flower bed.

When she was certain everything looked the way she'd found it, she returned to her coffee and Danish on the stone where she'd left them and then made her way back to the house. Her heart was pounding hard and her hands shaking. No matter the trouble she might be bringing upon herself, she had done the right thing. She was sure of it.

Eleven

ONE THING WAS INCREASINGLY CLEAR to Jackson—he was rapidly becoming obsessed with Sage. He'd only been able to sleep for a few hours last night since he'd been too restless from the dinner party and had wanted to be with her, and now as he paced the floor of his study, he still couldn't stop thinking about her, even though he'd tried working to get his mind on to something else.

He'd been enamored by her beauty from the very first time he'd seen her. But the more he'd gotten to know the strong yet compassionate woman she was inside, the more he liked her.

Then she'd given him the haircut and shave. After that, thoughts of her filled every waking and sleeping moment—thoughts of her fingers in his hair, on his neck, and against his scalp. Her fingertips gliding along his jaw, over his cheek, and so near to his lips.

The touching had all been innocent for her, but each stroke and caress had stirred the heat inside him until he'd become a boiling cauldron.

With a growl, he halted at his window, the morning light finally peeking through the draperies.

While the party hadn't been easy for him, the evening had proceeded more smoothly than he'd expected. Augusta had done her best to keep conversations from heading in the direction of his failed bridge project, and he'd only had to answer a couple of queries about his work. He'd done as Augusta had suggested beforehand and kept his answers succinct before changing the subject.

In reality, the dinner had been long overdue. He'd needed to mingle with society and push past the heavy guilt that had been chaining him and making him a prisoner since the accident.

The process of breaking free from all that had happened would take time. But at the very least, he was making progress—even if it was slow—in the right direction.

He might be returning to the land of the sane in some regards, but he'd never be completely like other men. He never had been. He'd always had a tendency toward being obsessed with whatever he was working on. It was just the way his mind worked, and he'd long ago stopped trying to be someone he wasn't.

Being obsessed over his projects, his studying, and his calculations was one thing. Being obsessed over a woman was a different matter. This had never happened to him before, not with Meredith and not with any of the other women who had shown him interest.

Maybe that was precisely the problem. Previously, other women had been the ones to show *him* interest. While he may have been flattered or even nominally attracted at times, he'd never been the one initiating the interest. This time with Sage, the roles were reversed. She remained aloof and professional, while he was turning into an infatuated imbecile.

He paused in his pacing and blew out a breath. If he was truly honest with himself, he suspected that even if Sage had reciprocated the interest, he still would have been an infatuated imbecile. There was just something about her that had snagged him and wouldn't let go, almost as if she'd gotten into his circulatory system and was running through his blood.

The soft patter of footsteps overhead was the sign that she was awake, likely getting ready before she went into Augusta's room.

The two women were leaving this morning to travel to Salt Spring Island to track down Sage's sister. He'd contemplated telling them that he'd take them since he was used to traveling around Vancouver Island, mostly by canoe with the aid of Native guides.

He'd done a great deal of exploring during his early months on the island to help the governor determine the best places for roads and bridges. During the past couple of years, more of his work had taken place up in the Fraser River Valley on the mainland. Nevertheless, he was still familiar with much of the coastline of Vancouver Island.

Even so, he didn't want to impose upon the two women. They would be fine hiring someone to take them to the island. It wasn't far from Victoria, and the ride would be easy, especially on a day with calm weather.

He turned to his desk, stalked around it, and plopped down into the chair. Moreover, he had work to do. Now that he'd started reviewing the older diagrams of his first few suspension bridges, new ideas were formulating, and he needed to capitalize on those ideas.

If only visions of Sage weren't interrupting his thoughts every few seconds . . .

He bent over the sheet he'd already tried studying and recalculating. He stared at it unseeingly, the numbers and equations swimming in his mind without any purpose.

With a frustrated sigh, he shoved back from his desk and stood. What was he going to do about his preoccupation with Sage? Normally, he embraced whatever his mind fixated upon. He let himself run with concepts and spend hours dissecting and discovering every nuance.

But he couldn't do that with her. Not only wouldn't that be

healthy for him, but he'd likely scare her onto the first ship sailing back to England, and he didn't want that to happen. Already, he was dreading the day when she'd walk out of his life—which wouldn't be long, just until Augusta got tired of being in Victoria and decided to move on.

How, then, could he restrain his growing desires for her without driving himself to the brink of insanity?

He sat back down, braced his elbows on his desk, and pressed his palms into his eyes. He had to get over Sage, that's what he had to do. And he had to learn to control his obsessions. That was all there was to it.

At the patter of footsteps—Sage's—coming down the stairway, he sat back up, combed his fingers through his hair, only to remember that it was short and manageable. He quickly attempted to straighten his cravat, then realized he hadn't donned one. He glanced down to find he was still wearing the same shirt from the party last night and that his waistcoat was gone and his trousers wrinkled.

He should have done a better job grooming himself this morning. But most likely Sage would pass by his study and not notice him.

As her footsteps drew nearer, he perched on the edge of his chair. Even though a part of him wanted to pretend he was busy, another part of him simply didn't care and only wanted to get a glimpse of her as she walked by.

When she appeared in his doorway and knocked against the doorframe, he jumped to his feet. He hadn't expected her to stop, and now he didn't quite know what to do with himself.

"Good morning, Mr. Lennox." Her pretty face with its dainty features was made all the prettier by her eyes, which were always so wide and blue and bright.

Today she was wearing a pale green gown which looked as though it had been made to fit her to perfection, showcasing her slender but womanly form. She'd fashioned her hair as she usually did in a chignon, which always seemed to draw his attention to her elegant neck and slender collarbones.

He knew he was being rude by staring so blatantly. He needed to greet her in return. But not only couldn't he think of what to say, he couldn't get his tongue to work.

"Augusta is still abed." Sage's lashes were long and only made her eyes more vibrant. "She would like to speak with you, if you would be so kind as to join her in her chamber."

"You may let her know that I shall be there shortly."

"Thank you." She gave a slight deferential bow of her head before turning and starting back to the stairs.

He waited until he heard her footsteps overhead again before venturing out of his study and heading to Augusta's bedroom. As he tapped lightly and was welcomed in, his gaze went first to Sage standing beside the bed, a worried line creasing her forehead.

"I'm just tired today, that's all," Augusta was saying. "It was a busy week and was busy last night."

"That's understandable." Sage lifted Augusta forward and plumped one of her pillows. "You should rest."

"You're sure you won't mind my not going?"

"As I said, we'll go a different day when you're not so tired."

Jackson's stomach tied in a dozen more knots seeing Sage again, although only five minutes had passed since she'd been in his study. Even in her role as a lady's maid, Sage was entirely too appealing from the way she moved, the way she spoke, and even the way she tilted her head.

Augusta situated herself more comfortably against the mound of pillows, as if she planned to stay a while.

He frowned. He couldn't remember the last time Augusta had ever stayed in bed. Was she ill?

"Jackson," she said as she closed her eyes. "I need you to take Sage to visit her sister today."

"No, Augusta." Sage spoke quietly, firmly. "I can wait."

"Nonsense. You've been looking forward to seeing Willow, and there's no reason Jackson can't make the arrangements and take you there. Right, Jackson?" Augusta cracked open an eye and pinned him with a glare that told him there was only one right answer.

"Of course I can take Sage—Miss Rhodes." He'd already wanted to go and didn't care if Augusta could sense his eagerness at her request.

Sage shook her head at him. "I wouldn't consider imposing on you. I know how busy you are."

Augusta closed her eye. "It would do Jackson good to take a break and get away for a day."

It would? She was probably right, just as she'd been right about everything else so far.

"I really don't mind waiting." Sage's voice was edged with a note of desperation.

Did she not want to go with him? "I'm probably not the best company."

"That's not it at all. You're fine company, and I'm sure I would enjoy a day with you as much as I would with Augusta, but . . . "

"But what?" Augusta persisted, opening her eyes and looking as wide-awake as if she'd already been up half the day.

"But I don't want to bother him," Sage half whispered.

"She won't be a bother, will she?" Augusta's gaze was direct, once again giving him no room to argue—not that he wanted to argue.

The prospect of spending the day with Sage, even just to take her to Salt Spring Island, was an opportunity he didn't plan to forego now that it had been given to him.

"I've been to Salt Spring Island many times during my explorations. I know where the settlements are, and I'm sure I'll be able to locate your sister without too much trouble."

Sage hesitated, her forehead still creased. "That's so kind of you, Mr. Lennox. I don't know what to say."

Augusta leaned back comfortably. "Just say yes."

"But what about you?" Sage tucked Augusta's blanket around her. "What if you're fighting an illness? I'd like to be here to watch over you today."

Augusta snorted. "I shall be fine. I'm just a little tired this morning and will be back to myself in no time at all."

She already seemed back to herself, but Jackson kept that piece of information to himself, not wanting to point it out and have her change her mind. "When would you like to leave?" He directed his question toward Sage.

She glanced at Augusta for an answer.

"You'll leave right away." Augusta's tone said she wouldn't be swayed.

As though recognizing the same, Sage nodded. "You're sure you'll be all right?"

"Of course." Augusta's thin lips curved into a satisfied smile that Jackson didn't understand, but that didn't matter.

He started to cross to the door. "I shall be ready to depart in no more than five minutes."

During the walk to the waterfront, Jackson was as nervous as if he were going courting for the very first time. But Sage wasn't awkward like he was and put him at ease with her casual questions and conversation.

As they reached the main wharf, the bay was already busy for a Saturday morning. A few straggling fishing boats were leaving for the day, and a couple of steamers were also preparing for departure with supplies and men heading up into the mountains for one last trip before winter.

The bellow of the steam whistles, the calls of stevedores, and the squawk of seagulls seemed to greet him and remind him of how much of life he'd missed over the past months. Even the cool October air with the hint of sea and salt reminded him of how much he'd grown to appreciate this new land.

He made quick work of tracking down Tcoosma, one of the Native guides he'd used many times. The short, brown-skinned man with his silvery-black braids and dark eyes never turned down an opportunity to shuttle Jackson around, primarily because Jackson paid him well, not only with the standard Hudson's Bay Company blankets with their red, yellow, and green bands, but also with flour, sugar, and tobacco.

Attired in his customary—albeit well-worn—breechcloth, leggings, and moccasins, Tcoosma settled into the front of his red cedar canoe in order to direct them. He wore no shirt beneath his cape, and the cold never seemed to bother him. His battered bowler was pulled low but did nothing to hide the large abalone shells that pierced his earlobes and made them sag.

Jackson assisted Sage into the spot at the center of the canoe and took up his place at the rear to help with the paddling. As they made their way out of the harbor and away from Victoria, the canoe glided swiftly through the calm water.

He was glad for his position at the back that allowed him to observe Sage. She sat quietly, taking everything in, clutching her cloak closed with one gloved hand while holding on to the side of the canoe with the other.

After the weeks of her being stuck in his house and trailing after Augusta around Victoria, the wilderness had to be different. It had been for him when he'd first arrived from London to Manitoba on the Hudson's Bay.

As they rounded the eastern bend of the island and started north, the distant peaks on the mainland came into view. The morning sunshine glimmered off a low mist, turning the reds and oranges and yellows of the trees into flames, making his heart swell with something that felt a little like peace—a peace he hadn't experienced in a long time.

At Sage's intake of breath, he could tell she was awed by the beauty too. With a fashionable straw bonnet tied beneath her chin and shading her face, she looked every bit as much a lady as Augusta did. Even so, he wished he could take off the hat and have a full view of her face and expression for the duration of the voyage.

He wanted to find something to talk about with her, but he didn't know where to start a conversation. Besides, she probably didn't want him intruding into her enjoyment of the scenery.

With the birds having begun their migration season, he was spotting flocks of them at every turn. As the canoe passed a rocky section of the coast where at least a hundred, if not two hundred, sandpipers were roosting and foraging, he drew his paddle out of the water to slow their progress.

"Sage," he called, "look to your left. Sandpipers."

Tcoosma slanted a dark glare his way, as if to tell him that he was in a hurry. But Jackson focused on Sage, waiting for her reaction to the sight.

She shifted her gaze and then drew in another breath at the shoreline full of the unique birds with their long, narrow beaks and skinny legs. "There are so many," she said after a minute, her voice tinged with awe.

"The island is a major migratory stopping point for many breeds." Jackson had already started paddling again, and they didn't have to go much farther before he pointed out a flock of Brant geese swimming close to shore amongst the eelgrass, their graceful black necks and heads shimmering in the sunshine.

He'd always had an interest in birdwatching, and it had only grown when he'd moved to Vancouver Island with the abundance of waterfowl, birds of prey, and songbirds. He'd once even kept a journal to record and draw the birds he spotted, but he'd become too busy and had neglected the journal over the past year or two.

Seeing the migratory birds now through Sage's eyes made him want to renew his journal. Maybe it was more that he wanted to see life again and appreciate the small things he'd started to take for granted.

Whatever it was, the ride along the coast passed too quickly, especially with Tcoosma attempting to keep a fast and steady pace, and they reached the southern tip of Salt Spring Island within an hour. Most of the island was made up of rugged rocky coastline, but Jackson knew of a place or two more hospitable to settlers claiming land.

He inquired at the first settlement while Tcoosma and Sage remained in the canoe. Her sister wasn't there, but the fellow and his family said that Willow and her husband had a farm farther west along the coast.

They paddled to the next area that consisted of a small pebbly beach with grassy banks rising into a woodland. An inlet with a rushing creek emptied into the narrow harbor. Other than a canoe propped against the bank, the area looked uninhabited and hilly, without any sign of land suitable for farming.

Sage was searching the shoreline eagerly, but no one was in sight.

"I shall follow the river and see if I happen upon anyone." Jackson was already climbing onto the bank. "Wait here until I return."

He easily found a trail that followed the river. It wound through the dense woodland before opening into a clearing that was littered with stumps but also was being cultivated to grow crops. Jackson was no farmer, but amongst the stumps he recognized some potato plants that had yet to be harvested.

On an incline above the cleared land stood a rugged log home with a lean-to. A thin line of smoke trickled out of a stove pipe in the roof made of handcrafted shingles.

A single-story barn had been built in the open area beyond the house. Like the cabin, it was made of hewn logs and solid chinking.

The corral off to one side housed a cow and a couple of pigs, along with a smattering of chickens.

At a laundry line that ran from the log cabin to a nearby tree, a young woman with a turban on her head and a bundle in a sling—likely a baby—paused in hanging a man's shirt to peer down at him.

"Elijah!" she called toward the barn. "Someone's here!"

Jackson halted. The folks out in the remote areas were cautious with strangers, sometimes overly so. He didn't blame them, not with so many newcomers coming and going.

It was obvious this wasn't where Willow and her husband lived. But he wasn't about to leave without getting more information. "I'm looking for a woman named Willow," he called. "Any idea where I might find her?"

The woman scowled at him like a mother bear protecting her cub. "Who wants to know?"

"Her sister Sage."

The woman made a point of scanning the trail behind him. "I don't see no sister."

"She's in the canoe."

At that, the woman froze. "Here? Now?" Her voice wobbled with emotion.

"Yes. I'm trying to locate her sister Willow. Do you know where she lives?"

A man ducked out of the low barn door in simple garb and a neckerchief tied over a shaven head. Shielding his eyes with a hand, he straightened to a full, towering height. He glanced first to the woman with the baby in the sling, then his attention narrowed upon Jackson.

"Elijah!" the woman called again. "Go get Willow."

"Why?"

"Just go on now and do as I say."

The man with the neckerchief—Elijah—hesitated a moment, then began to cross his farmyard toward a bridge that spanned the river. A trail cut through the woodland on the other side. Did Willow perhaps live here after all?

With his muscles tensing with sudden anticipation, Jackson turned and made his way back along the path toward the shore to fetch Sage. The thought of her elation at finally being reunited with her sister brought him a sweet sense of satisfaction. He wanted Sage to be happy today and always. In fact, for a reason he couldn't explain, her happiness meant more to him than anything else.

Twelve

FROM HER SPOT IN THE CANOE, SAGE'S heart gave an extra beat as Jackson hiked out of the woodland. Even as a wealthy gentleman, he seemed so at ease in the wilderness, his footsteps certain, his stride unwavering.

He made a dashing picture in his blue suit with his gold watch chain hanging from his waistcoat pocket, his fine felt hat, and his polished shoes. Although he had changed his clothing before leaving on their trip, he hadn't shaved, and now a dark layer of stubble coated his jaw and chin, making him look only more darkly handsome in that brooding, moody way of his.

Not that she minded his brooding, moody way. In fact, the more she got to know him, the more she appreciated how his mind worked. She was coming to realize that sometimes his silence meant he'd retreated into his brain and was likely solving a complex problem, coming up with a new invention, or figuring out details that she couldn't begin to understand.

At other times, his silence meant he was probably thinking too deeply about past pains and problems. For as intricately as he thought about the positive things, he also apparently thought just as intricately about all the negative, making it difficult for him to move on.

She appreciated that he was complex and deep and emotional. During his especially quiet moments, she didn't feel the need to fill the silence with idle chatter and instead was content to let him speak when he had something to say.

Regardless of his shifting moods, he'd been kind and polite to her since leaving Victoria, so much so that she felt like a real lady and companion, not the maidservant she really was.

Although she hadn't wanted to leave Augusta behind, Sage could admit she was glad to have Jackson accompanying her.

It was possible Augusta was trying to facilitate something between her and Jackson. After all, Augusta's behavior had been odd since awakening. Had she feigned tiredness so that Jackson would have to step in and do the gentlemanly thing and travel with her? After the conversation the previous day about Jackson, Sage wouldn't put it past Augusta to start meddling.

In spite of Augusta's possible scheming, Sage had no intention of letting herself get carried away by the trip with Jackson. She also wouldn't let herself get carried away by his intensity toward her at times. She had to remember that was just the way he was and that it didn't mean he was attracted to her.

Well, maybe it did hint at some attraction. She would be naïve to deny the measure of awareness that had developed. But just because desire was developing didn't mean they needed to act upon it.

No, they would both remain professional and polite.

Even so, as he crossed the embankment toward the canoe, she admired his handsomeness once again. There was nothing wrong with admitting to his good looks. It was an undeniable and undisputable fact that everyone could see, and she was merely acknowledging it.

He reached the edge of the canoe and nodded at their guide, the quiet Native who'd expertly handled the canoe and was now sitting with his paddle across his lap.

"Any news of Willow?" She couldn't hold back the question any longer. The anticipation had been building inside her with every passing mile. When they'd first stopped on the island, she'd nearly gone faint with the possibility of seeing Willow. After they'd started on again, she'd realized that finding her sister might not be as easy as she'd first believed and that she needed to be patient.

But patience was difficult to facilitate today. She'd been so excited to get going this morning, that she'd almost decided not to pay a visit next door to the Firths' and try to restore the jewels to their rightful owner. While Jackson had been getting ready, she'd gathered the bracelet, the hairpin, and the brooch and placed them into a velvet pouch that Augusta had discarded after the purchase of a new necklace.

With the velvet pouch containing the pilfered jewelry, she'd been bold enough to knock on the Firths' front door rather than the servants' entrance, mainly because she'd wanted an audience with Mrs. Firth and not any of the servants.

As it turned out, the butler had sent her away without letting her step a foot inside. Even though she'd indicated it was a matter of great importance, he'd frowned and told her coldly that the lord and lady of the manor were still slumbering and could not be disturbed.

From the disdain in the butler's expression, he'd made it obvious she'd overstepped the boundaries of propriety. Perhaps she'd begun to think too highly of herself after the kindness Augusta had shown to her.

Sage had tucked the jewelry away in her chamber until she could enlist Augusta's assistance in returning the pieces. Augusta would be able to speak directly to the Firths and relay everything Sage had witnessed in the backyard. The sooner the better so that the thief wouldn't be able to take anything more.

Jackson tugged at the canoe, swinging it around so that the side landed in the sandy stretch of the beach. Then he reached a hand out to her.

Her heartbeat gave a quick thump against her ribs. Did this mean what she thought it did?

His eyes met hers, and the gray-blue was light and clear as if reflecting the sunshine on the water.

"She's here?" Sage whispered as she placed her hand in Jackson's.

"I believe so." His fingers folded around hers, his touch firm, solid, and steady.

With a gentleness and carefulness that made her feel like she was a fine crystal vase, he assisted her out of the canoe and helped her to plant her feet firmly on the beach. Even after she was grounded, he held on to her hand. He was staring at where their hands connected as if he was searching for the answer to a riddle, likely getting lost in his thoughts.

The excitement inside her was swelling. What if Willow really did live here? "Jackson?" The informal address slipped out before she could stop it.

It clearly surprised him as much as it did her, and his gaze darted back to hers. Thankfully, he didn't seem irritated by her crossing the class boundary with him.

"Will you take me to her?"

He nodded and started to tuck her hand into the crook of his arm as if he intended to walk by her side and assist her as if she were a proper lady. She couldn't let him do that, could she?

Before she could offer an objection, the shout of her name sounded from somewhere up the trail. "Sage?"

It was Willow's voice.

"That's her." Hot tears sprang to the backs of Sage's eyes.

Jackson squeezed her hand, as if sensing the emotion of the moment.

In the next instant, Willow broke through the woodland at a run. Her face was flushed, her blue eyes bright, and her face wreathed with a smile. She was hatless, with strands of red-blond hair having come loose from her braid. Her garments were faded and worn. And her skin was brown from the sun. But never had a face been more beautiful than the one across the beach.

At the sight of Sage, Willow shrieked even as tears coursed down her cheeks. Picking up her pace, Willow crossed the last of the distance. Before Sage could break away from Jackson and take a step, Willow flung herself forward.

With tears now sliding down her cheeks, Sage embraced her sister tightly, clinging to her as they both cried.

Finally, Willow pulled back, sniffling and laughing. She held Sage at arm's length, sweeping her gaze over her. "Look at you. You're a real fine lady." In Augusta's cast-off garments, Sage supposed she did look like a fine lady, and she didn't mind that she did.

Sage examined Willow in the same measure, and this time confirmed what she thought she'd felt during the hug—a gently rounded abdomen. "And look at you. You're expecting." At the same moment, she caught sight of Caleb, who'd obviously followed Willow down to the beach. He stood near the trail, holding himself back, obviously not wanting to interrupt their reunion.

He was as brawny and muscular as he'd always been and just as stoic. He nodded at her, his eyes holding welcome. He wore the same flat-brimmed hat that he had in Manchester, and the clothing was the same too, just more frayed. His skin was sun-bronzed, especially his hands and arms where his sleeves were rolled up.

"Hi, Caleb," Sage said, still not sure what to think about Willow and Caleb being together after so many years of the two of them insisting they were only friends.

Caleb crossed toward her. "It's good to see you, Sage."

"It's not only good"—Willow gave a small hop of happiness before throwing her arms around Sage again—"it's absolutely wonderful!"

They hugged again for another long moment before Willow pulled back abruptly and looked directly at Jackson, who had released Sage's hand for all the hugs, but who was still standing next to her.

Jackson was watching the interchange with his usual intensity and brooding eyes. He snagged Sage's gaze, his eyes seeming to ask her if she was okay.

She offered him a happy smile in return.

"And who is this?" Willow's gaze was bouncing back and forth between Sage and Jackson.

Before Sage could think of a way to graciously introduce Jackson and explain who he was, he made his own introduction. "I'm Jackson, a friend of Sage's. I'm pleased to meet you." He reached for Willow's hand, bowed, and placed a polite kiss on her hand.

Then he turned to Caleb and thrust out his hand. Caleb took the offering in a firm shake, all the while studying Jackson and probably noting that Jackson was in a class far above them. It was all too easy to see by the way he spoke, his mannerisms, and his clothing.

"It's good to meet a friend of Sage's," Willow said, glancing now at Tcoosma in the canoe. The older man had leaned back, pulled his hat over his face, and seemed to be resting. "I'm assuming David decided to come with you?"

Sage's smile faded. This was the crushing moment she'd dreaded the whole voyage over from England, the moment when she had to admit her life had fallen apart and nothing had turned out as perfectly as she'd planned.

Jackson slipped his hand to the small of her back. The touch of his fingers was light, as if to reassure her—or perhaps remind her—that he was by her side.

He was looking at her with his jaw rigid and his eyes hard with anger—toward David? He already knew she avoided talking about David. Maybe he'd drawn the conclusion that David had hurt her. If so, he was right.

His fingers pressed into her back gently again.

Some of the tension inside her eased, and she returned her focus on to Willow. She may as well tell her sister the truth. It would come out soon enough. "David fell in love with someone else and broke our engagement so that he could marry her."

"Oh, Sage." Willow's face didn't hold pity, only compassion.

Caleb was standing beside Willow and wrapped his arm around her. She leaned into him, clearly finding her support in him just as she always had. Was that what made their relationship work? That they were there for each other during the hard times?

Sage had never had that kind of relationship with David. They'd always known each other, since they'd grown up in the same neighborhood. But David hadn't started showing an interest in her until after she'd matured into a woman, the year she'd turned sixteen, when she'd begun to draw the attention of plenty of young men in the area. She'd picked David because not only had he been good-looking, but he'd had a steady job at the catgut factory and had ambitions to rise in the ranks at the factory, would be able to afford their own flat, and could take care of her and their children.

Everything had seemed perfect with their relationship. They'd gotten along well and enjoyed spending time together. She'd even thought she was in love with him.

After she'd been let go at the mill, he'd claimed that her lack of a job hadn't mattered, and she'd believed everything would be okay. But the truth was, her life and her family's had only gotten harder with the unemployment, especially after Dad was laid off. They'd struggled with finding food and fuel and hadn't even been sure they'd be able to stay in their tenement.

As the situation worsened, she'd suggested moving up the wedding date to take the burden off her family, so that they would have one less mouth to feed. But David hadn't seen the need to change their plans. Maybe his lack of compassion in her hardships—even his disinterest in Willow's leaving and Mum's death—should have been a warning that he wasn't the right man. But she'd ignored the signs.

"I'm fine, truly." Sage forced a smile. "Everything has worked out as it should."

Willow studied Sage's face for a moment as though trying to see the truth. Then she glanced at Jackson again before her lips curled up into a smile. "It sure looks that way."

Sage shook her head. She couldn't let Willow assume Jackson was a suitor. Before she could explain, Willow was tugging her into another hug. Then she began to guide her toward the path in the woodland.

Arm in arm, they made their way to Willow and Caleb's home which was situated a short distance up the river trail and adjacent to another farm. Willow was excited to show Sage everything—the cabin with its addition, the new barn, her large garden, the land cleared for crops, the bountiful harvest, the bushels of food in the cellar along with dried and canned goods.

Willow and Caleb had worked hard to carve out their farm in the wilderness, and Sage was proud of her sister for all she'd accomplished. The roughness and simplicity of their log cabin and the log barn couldn't compare to the fancy home she was living in with Augusta and Jackson. But it was more than either one of them could have dreamed of having back in Manchester.

At one point, Caleb returned to the portion of the interior of the barn where he'd been building a stall for their new dairy cow. Jackson offered to assist and went with him.

Time got away from Sage as she and Willow sat in chairs in the warm sunshine outside the cabin door, first sewing the curtains for the new addition and then plucking a chicken to set to roasting.

Willow was eager for news from home and wanted to hear all about everyone, not allowing Sage to leave out a single detail. They talked about their mum's passing, how Dad's health was deteriorating, what their sisters were doing, and what life in Manchester had been like before Sage left.

Willow also queried more into what had happened with David and what had led Sage to come to the colony ahead of their family. Sage didn't hold anything back and told Willow about meeting Augusta, their voyage across the world, and what her life had been like as a lady's maid.

In turn, Sage asked Willow about her voyage and all that had transpired when she'd arrived in the colony. Willow told her about the friends she'd made—including Juliet and Daisy—and how they'd become like family to her.

She also shared the whole exciting tale about working for the Manns at White Swan Farm, the key to the buried treasure, the danger she and Caleb had been in, and how they'd run away and hidden on Salt Spring Island to protect Caleb from Mr. Mann. She explained how they'd gotten married for convenience's sake but how it hadn't taken long for each of them to confess their true feelings and stop pretending that they didn't love each other when they'd been in love for years.

"So," Willow said, leaning back in her chair and studying the two men who'd stepped out of the barn and were conversing. "I know you said you're not planning to get married and that Jackson is just a friend. But he definitely doesn't see you as just a friend."

Sage was taking out the seam in the waist of one of Willow's skirts in order to give her more room for the baby growing inside her. At Willow's statement—spoken much too loudly—heat rushed to Sage's face. "Hush now, Willow."

With both hands resting on the swell of her abdomen, Willow just laughed. "The fellow obviously can't keep his eyes off you anytime you're near."

Sage cast a glance Jackson's way. He was leaning casually against the split rail post of the corral. Sure enough, his gaze was riveted to her even as Caleb spoke to him. The moment their eyes connected, she expected Jackson to glance away, perhaps pretend he'd been busy with something else. But his attention didn't waver. He even raised a brow as though to ask her how she was doing.

When had David ever asked her if she was okay? When had he ever raised a brow to see how she was doing? When had he ever really seen or known her—other than for admiring how she looked?

Here was this wealthy gentleman who had the temperament of a troll, yet he'd shown her more consideration and kindness in the past few days than David had in the years they'd been together.

Even so, nothing could come of the connection she and Jackson were forming. "I'm not interested." She spoke in a hushed tone.

Willow snorted. "Oh yes you are."

Jackson was still watching her, obviously not caring—as usual— that everyone could see him staring and that they were assuming things.

"Even if I were to find myself interested—which I won't—I could never have all the qualities that he'd need in a wife. I would never be good enough."

Willow's smile faded, and she grew suddenly somber. "That's not something the Sage I used to know would have said."

"The Sage you used to know was prideful and thought she was better than everyone else." Sage sat forward and turned her full attention on Willow, whose heart-shaped face with high cheekbones resembled hers in so many ways that they could have been twins.

Willow didn't say anything, but a sad shadow fell over her eyes. Even so, she'd never looked more vibrant and whole and healthy than she did sitting in her chair with the sunshine browning even more of her skin, giving her a glow and life that had never been present in Manchester.

"I was filled with pride even with you." Sage forced herself to say what was long overdue. "I compared myself to you, I believed I had the perfect life."

"It's in the past—"

"No, Willow. I was wrong to compare us. I was wrong to be prideful. I was wrong to make you feel as though you were less than me." She reached across the short distance between their two chairs and took hold of Willow's hands. "I've learned that I'm far from perfect."

"Nobody ever said you had to be."

Sage wasn't sure why she'd started to feel the pressure toward perfectionism. But it was still there, and she didn't know if it would ever go away.

"I've only just met Jackson," Willow said, watching Jackson, who had finally pushed away from the railing and was crossing toward them. "But I doubt he'll want you to be perfect. In fact, I think he finds you pretty appealing just the way you are."

It didn't matter what Jackson thought. All that mattered was that Willow understood how sorry she was. "Will you forgive me, Willow?"

"Already done. It's in the past."

"You're sure?"

"Yes, I'm just glad you're here and that we can start again."

"Me too."

Jackson was only a few feet away now. The afternoon would soon pass into evening, and no doubt he was ready to return to Victoria.

She gathered the mending in her lap and stood. "Is it time to go?" She wasn't ready to depart yet, but she'd imposed upon Jackson longer than necessary.

He halted but a step from her. "No." He reached out a hand as though he might touch her arm, but then he stuffed both hands into his trouser pockets.

"I can't keep you any longer—"

"I'm thinking we should stay overnight and leave in the morning." He spoke as if he'd already made up his mind.

"Stay? Here?" Hope swelled swiftly at the prospect of a little more time with Willow.

"Caleb indicated that his friend Jonas could take us back to Victoria in a steamboat tomorrow morning."

"Really?" Sage couldn't hold in a smile for another second.

Jackson took in her smile, and the tightness in his expression softened. "I'll go tell Tcoosma he can go." Without waiting for her to say anything more, he strode away on the path that led to the adjacent homestead belonging to Elijah and his wife Frannie and Elijah's brother Jonas.

Jackson was a striking contrast of opposites. He was the epitome of an English gentleman but as experienced and comfortable in the wilderness as a fur trapper. He was more intelligent than any person she'd ever known but also the most disorganized. He was consumed with his work but was also deeply caring about the people in his life.

"Oh, luv," Willow said with a soft laugh. "You can protest all you want. But you won't be able to resist that man for much longer, not when he treats you like you're the only thing that matters in his life."

Sage quickly tore her attention from Jackson's retreating form. He didn't treat her that way. But even as she tried to deny Willow's observation, a part of her wished it were true.

Thirteen

J ACKSON STARED AT THE CEILING BEAMS
of the barn, swiftly calculating the degrees of the angles needed
to build a loft.

After working with Caleb throughout the day on the barn, his
mind had begun to design the rest of the interior to make it as
efficient and productive as Caleb needed. Now that Jackson had
allowed his thoughts to go that direction, he couldn't stop them.

"Jackson?" A woman's voice came from near the barn door.

It was Sage. Only her voice had the power to interrupt his calculations and draw him back to reality. No one else had ever been
able to do that.

He liked that she'd started using his given name, doing away
with formality. It felt right.

He moved out of the corner stall he'd helped Caleb build. The
darkness of night had fallen, and Caleb had lit a lantern that hung
from a rafter at the front of the barn. The young man had been
quiet company for most of the day, just the way Jackson liked it.

Now that they were retiring—the men sleeping in the barn and

Sage and Willow taking the bed in the cabin—Caleb had disappeared to say goodnight to his wife. Jackson had no doubt that Caleb's goodnight involved some fairly passionate kissing, having already caught Caleb sneaking kisses with Willow whenever he thought no one was looking.

It had been obvious Caleb was in love with his wife and that he couldn't keep his hands off her. It had also been obvious Willow adored Caleb in return and relished his stolen kisses and couldn't get enough of them.

Watching the two interact had only made it all the harder for Jackson to hold in check the feelings for Sage that were growing exponentially. Since first meeting her, his affection may have started slowly, but now it was multiplying with every passing hour so that it felt like it was already at ten to the power of twenty. Soon it would border on infinite, beyond the capability of counting or equations.

As she stepped inside the barn, she was clutching a shawl over her shoulders . . . and her hair was unbound. He'd never seen her hair down before, and now it swirled in long waves, falling nearly to her waist. The faint lantern light cast a shimmer over her, turning the strands into burnished gold, warming her face, and brightening the blue of her eyes.

His breath snagged in his chest, and every single thought fled from his mind except for her. Nothing else compared. Nothing else was worthwhile. She was all he needed and wanted. There was even a part of him that didn't know how he'd ever survived without her.

"Jackson?" She paused and searched the spacious area at the front of the barn. It was sparely furnished, with only a few tools. The dairy cow was resting already on one side and lifted her head and turned curious wide eyes upon Sage.

Jackson stepped away from the new stall. "I'm here."

Her gaze swung toward him, landing upon him with a force that once again sucked the air from his lungs. How had this happened that he was so consumed with her? Yes, partly the consuming thoughts were the way his mind always worked. But why now, when he'd all but given up on relationships? And why was he so attracted to her more than the other women he'd known?

She was different, that's why. She was simple and straightforward with him, genuinely interested in what was important to him, accepting of who he was, and yet unwilling to coddle him.

He liked those things about her. Actually, he could probably list at least two dozen things about her he liked. Near the top of that list would be how beautiful she was.

She started toward him, a smile beginning to curve her lips.

He could only watch her approach with a sense of reverence. She was incredibly beautiful, so much so that he couldn't even put into words how to describe her.

She stopped when she was several feet from him. "I stepped out of the cabin to give Willow and Caleb some privacy."

"Excellent choice."

Her smile crept higher. "I love seeing her so happy, and I've loved being here today."

Did she want to stay permanently? "Then you want to stop working for Augusta and move here?"

"No, not at all. I couldn't move here. I would just be imposing on them and the life they're making."

He breathed out a tight breath. He didn't want her to move either. But he'd also seen a side to her today that he hadn't witnessed before—emotional and happy and relaxed. If living with Willow would fulfill Sage, then how could he oppose that?

"Besides, Augusta needs me." Sage clutched her shawl tighter.

"I need you too." He tried to keep his voice light, knowing he had to hold back his ardor.

"You need my organizational skills."

"Yes. Desperately."

"And you need me to continue to make sure you're well groomed." She looked pointedly at his unshaven face.

He reached up and scrubbed a hand over the day's worth of scruff. "Yes. I shall easily turn back into the beast without you around."

"Then that settles it." Her eyes held a twinkle. "I must go back to Fairview to keep you tamed."

"I agree wholeheartedly." This bantering between them was new, and he liked it. Not as much as serious conversations, but it was a side to her that being around Willow possibly brought out.

She studied his face for a moment. "Thank you for bringing me. Even more, thank you for giving me the opportunity to stay tonight."

"We're not in a hurry to return."

"Except that Augusta might be worried about what became of us."

"She will understand we decided to stay longer."

"I hope so. I don't want to neglect my duties."

"Augusta is perfectly capable of taking care of herself when necessary."

"She is quite capable." Sage's tone held admiration. "But I have pledged to be there for her."

"She knows you won't be her lady's maid forever."

"I would like that, though."

His thoughts went back to what he'd heard in bits and pieces today about her previous relationship with David. While Sage hadn't come out and said so, David's quick engagement to another woman so soon after ending the relationship with Sage hinted at unfaithfulness.

Whatever the case was, she needed someone to show her she would be safe in a new relationship and that not all men were like David. Could he be that someone? Was that even possible?

She glanced back at the door. "Have I given them enough time?"

He knew she was referring to Caleb and Willow and their saying goodnight. "Probably not." She'd likely given them plenty of time, but he wasn't ready for her to leave yet.

"He adores her," she said almost wistfully.

"I noticed."

Once again her smile crept up.

Jackson couldn't keep from staring at her smile. Her lips were so perfect, so full, and so symmetrically shaped.

She shifted back a step, her gaze darting around, her cheeks turning rosy.

He was embarrassing her with his stare. Quickly, he looked away and cleared his throat. "They have done well here."

"Very well. My mum would be so proud of Willow." She'd mentioned to him that her mum had passed away last winter and how much she'd missed having her mother's presence in her life. But she hadn't talked much more about her, as if the grief was still too tender.

"Your mum would be proud of you too."

"I'm not so sure." Sage released a sigh, and then her shoulders slumped. "Sometimes I think I've disappointed her by leaving my family behind."

He knew a great deal about being a disappointment. All his life he'd felt like he was disappointing his father, falling short of what the great man wanted him to be. It was difficult to live up to someone with the kind of reputation his father had—the daring, adventurous explorer who had accomplished so much and who'd even been knighted.

Jackson could admit to his many shortcomings and being a disappointment to his father. But Sage? She was admirable for what she was doing for her family—saving for their passage and trying to provide a new life for them.

"You're not a disappointment." He took a step closer to her, needing to reassure her. "You and Willow are brave for coming here." He wanted to offer to help pay the passage for Sage's family again, but he was also learning she was a strong woman who didn't want to be reliant upon others.

"I'm actually a coward," she whispered, dropping her gaze to the hay scattered on the dirt floor of the barn. "David was getting married, and I ran away so that I wouldn't have to see him and his new wife."

"David is a dolt." The criticism slipped out before he could censor himself.

She shook her head. "I clearly fell short somehow—"

"No," he whispered harshly as he gently took hold of her chin and tilted her head up so that he was looking into her eyes. "He fell short. Not you."

"You don't know—"

"Yes, I do know. He was a fool to ever let you go."

"You're just saying that . . ."

He skimmed his thumb up her chin, silencing her.

Her eyes widened and filled with questions—questions he wasn't sure he could answer, like what did his touch mean? What was happening between them? What were his intentions?

He didn't know. All he did know was that his attraction was powerful and undeniable.

He shifted his thumb from her chin to her bottom lip. Before he could stop himself, he grazed her lip, the fullness as well as the firmness fanning a blaze low in his gut.

She released a quick exhale, the warmth caressing him. Was it a breath of anticipation? For what he'd do next?

What exactly would he do next? He didn't have to think about the answer. He already knew and was reaching for her with his other hand. His fingers wrapped around her arm and tugged her. The movement was gentle and yet determined enough that she stumbled forward against him, bumping him lightly.

At the contact, her eyes widened, but she didn't push away.

That was a good sign, wasn't it?

He slid his thumb across her lips again, and this time her lashes fell, and her lips parted just slightly—enough to sense that she was taking pleasure in this moment.

More heat sparked inside him, and he bent down, his heart thudding with a need for her that pushed aside all other rationale. His hand cupped her chin so that he could direct her. In the next breath, his mouth connected with hers in a sweet, delicate kiss where his lips clung to hers for a long second.

Her response was just as soft and short, the kiss hardly beginning before it ended. She took a tiny step back, as though the short kiss was enough to satisfy her.

But it didn't satisfy him. Instead, it only seemed to set his attraction loose like a wild beast now uncaged. Desire leapt through him, and a low growl formed in his throat.

He snaked a hand around her to the small of her back and captured her there and pressed her closer. At the same time, he lowered his mouth to hers with a surge of passion, this time taking her lips fully and completely with his.

She didn't quite seem to know what to do with this kiss. He actually didn't either. But the swell of powerful attraction to her had a mind of its own, leading him onward, propelling him faster, driving a strange urgency through him.

As he slid his other hand from her chin to the back of her neck, she rose into him and into the kiss, almost as if she was afraid he was ready to break away.

But he was just getting started. He pressed in more hungrily, greedy for more of her. And she swelled into him, meshing her mouth with his in a give-and-take that rendered him nearly senseless.

He loved that she was relishing the moment and participating, and he would have stopped in a heartbeat if he'd sensed otherwise.

As it was, kissing her needed to become his new occupation.

Why bother with roads or bridges or anything else when he had Sage in his arms and her lips tangled with his. There was nothing and no one else he needed. Only her.

It was almost as if everything else in his life had been leading him up to this moment, conspiring to draw them together, and now intertwining their breaths, and their very souls.

Were his thoughts too intense? Probably. Was he being obsessed with her at the moment? Most definitely.

All he knew was that he had to go on kissing her forever and ever.

At an exaggerated cough near the barn door, Sage broke from him, dragging her mouth away and pushing against his chest.

She was straining hard enough to waken him from his passion-induced delirium, and he quickly released her.

She scampered away while pivoting to face whoever had stepped into the barn and witnessed their moment of passion.

Of course it was Caleb. Holding blankets and pillows, he wasn't looking at either one of them but was instead staring at the cow.

Sage ducked her head and retreated several more steps, but not before Jackson saw the rosy stain on her cheeks. She finally turned and raced across the barn, sidling past Caleb and out the door into the night.

As soon as she was gone, Caleb shifted enough to watch her as she crossed the yard. When he was obviously assured that she was safely ensconced in the cabin, he closed the barn door. Without a word to Jackson—or even a glance his way—Caleb stalked toward the mound of hay against one wall.

He split the pile into two heaps before tossing a pillow and blanket onto each. Still silent, he turned out the lantern overhead, casting the barn into darkness.

From the tension that seemed to be radiating from the young man, Jackson guessed Caleb wasn't too happy about the kiss, which was only natural. After all, Sage was Caleb's family now, and he likely felt responsible for her.

At the crackling of hay, Jackson could tell the fellow had dropped into what was apparently his bed for the night.

With only a faint outline in the darkness to guide his way, Jackson shuffled to the second hay pile, blanket, and pillow. He lowered himself, draped the blanket over his length, then situated himself on the pillow.

When he finished, a heavy silence settled over the barn except for the distant honking of migrating geese. He had the feeling it was only a matter of time before Caleb said something. And he was right.

A moment later, the young man's tight voice broke the darkness. "With that kind of kissing, you better be planning to marry Sage."

Marry Sage? Jackson pushed up, letting his blanket fall away. While thoughts about Sage had filled his head to capacity lately, he hadn't stopped to consider what the future would hold for them. After all, they hadn't known each other very long.

She'd insisted she wanted to remain a lady's maid and had even claimed she wanted to be a spinster. While he hadn't believed she would do either, he hadn't made plans or considered the possibility that he might be the one to take her firmly out of the lady's maid and spinster categories by marrying her for himself.

"Well?" Caleb's tone held a threat that hadn't been there earlier in the day.

Jackson stiffened, preparing himself for a fist into his stomach. He'd learned today that Caleb had once been a knuckle-boxing champion. Jackson had learned to proficiently wield both a knife and gun during his early days in the wilderness of Rupert's Land. He'd needed to for self-preservation. Even so, he didn't want to get into a fight with Caleb.

"I don't intend to hurt Sage." He couldn't promise he wouldn't kiss her again. With the way his blood was still heated and pulsing through him at double the speed, he guessed he would need to kiss her again.

But how could he take that liberty when he wasn't ready to offer her more? It wasn't fair to lead her on and to take kisses when he wasn't able to offer her a relationship in return.

No, he couldn't. He had vowed to Augusta he would respect Sage, and stealing kisses would only fuel his consuming desire for her. With the way his mind worked, he was already having a hard enough time keeping proper boundaries in place.

"She's been hurt by one man," Caleb said. "She doesn't need to be hurt by another."

Jackson didn't want to hurt her, not even in the tiniest amount. "I'll be careful."

"Then don't kiss her again until you're willing to marry her." Caleb's statement was less of a suggestion and more of a command.

Jackson blew out a tense breath. Would he ever be willing to get married? He'd once thought he was ready with Meredith. But since calling off their engagement, he'd decided that he didn't deserve happiness or a future with Meredith or anyone, not when the men he'd killed on the bridge hadn't gotten happiness or a future.

The terrible images flashed through his mind again. With a shudder, he reclined into the hay, drawing the blanket up to his shoulders.

"If you kiss her again and don't marry her," Caleb continued, "I'll track you down and make you do it."

"Fair enough." In his mind, Jackson could see the rationale behind everything Caleb was saying, and he agreed. If only he could convince his heart to follow suit.

Fourteen

SAGE COULDN'T LOOK AT JACKSON WITH-out thinking about their kiss from last night. As she walked hand in hand with Willow along the short section of beach toward the steamboat, she kept her gaze from straying to him. He'd already boarded and was standing on the top deck next to the pilot house and Jonas, the captain of the steamboat.

Jackson was studying a new whistle that Jonas had installed, as engrossed in the new device as he was everything that fascinated him. He was probably trying to figure out how it worked, as curious as always, his mind busy, his thoughts preoccupied.

She was glad he was distracted so that she didn't have to face the full effect of his intense gaze as she drew near.

Besides, she'd wanted to focus on Willow and the little time they had left. They'd lingered in bed in the early morning hours because Willow had been sleepier than usual now that she was with child. They'd whispered and laughed and cried together about everything. They'd also plotted and planned for how they could save more money to send home to their family. Between the two of them, they might have enough to pay for two ship passages. But they weren't sure if they should split up the rest of the family or wait until they had enough to send for everyone all at once.

Finally, they got up and made breakfast for the men, who'd already awoken and were doing chores. Even though Willow seemed more tired than usual, she was decidedly healthier than she'd ever been in Manchester, her breathing issues all but gone, only surfacing on rare occasions.

Sage hadn't told Willow about the kiss with Jackson. Since it was so new and so delicious, she hadn't been quite ready to talk about it, had wanted to tuck it away and remember it at her own pleasure.

And pleasure it had been.

Sage lifted her free hand and fanned her face, warmth pulsing into her cheeks just thinking about having Jackson's mouth on hers. The first soft kiss had been only an introduction, as if he'd opened the door and invited her in. When she'd stepped over the threshold, he'd ushered her in fully with the next kiss, enveloping her with a passion she'd never experienced before.

His hands had set her body on fire and his mouth had incinerated her, leaving only smoldering ashes behind . . . and a heat that still glowed deep inside. Even now, that heat pulsed in her blood, sending remnants throughout her, making her fingers and toes tingle with the need to kiss him again.

She would kiss him again, wouldn't she? Now that she'd experienced his passion, she couldn't deny that she wanted to have it more. Preferably soon. Was that wanton of her?

She'd never had such a strong experience with David. Yes, they had exchanged kisses once in a while, especially after they were engaged. But the kisses hadn't evoked anything inside her, mostly had been perfunctory. They'd been nothing like the one she'd shared with Jackson. Not even in the same hemisphere.

Expelling a taut breath, she halted beside Willow near the dock.

Willow's brows lifted to reveal sparkling eyes. "You're thinking about your kiss with Jackson last night, aren't you?"

Of course Willow already knew. She'd probably learned of it from Caleb.

"Hush now." Sage glanced at Jackson still tinkering with the whistle on the steamboat a dozen paces away.

"You can't deny," Willow whispered with a mischievous smile. "Caleb told me he walked in on the two of you kissing very passionately."

Sage pivoted swiftly and cupped a hand over Willow's mouth. Behind the gag, Willow's laughter was muffled.

Sage leveled a stern look at her sister. "Don't say another word about it."

Willow mumbled something that sounded like, "I know you like him, and it's obvious he loves you."

Loves? Sage couldn't hold back a soft snort. Jackson was attracted to her, but that didn't mean he loved her. "It doesn't matter. I'm not ready to be in another relationship."

Willow broke free from Sage's hold. "Learn from me and don't push him away."

Sage had enjoyed getting to hear all the details about Willow's love for Caleb and could see that her younger sister had indeed learned a lot over the past year about love. Even so, Jackson was different.

Willow's smile faded, replaced by seriousness. "Listen, Sage. You don't have to be perfect to be ready for Jackson. And your life doesn't have to be perfect to have a relationship."

"I know I'm not perfect and never will be." Maybe she'd once thought she could reach a certain standard of perfection in order to attain the perfect life, but she'd given up that aspiration. "I'm actually a failure."

"That's just it." Willow pressed a hand to Sage's cheek, warmth and love in her eyes. "You may have failed at one relationship, but that doesn't mean *you* are a failure and that you should punish yourself for the imperfections."

"I'm not punishing myself." But was she?

"Sometimes God works best when we're imperfect. As our reverend likes to say, 'His strength is made perfect in weakness.' We just have to jump into a relationship with all our imperfections and pray that God would step in and be our strength through our weaknesses."

Sage didn't quite know how to respond. She'd always been the one giving out advice over the years to her sister. How had their roles reversed? In some ways, it just showed again how much Sage had failed to be everything she'd aspired to be.

Sage wasn't ready to leave Willow behind, not after just being reunited. But with Jonas wanting to make the trip to return in time for the local church service, she didn't linger any longer. She waved at Caleb, who was standing a distance back, giving her and Willow privacy for their goodbye. Then she hugged Willow tightly before boarding.

When the steamboat chugged away from the island toward the south, she stood at the deck and watched Caleb cross to Willow and slip his arm around her. Neither Caleb nor Willow was perfect, but they'd made a happy marriage anyway. Was it possible that even though she was imperfect, she could do the same? That she could rely on God to be her strength during her weaknesses?

As the steamer veered out of sight of the island, she waved a last time. Then she turned back to the deck, hoping to find Jackson nearby. But he was nowhere in sight. Either he was still caught up in analyzing the whistle or some other part of the steamer, or he was avoiding her.

She'd thought she'd been the one staying away from him so far this morning, but maybe he was also doing the same. Was he embarrassed about the kiss? He hadn't seemed so last night. In fact, he'd seemed to relish every moment, had even seemed reluctant to let go of her after Caleb interrupted them.

Maybe he was as confused about everything as she was. He'd never made mention of wanting a relationship with her, never hinted at a future, never suggested there could be more between them.

But with as ardently as he paid her attention, was he wondering what the next step was for them? Was there a next step? After all, she was a poor lady's maid, and he was a wealthy gentleman.

So far, except for the initial rebuff that first night at dinner, their class differences hadn't seemed to matter to him—although she wasn't entirely sure. He'd also seemed to want more in their relationship than simple friendship. Surely he wouldn't have kissed her the way he had last night if that weren't true.

With a man like Jackson, she didn't feel comfortable bringing up the relationship issue, and she decided to wait for him to initiate a conversation about the kiss. By the time the steamboat reached Victoria a short while later, and she still hadn't seen or talked to Jackson, a strange anxiety gripped her chest.

They disembarked on the wharf in James Bay, thanked Jonas, and began to walk back to Fairview. With the Sunday morning bright and sunny and containing a hint of warmth, it was turning out to be a lovely day. If only Jackson would say something—anything—to diffuse the growing tension.

As she strolled beside him, she tried not to keep glancing his way. He'd slung a grain sack of items from Caleb and Willow over his shoulder—mainly produce from their garden to give to Gustave. After a second morning without shaving, the stubble on his jaw was even darker, making him more broody-looking than usual.

By the time they reached Fairview's front gate, she was almost desperate for him to speak, and her stomach was in knots.

When they stood before the door, Jackson paused. "I apologize if I overstepped myself last evening in the barn."

She let herself take a full breath, relieved he was finally bringing up the matter even if he was staring at the door and avoiding her gaze. "You don't need to apologize."

"I do." He fiddled with the door handle but didn't open it. "I shouldn't have kissed you in the first place. Then I was remiss in getting carried away."

He was apologizing for kissing her? She shouldn't have kissed him either. They were from two different worlds, going two different directions. Just because they'd felt some attraction to each other didn't mean they should have acted upon it.

Besides, Willow had been wrong to suggest that Jackson loved her. What did Willow know after seeing Jackson for less than twenty-four hours?

"Please forgive me," Jackson persisted softly.

"There's nothing to forgive." An ache settled in her heart, one that felt an awful lot like what she'd experienced with David. "We got caught up in the moment. It was a mistake, and we won't let it happen again."

"It was a mistake?" His gun-metal blue eyes regarded her almost as if he was surprised by her statement.

It had been a mistake, hadn't it? Wasn't that what he'd implied by apologizing? "It won't—it can't lead anywhere." Embarrassment flooded her as she spoke the bold words. She needed him to know she wasn't the type of woman who would ever consider illicit relations. She didn't think he was that kind of man either. Nevertheless, she had to make that clear.

He sighed heavily. "You're right. I am unable to offer anything, and I shan't make promises that I cannot keep."

The ache inside her heart swelled. What had she expected? That he'd contradict her and tell her that he wanted more? That they'd go slow and work things out? That they'd overcome all the obstacles to find a life together?

After what Willow had said about not pushing Jackson away,

Sage could admit that secretly and for half a minute she'd entertained the idea of having a relationship with him. But that wasn't what he was thinking in return. He didn't want anything with her. And he obviously didn't want to disrespect her by pursuing a short-term dalliance.

She stiffened her shoulders against the turmoil rolling through her, the feelings reminding her again of all she'd gone through with David. She didn't want to experience that kind of rejection again. Once had been enough. That was one reason why she'd resolved herself to being a spinster, because the endless ache in her chest was too much to endure.

She was better off staying away from relationships altogether and focusing on being a good lady's maid.

"I suggest we forget the kiss ever happened." She scanned the wide street lined with the finest homes in Victoria, all of them with sprawling yards and lovely landscaping. Although no one else was out on the street at the Sunday morning hour, the conversation was still mortifying, and she didn't want anyone to hear it. She just prayed Augusta was away at church and hadn't been listening to them from inside the house.

Jackson stared down at the front stoop, his jaw flexing. His back was rigid, and he seemed to be fighting a battle within himself.

Could he really forget their kiss? She never would, not as long as she lived. But she would never admit that.

After a moment, he nodded. "I shall try to do as you have suggested." With that, he turned back to the door and opened it. He waved her to go ahead of him as any polite gentleman would do.

More rejection knocked against her heart, but she tried to ignore it, held her chin high, and stepped forward.

He focused inside the house until she was adjacent to him. Then his gaze dropped to her face and to her lips for the briefest of moments.

As much as she wanted to deny their kiss, the memory flashed into her mind unbidden and unfiltered, taking her right back to the moment his mouth had crushed hers with a power that had swept her away.

But she forced herself to not look at his lips in return, forced her feet to keep moving, and forced herself to walk past him. Even though Willow had warned her not to push Jackson to arm's length, that's exactly what she needed to do. It was the only way to survive being around him.

He obviously had his reasons for holding her at arm's length too. Certainly, he'd shown that he desired her. But desire wasn't enough to build a relationship.

As he closed the door, she untied the silk ribbon under her chin and lifted the hat from her head. The silence of the home indicated Augusta had gone to church.

Sage hung her hat on the coat-tree just as the servants' door at the long end of the hallway burst open and Gustave rushed out.

"There you are, Monsieur." The cook's orange-red hair sprang out in curls around his plump face, which was also a shade of splotchy red. His rounded stomach heaved up and down, and he was breathing hard, as if he'd run all the way up from the kitchen in record time.

Jackson didn't seem to notice the cook, was already stalking toward his study, clearly wanting to escape from her or from whatever turmoil was going on between them.

"Something has happened to Miss Lennox," Gustave managed between gasps.

Sage slipped out of her cloak, alarm racing through her. What if that's why Augusta had stayed abed the morning they'd left?—because she'd been ill and hadn't wanted to alert them.

Jackson halted and gave the cook his attention.

"What is it, Gustave?" Sage asked. "Is she sick?"

"No, she's gone. She's been kidnapped."

Fifteen

"KIDNAPPED?" THE ENDLESS RACKET IN Jackson's head—the constant wrestling with himself over what to do about kissing Sage last night—came to a halt.

"What do you mean?" Sage's voice filled with alarm. "That someone came into the house and took her against her will?"

"Aye, I believe so." The cook's French accent had disappeared, and a thick Scottish brogue rolled off his tongue.

Sage clutched at her chest, her face pale. "When?"

"It happened yesterday, not long after you left. I heard a screech followed by commotion upstairs, and by the time I came to check on Miss Lennox, a fellow was carrying her out to a waiting carriage."

"Oh my." Sage let her cloak sag to the floor. "Who would have taken her? And why?"

The same questions were swiftly rising inside Jackson, and his body was growing more tense with every passing moment.

"I don't know. I tried to follow her, but the carriage was too fast, and I lost track of where it went."

Sage's eyes widened with growing horror at the unfolding situation.

"I went to the police station and asked for help," Gustave continued. "They searched around Victoria, but they couldn't find Miss Lennox either."

"Perhaps you should start at the beginning, Gustave." Jackson needed to remain calm, not just so that he could think straight but so that he could be there for Sage.

"That's all I know." Gustave shook his head sadly. "I'm sorry I don't have more to share."

Jackson scrubbed a hand over his jaw. "Did you get a look at the kidnapper's face?"

"Not much. From what I could tell, he may have been a fellow in his forties or fifties, with fair hair, maybe some gray. Long sideburns and a long nose. A real big guy and hefty, strong enough to hoist up Miss Lennox."

"And you didn't recognize him?" Jackson persisted. "He was no one you'd ever seen before?"

"I know plenty of the locals, but never once have I seen the likes of him in town."

"Who would do this?" Sage cut in, her tone laced with angst. "Poor Augusta."

Jackson hadn't kept abreast of the Victoria news or his social circles to know if there had been dangerous criminals in town recently. But why would anyone want Augusta? Unless, of course, they knew about his family's wealth and prestige and hoped to capitalize on that. "Do you think the fellow took her in order to get me to pay a ransom?"

Sage glanced around the hallway. "Maybe he left a ransom note."

"I didn't see anything," Gustave responded. "But I wasn't specifically looking for a note."

Without a word, Sage crossed to the stairway and raced up, the tapping of her footsteps filling the silence of the home.

Jackson watched her climb all the way to the top until she disappeared from sight. No doubt she intended to search every inch of Augusta's room to look for clues.

With a grave expression, Gustave waited, clearly expecting some direction or plan of action. But Jackson didn't know where to even begin searching for his sister. Their only hope was that the kidnapper had left them some kind of explanation, his motivation, and what he would expect for Augusta's return.

"Is there anything else you noticed?" Jackson had never paid sufficient attention to his surroundings and wouldn't be able to tell if anything had changed between now and when he left yesterday. "Any other information that would be helpful as we try to determine what may have happened?"

"I'm sorry, sir." Gustave shook his head. "I wish I did. But I'm baffled, that I am."

As Jackson ascended the stairs, his feet dragged. His heart was already heavy from his thoughts regarding Sage. Now with Augusta's kidnapping, his chest felt flat, as if his heart had fallen and been trampled.

If only he could find a way to ease the tension with Sage and go back to their previous friendship.

He sighed. After kissing her the way he had, he doubted he'd ever be able to return to thinking about her as just a friend—not that he ever really had considered her *just a friend*. He'd already been hopelessly enamored with her, and now he was even more so.

Yet after Caleb's rebuke in the barn, he'd known he couldn't pursue Sage. He'd had a restless, sleepless night, analyzing the possibility of having a relationship with her. Every equation added up to the same answer—he was no good for her. His personality was odd and unstable at times. He got too wrapped up in his projects. As a result, he invariably ended up hurting people.

He had only to review his relationship with Meredith to confirm that truth. From the start, he hadn't been the kind of man she wanted. He'd tried to accommodate her by taming some of his eccentricities. Ultimately, however, he hadn't been able to change enough about himself to satisfy her, just like he'd never been able to satisfy his father.

After the bridge accident, he was even more broken. Even if he was starting to emerge from the cave that he'd crawled into, he still felt like a monster. Guilt and fear and insecurity from all that had happened shackled him. And maybe those emotions would always be his burden to bear.

As much as Sage had brought light and hope into his dark world, she deserved a much better man than him, someone wholesome and solid, not one who could easily revert back to a beast at any moment.

He'd told himself over and over all last night and all morning that he had to let her go, that he would be selfish to hold on to her. He'd tried to convince himself they couldn't have a life together, that they wanted different things, that they were from two different worlds. He'd even tried to persuade himself she'd be better off as a lady's maid and as a spinster. She'd be happy enough, and Augusta would be good to her.

But whenever he looked at Sage, all his excuses kept collapsing like a bridge held up with rope instead of iron rods. The truth was, he was still obsessed with her, and after kissing her he was even more so.

She'd suggested they forget the kiss had ever happened. But that kiss was welded into his heart permanently. It was now a part of him.

As he reached Augusta's chamber, the door stood wide, revealing a room in complete disarray. Sage was searching frantically through every item, picking things up and then dropping them. Clothes were strewn over the bed and floor, the bed was unmade, the stool at the dressing table was tipped over, and the dresser drawers were pulled out with items hanging from them haphazardly.

Augusta was normally a tidy and responsible person. She never would have left her room in such a state of disorder. Had the kidnapper rummaged through everything, looking for something that Augusta had that was valuable? "Do you know if Augusta was traveling with anything that was rare or costly?"

Sage paused in throwing back the covers on the bed, as if that would somehow reveal what had happened to Augusta. Her face was flushed from her efforts and her eyes wild. "She brought some of her jewelry on the voyage here, and most of it is still on her dressing table." Sage nodded toward the elegant table where items were strewn. "So the kidnapper wasn't interested in the thievery."

"It would appear that way."

Sage pressed her pretty lips together—pretty lips that had meshed with his so perfectly and so passionately, pretty lips that he loved seeing curled up into a smile, pretty lips that could also tell him hard truths he needed to hear.

He gave himself a shake. He couldn't let himself start thinking about her lips. Not now, not when Augusta was in trouble and needed their help. He had to focus on rescuing her.

Sage righted the stool. "It doesn't look like anything was destroyed."

"I concur. It simply looks messy."

"Like Augusta was in a hurry."

"Perhaps."

"But in a hurry for what?" Sage crossed to the armoire and rummaged through it. "Was she going somewhere? Did she take anything with her?"

He liked the logical way Sage's mind worked. It was almost as if she was solving the mystery around Augusta's kidnapping the same way she'd organized his study.

Sage moved to the bed again, knelt, and dragged out several pieces of luggage. She studied them then paused. "Her red floral-print carpetbag is gone."

"You're certain of it?"

"I think so." She stood and once again searched the room. After a minute of retracing her steps through the mess, she halted. "It's not here, which means she must have taken it with her."

"In addition to the carpetbag, are you able to deduce if anything else is missing?"

Sage studied the dressing table, then the dresser, before shifting to look at the contents of the armoire. "Her lavender and rose gowns are gone, her nightgown, some of her personal hygiene items, at least one handkerchief, and her extra pair of gloves."

"The items sound ordinary and necessary."

"Her kidnapper clearly gave her leave to pack what she needed. We can be grateful for that."

"But why would he take her?"

Sage's forehead was wrinkled with worry. "What could she possibly have that anyone would want?"

"Unless he intends to hold her for ransom." Jackson circled back around to the only reason that made sense, that someone wanted a share of his family's wealth.

"If so, then there should be a note explaining the demands. But I've found nothing."

"Maybe the note is in my bedchamber or my study?"

Together they searched his chamber and then went down to his study, but they didn't find anything in either place. They scoured the hallway and the dining room and every other possible place where the culprit might have left a note itemizing his demands.

After they'd concluded that perhaps the kidnapper would send them a letter in the mail, Jackson returned to his chamber to change his clothing and freshen up after having slept in his current garments. Sage also reluctantly gave up the search for the time being to change.

He'd barely had time to unbutton his shirt when her voice came from down the hallway. "I found something on my bed."

He threw open his door and stepped out of his room and nearly bumped into her.

Her eyes were alight, and she dangled a piece of jewelry from her finger. "It's Augusta's charm bracelet, and it was on my pillow."

"Maybe she dropped it there in her haste?"

"No, it was positioned too neatly and strategically to be accidental."

"Then you conclude that it is a clue to what happened to her?"

Sage held up the bracelet. All the charms were jewels except for the one Sage was fingering. "Look at what this charm says."

He took it and read the neat print. It said only one word. "Hope."

"Hope," Sage repeated. "What does it mean? Is she suggesting we have hope that we can find her? That she'll be okay?"

Why would Augusta leave a bracelet with the word *hope* on Sage's pillow? Why not leave a detailed note? Unless the kidnapper hadn't given her the time. Perhaps she'd only been able to sneak the bracelet into Sage's room before being whisked away.

He could feel Sage watching him, waiting for him to analyze the word and draw his own conclusions. She was standing close enough that he could hear her exhalations and feel the tension radiating from her body.

Her proximity reminded him again of the previous evening in the barn, feeling at ease with her, as if he didn't have to pretend to be someone he wasn't. She accepted him for who he was, which wasn't something many people had ever been able to do, especially not his father.

In fact, Sage had not only accepted him, but she'd also seemed to be able to step in and help him in his weaknesses, as though she was a piece of him that had been missing and now was found.

Why was he so set on keeping her at arm's length and remaining alone and single? He'd had reasons a moment ago, but he couldn't think of what they were now that she was so near.

"This is all my fault." Her voice trembled.

"Your fault? Of course it's not your fault. Why would you think so?"

"If I'd been here to watch over her—if we'd both been here—then maybe she'd still be here. At the very least, we would have been present when the fellow came into the house, and we could have tried to stop him."

While Jackson wished he would have been home to help Augusta resist the intruder, he was relieved Sage hadn't been present, that she hadn't been taken too.

"Don't blame yourself," he said almost too severely. "She could have been kidnapped anywhere, even off a street."

"But it's my job to be at her side and help her."

"It's not your job to remain with her every second."

Her head drooped. "Why, Jackson? Why her? She's a wonderful woman—so kind and generous and helpful."

He wanted to give Sage an answer and felt suddenly helpless that he couldn't. "We'll find her. I promise."

She nodded gravely.

He had the strongest urge to pull her into his arms, hold her close, and simply embrace her. But he knew he couldn't, not if he hoped to stay rational and level-headed.

She was quiet a moment before looking down the hallway past him. "Should we meet with the police and see if they've discovered any witnesses who saw her? They might have an idea of where the kidnapper took her."

Where. Jackson looked at the charm dangling from the bracelet again.

Hope.

What if that was why Augusta had left the bracelet for them? Because she'd known the kidnapper was taking her to Hope which was on the mainland of British Columbia?

Was that it?

Maybe he was only imagining a connection. But it was worth exploring. "I have an idea of where she may have gone."

"You do?" Sage lifted her beautiful wide eyes, and they practically pleaded with him to find Augusta.

"Hope is a little town up the Fraser River in the mountains."

"Do you think that's where her kidnapper took her?"

"It's possible." What if he was wrong? What if Augusta had left the bracelet as a gift for Sage and it wasn't a clue?

"How far is Hope from here?"

"At least a day by steamboat."

"Should we go look for her there?"

He wanted to say no, that he couldn't do it, that it simply wasn't possible for him. He hadn't ventured up the river on the mainland since the accident. He hadn't wanted to go back anyplace near the bridge, not until he had a solution to the engineering problem and could fix it.

Even as protest pulsed through his muscles, his love for Augusta pulsed harder. She was in trouble, and she'd possibly left the clue for them so that they would be able to help her. Although he wasn't ready to return anywhere near the site of the accident, he had to do it for his sister's sake.

With Sage watching him expectantly, he finally nodded. "Let us pack our bags, and we shall attempt to find a steamer that is leaving today."

As it was Sunday, the task would be difficult, since most of the commerce was at a standstill on the day of rest. Perhaps he'd have to hire a captain to privately take them. If only Jonas was available for the job, but the young captain had probably already returned to Salt Spring Island.

Whatever the case, they would have to pray that they could rescue Augusta from danger before it was too late.

Sixteen

S AGE COULDN'T SHAKE THE FEELING that something terrible had happened to Augusta. Before leaving for Salt Spring Island, she'd known something was wrong. Why hadn't she pushed for answers?

As she stood at the railing of the hurricane deck of their steamboat and let the evening breeze blow against her face, she hugged her cloak around her arms to ward off a chill that didn't come from the wind.

Behind them in the west, the sun had already finished its descent, and now darkness was settling around her. After spending the day traveling up the Fraser River, she and Jackson would only make it to Centreville—not far enough, but the captain had informed them he would be stopping for the night and that they would continue to Hope in the morning.

She tried to quell her frustration that they hadn't reached Hope today. But Jackson had warned her they might not since they'd gotten a late start leaving Victoria.

Jackson had done the best he could earlier in the day to find a steamboat captain who was available and didn't already have other obligations. That task had been daunting, but the sizable payment Jackson offered had helped them secure passage on the *Widower*, a small but tidy steamboat whose captain claimed he'd made hundreds of trips up and down the Fraser River.

While waiting for the steamboat to be ready to leave, Jackson had investigated along the waterfront, trying to discover whether anyone had spotted Augusta yesterday. But he hadn't found any information about her, and no one had seen a woman who matched her photograph. Without a definite sighting of Augusta, Jackson had questioned the wisdom of traveling all the way to Hope. But they hadn't found any other clues, which left them with no other recourse but to visit Hope and pray she was there.

Finally, shortly after noon, she and Jackson, with their bags, had boarded the *Widower*. The trip across the Strait of Georgia and up the Fraser River had been uneventful, even peaceful. They'd spent most of the afternoon lounging in deck chairs, watching the scenery and talking.

They'd discussed every reason why Augusta was in trouble, and Sage had made a list of the possibilities, including unpaid debts, other financial problems, family enemies, a personal enemy, revenge, and greed.

Sage had even added the chance that the kidnapper had taken Augusta because he wanted a wife. In the colony where men outnumbered women, it was certainly an option, even though Jackson didn't think so.

She'd told Jackson about the jewels she'd uncovered in the Firths' yard. While the velvet bag with the jewels was still in the drawer in her room, they'd discussed the option that the kidnapper had wanted them back and would hold Augusta as a prisoner until they handed the jewels over.

Sage could admit the conversations with Jackson had been the highlight of the trip, even more so than getting to see the stunning mountain vistas on all sides. When they'd exhausted their discussion of Augusta, they'd found other topics to chat about. As usual, Jackson was a fount of knowledge about everything, going into great detail for most subjects, whether the history of the area, rock formations, salmon fishing, Natives, and even the process of gold mining.

She didn't mind that he got carried away with complex and intricate details. Even if she didn't always understand what he was telling her, she loved that he was so intelligent and interesting.

He was attentive to her too, making sure she was warm and comfortable and had something to eat and drink. Even now, as he spoke with the captain in the pilothouse, he was watching her in that keen way that told her he was attuned to her every need.

He'd proven himself again today to be a good and honorable man, not only toward Augusta but also toward Sage, treating her with the utmost of respect. In fact, he was so gentlemanly that at times she almost wished he would cast aside all reason and manners and just pull her back into his arms. But he'd kept a respectable distance and hadn't touched her, except when he'd assisted her now and then.

They hadn't discussed the kiss again. And they hadn't discussed the nature of their relationship—or lack thereof—either. A part of her wanted to push him to discover why he'd kissed her and what it meant, but she didn't want to upset the peace that had settled between them.

He ducked out of the pilothouse and crossed the promenade toward her. The light gray of his suit and the white shirt contrasted with his dark hair, lending him a shadowed, haunted look, especially with the dark blue evening hues surrounding him.

As he drew near, he lifted his hat and combed his fingers through his hair. He'd neglected to shave again today—hadn't made the time with their haste in searching for Augusta. Now the scruff on his face was more defined, making him all the more appealing. So much so that a strange sizzle of heat burned through her abdomen, followed by the overwhelming urge to cup both scruffy cheeks and press her lips to his.

He had such a fine mouth, such firm lips, such perfect teeth.

Oh dear heavens. Why did he have to be so attractive? Resisting him would be easier if her body didn't react so strongly every time he was near.

He halted a foot from her, regarding her with his usual seriousness.

"We have just a couple of minutes left before we arrive in Centreville." He studied her face, seeming to take her in as much as she was taking him in.

Their focus on each other didn't mean anything. It was just that they were the only two around—except for the captain. At one point they'd passed by a group of Natives fishing from their canoes. They'd also seen men on a sandbar who'd waved as they'd passed. But otherwise they'd been alone. Regardless, she had to stop looking at him so much.

Ahead on the shore, a whole herd of deer—or perhaps elk—grazed in an open field not far from the riverbank. Some had lifted their heads and were peering back with wide eyes, their ears flickering. "Look." She pointed in their direction. "Aren't they beautiful?"

Jackson followed her gaze and nodded. Although he'd been living in the New World for the past eight to nine years, he'd told her he never tired of seeing the beauty and that he never would. He made no secret of the fact that he planned to remain in the colony for the rest of his life and had no aspirations to return to England to be with his father and mother.

As with other times when he mentioned his parents, Sage hadn't wanted to pry into the past issues. But she also longed to know more about him. In fact, there were times when she wanted to know everything about him.

Jackson leaned against the railing. "I regret I've put you into an awkward situation."

"I don't find it awkward." She'd actually had a lovely afternoon. If she hadn't been worried about Augusta, she would have enjoyed it even more.

Jackson cleared his throat. "I'm afraid I truly have made our situation awkward and did not realize my mistake until too late."

At the distress in his tone, she shifted and gave him her full attention. "What mistake?"

He blew out a breath. "I didn't realize the captain . . . well, he assumed that we are . . . he still believes you and I are . . . married."

"Oh." The same heat from moments ago swirled inside her. "We can set him straight and let him know I'm your servant."

"We shan't do that, Sage. Because you are not my servant."

"Then we'll let him know I'm your sister's servant."

"Afraid not. We shan't do that either."

"It's the truth."

"Not entirely, and we both know it." He didn't meet her gaze, but something about the way his jaw flexed told her he was serious.

She supposed she always had been more of a companion to Augusta than servant.

"The truth is"—Jackson blew out another breath, more exasperated than the last—"I should have realized how inappropriate our traveling together alone and unchaperoned would be."

"We're not alone." She nodded toward the pilothouse. "We've been sitting in sight of the captain all day."

"We are still taking this trip alone, which is unsuitable for a single man and single woman. If I admit to the captain—or anyone in Centreville—that we aren't married, then I shall likely tarnish your reputation."

"We took the trip to Salt Spring Island, and no one thought anything of it."

"That was to visit your family. Your sister and Caleb were our chaperones, and we weren't alone there. But here, we shall be alone for most of the voyage with no one to oversee us."

She hadn't really thought about the ramifications of traveling with Jackson. But was he right? Would people think the worst? And by worst, would everyone assume she was Jackson's kept woman, his mistress, a lover?

Mortification rushed through her. Rumors would certainly spread and hurt not only her reputation but also Jackson's, possibly even Augusta's. With such a scandal, the dear woman would be left with no choice but to terminate Sage from her position as lady's maid.

"When the captain made a comment about us being married," Jackson continued softly, "that's why I didn't correct him."

"I see."

The steamboat veered toward the shore where a wharf and a warehouse stood, both containing stacks of corded wood. Several weathered gray clapboard establishments faced the river, their windows shining with welcome warmth and light. A couple of simple log cabins sat a distance back, along with a barn and corral. Stumps littered the cleared area where tents were propped up and a cluster of men congregated around a campfire.

"This is Centreville?" It was much smaller than she'd anticipated.

"This is it, primarily a place for steamboats to refuel."

This was the wilderness of British Columbia, a place as far from and as unlike Manchester as any place on earth. At least she had Jackson by her side . . . as her pretend husband.

"So," she said, "do you think it's best for the duration of our trip that we carry through with the pretense of being man and wife?"

He hesitated. "If you're not agreeable to it, I shall set the record straight with the captain and do my best to uphold your reputation in spite of the unfortunate circumstances."

What else could they do? She honestly didn't know. "I never like to speak falsehoods, and I would hate to do so now."

"I respect that." He sighed and then was quiet as the steamboat whistle blasted in the quiet, alerting those on shore of its approach.

If the captain already had assumed they were together, then most people would, and how would they be able to explain to everyone the nature of their relationship without casting doubt onto both of them?

After all the gossip Jackson had already experienced as a result of the bridge collapse and because of his failed engagement, she couldn't subject him to more gossip about having an illicit affair with her.

The only thing to do was let people believe they were married. "What if we refrain from outright lying about our relationship but just neglect to correct wrong assumptions?" It would still be deceptive, but was it the lesser of two evils?

His expression was grave. "I don't want to do anything you're uncomfortable with."

"It will be an awkward situation either way, but more damaging if people think I'm your mistress instead of your wife."

"That was precisely my conclusion."

"Then we'll be *married* for a day or two. It won't be long. And when we return to Victoria, no one needs to know, right?"

Again, he hesitated. "Let us hope so."

His answer wasn't reassuring. "Is there a chance your friends and acquaintances in Victoria might hear of our pretend marriage?"

"Anything is possible."

"Is it likely?"

"If by chance any acquaintances of mine spot us together, I shall privately explain the situation in more detail and hopefully curtail any problems."

It seemed like a good plan. "This shouldn't be too difficult.

Let's pray we find Augusta quickly, and then she can act as our chaperone on the return trip."

The steamer was nearing the wharf, and a dock worker had come out of the nearby warehouse and was standing ready to secure the *Widower*. Within minutes the boat came to a standstill, the landing stage was lowered, and Jackson carried both of their bags from the steamer, not intending to spend the night on the steamer since it had no private cabins.

Among the scant buildings that made up the town, Sage didn't see any that looked like a hotel or inn, and she couldn't imagine setting up a tent and camping.

She followed Jackson to the closest building, a simple two-story structure that had a wooden sign extending from above the door that read *The Golden Acre*. As Jackson opened the door and waved her inside, the waft of roasting game and herbs awoke the gnawing inside her stomach. After having eaten very little all day, she was ready for a meal.

A scattering of men with mugs of ale sat at the plank tables that were crowded together in the front room. Low lantern light filtered over the dark paneling, highlighting elk antlers on one wall, a stuffed raccoon on another, and an owl on the opposite.

The conversations around the dining room puttered to a stop, and all eyes turned their direction. The faces staring at them were worn and grizzled and filled with lots of facial hair, reminding her of how Jackson had looked when she'd first arrived. The expressions were mostly curious and thankfully not hostile.

"Good evening," Jackson said with a glance toward the far door that seemed to lead to a kitchen. "May I speak with the owner of this establishment, please?"

"What fer?" called a fellow at the farthest table. Although his skin was white, his brown hair was slicked back into a long braid in a fashion similar to the Natives. He had a bright neckerchief rolled up and tied around his head, and he wore an equally colorful beaded necklace.

Jackson gave the fellow a nod. "I would like to rent a room for the night."

"Sorry." The fellow stood, revealing leather buckskin trousers of some kind. "Got nothing available."

"Free up a room." Jackson didn't appear to be taken aback by the fellow's unfriendliness. Instead, he dug into his coat pocket and pulled out a leather pouch that clinked with coins. "I shall make the effort worth your while."

Every eye in the room now centered upon the bag.

Jackson also swept back one side of his coat to reveal the handle of his pistol—a pistol Sage hadn't realized he carried.

"How worthwhile?" The fellow with the braid was looking at the bag too.

"Very." Jackson spoke the one word with a curtness and authority that no one could ignore. He was leaving little doubt about how powerful and wealthy and formidable he was.

The fellow surveyed Jackson for a moment then shifted to look at Sage. As his eyes rounded, he gave a low whistle of appreciation. "You got a fine-looking woman—"

"She's my wife." Jackson spat the word with enough venom to make the man take a rapid step back. "Nobody better look at her except for me."

Sage guessed Jackson was simply doing his best to protect her, but all it had taken was one interaction for him to spew the falsehood about them being married. Even though she didn't like that they were getting more tangled into the lie, she couldn't deny how much she liked Jackson's possessiveness, as if he was claiming her and didn't intend to give her up. That was a wild dream, wasn't it?

"Do you comprehend?" Jackson's gaze was as hard as steel as he surveyed the men. Gazes dropped away under his severity.

"You newly married?" the fellow with the braid asked without looking at Sage.

"Yes. Today."

"I could tell." The fellow cracked a grin, one that revealed discolored teeth.

Jackson ignored the comment and set down their bags near a narrow set of stairs. Then he slipped an arm around Sage, gently resting his hand on her back while he addressed the fellow again. "If you'll be so kind as to provide us with a meal, we shall partake of it while you ready our room."

Maybe he wasn't being possessive and was merely trying to scare the fellows away from making advances toward her. As usual, she had to be careful about reading more into Jackson's actions.

"Course. Sit right here." It was amazing what the promise of money could accomplish. Gone was the antagonism. Instead, the fellow—clearly the proprietor—shooed at the other men who were still sitting at his table. They rose from their spots and began to make their way to other tables while the proprietor hastily finished clearing theirs.

Jackson guided her to the table. Even after they were both seated across from each other, she could feel everyone discreetly watching them. Only after the proprietor disappeared into the kitchen with his arms and hands full of dishes did the others in the room resume their conversations, although in much quieter tones, as if they didn't want to miss out on anything she and Jackson might say.

"Are you all right?" Jackson murmured, shooting a glare at one of the men at the table next to theirs who was still staring.

"I'm faring well enough." The option of pretending to be married was looking better with every passing moment. Not only would it keep rumors at bay, but hopefully it would squelch unwanted attention. She just prayed all the more that Augusta would be safe.

Jackson had tucked his money bag back out of sight, but his hand still rested on his revolver. Although he was bookish and intelligent and scientific, he also had an air of danger about him, one that he'd no doubt fostered during his years of living in this uncivilized land.

The proprietor—who introduced himself as Rawhide Ralph—brought them plates filled with a simple fare of roasted hare along with a surprisingly delicious dish of potatoes with herbs. The bread was thick and tasty too, and by the time she finished, she was grateful for the full stomach—something she didn't take for granted, not after the hunger she'd experienced in Manchester.

As she pushed away from the table and stood, everyone in the establishment quieted again. Rawhide Ralph, with their luggage in hand, started up the steps. "This way."

Jackson scowled around the room again as he lightly rested a hand on Sage's back and guided her toward the stairs.

"Had my woman tidy up the room," Rawhide Ralph was saying as he tromped loudly on the simple plank stairway. "Ain't fancy and the bed ain't big, but it'll be real nice for your wedding night."

At the insinuation that she and Jackson would be engaging in marital intimacies, fresh mortification shot through Sage, and she stumbled.

Jackson drew her closer, likely in an effort to steady her steps. But as her body connected with his, all she could think about was the fact that she would be sharing a room with the most attractive man she'd ever met.

Seventeen

T HE COMING NIGHT WOULD BE A VERY long one.

Jackson stood at the window of the room Rawhide Ralph had given them and peered through the darkness toward the river. Although he couldn't see the steamboat, he knew it was secured at the wharf, and it was beckoning to him, even chastising him, to bed down on one of the decks. The autumn night would be cold, but the frigid temperature would surely cool down his overheated body and keep him from doing something with Sage he'd regret in the morning.

Not that he had any intention of taking advantage of her or the situation. But the entire marriage charade had gone from bad to worse with every passing hour.

The moment he'd stepped inside the room that was no bigger than a closet, he'd halted abruptly and nearly demanded more spacious accommodations. But Rawhide Ralph had been waiting in the hallway for his reaction with such anticipation, Jackson had known that this was the best the fellow had to offer.

Now Jackson was stuck for the night in a tiny room with a bed that could hold two people ... if both people were small children. With the night table, a dresser, and a trunk filling the rest of the room—along with their luggage—there was no floor space left available for a man of his size.

Behind him, Sage was attempting to change out of her garments into her nightgown. But from all her shifting and rustling, he guessed even the smallest movement in the tight confines was challenging.

He'd wanted to step into the hallway to give her more privacy, but with the sound of footsteps coming and going outside the door, he refused to leave her alone for even a few seconds.

"I'm almost done," she said breathlessly, as if she was hurrying.

"I beg your forgiveness that I am not able to give you more privacy." He apologized again as he'd already done several times.

"We'll make do." Her whisper held a note of embarrassment that hadn't gone away since they'd entered their room and Rawhide Ralph had wished them a good night with a vulgar wink.

"I can put out the lantern," Jackson offered once more.

"I trust you, Jackson."

He was glad she'd kept a level head throughout the whole ordeal, explaining to him several times that she wasn't bothered by the accommodations, that she'd had far inferior sleeping quarters during her life.

The real issue wasn't the tight space or small bed. The real issue was that they were not man and wife and shouldn't be in the compromising situation at all.

But what choice did he have? He couldn't very well go out and confess that he and Sage were traveling companions and friends and nothing more. They had already established that fabricating a marriage was the best option available to them at this point. And after the men's reaction to her beauty earlier—the way everyone had stared at her in the dining room—he felt even more responsible for her well-being and making sure she wasn't sullied.

Caleb's warning from the previous night echoed in his head. *If you kiss her again and don't marry her, I'll track you down and make you do it.*

Staying together like this ranked with kissing in terms of intimacy. If Caleb could see them now, he'd make them get married.

Jackson's chest tightened. Should he just wed her? Would that be best? He doubted she would agree to it. Besides, he didn't want her to feel coerced into being with him.

Behind him, the bed creaked.

The very idea of her sliding onto the mattress and between the sheets in her nightgown sent a shot of heat into his blood.

With a rapid shake of his head, he closed his eyes against any desire for her. He couldn't let himself think about her as a beautiful and desirable woman. Not only wasn't it appropriate at a time like this, but it wasn't appropriate ever.

He had to think of Augusta and how to find her. He'd let it be known that he was searching for his sister and was offering a reward for any information about her. But no one recognized the description he'd given of Augusta.

"I'm done," Sage whispered.

He blew out a breath and straightened his shoulders before turning around. He looked everywhere but at her in the bed. His gaze bounced to the door, to the neatly folded stack of her clothing on the dresser, to the hairbrush next to it, and to her shoes lined up next to her bag.

He allowed himself a short glance at her.

She was sitting against the metal headboard, the covers pulled up to her chin and her eyes wide upon him—those beautiful blue eyes that were so perceptive, that saw him for who he was and accepted him with all his flaws but also challenged him to be better.

"You have such pretty eyes." He blurted the words before he

could stop himself. The moment they were out, he bent toward the lantern on the bedside table and snuffed it.

Blessed darkness descended over the room, hiding her, hiding him, hiding all the emotions he didn't want her to see. The truth was, no matter how much he might be telling himself that he wasn't interested in Sage and couldn't be with a woman anytime soon, he wasn't listening to the messages. His interest in her continued to manifest itself every time he looked at her.

He hovered beside the bed, both angst and anticipation swirling low inside him. What should he do now? She'd said she trusted him. The question was, did he trust himself to lie down on the bed beside her and sleep the whole night through without touching or reaching for her even just a little?

With as attracted as he was to her, he wasn't sure he could do it.

But he had to. He needed to prove to her and to himself that he was a man of honor, that he respected and valued her enough not to use her in any way at all.

"You may as well lie down," she whispered, her voice strained. "You can't stand there all night."

"Perhaps I can."

She huffed out a small laugh. "I won't let you. If anyone should be giving up the bed for the night, it should be me. I'm only the hired help."

At her self-deprecation, irritation rose swiftly inside. "Don't say that." His whisper came out harsh. "I thought we already established that you are more than a servant."

"Let's be honest, Jackson." She spoke in her no-nonsense way. "I'm of the laboring class and you're practically nobility. Pretending otherwise won't change the way of things."

The social hierarchies had been transplanted from England to the colonies, and he'd lived a distinguished and privileged life during his years in North America the same way he had in England.

He'd never once even thought about the class distinctions, and he certainly hadn't challenged them the way Augusta had. Why hadn't he?

Maybe it was past time to do so. His mind raced in a dozen different directions at the implications of living more simply and fairly and without the airs of his class.

The bed squeaked again. Was Sage getting up in order to give him the bed? He'd never allow it. "No!" The one word came out a whisper-roar as his inner beast reared up in protest.

The shifting halted.

"You must not vacate the bed for me. If you do, I shall toss you right back."

"Toss me?" Her whisper held the note of sassiness he liked. "You wouldn't dare."

"Would you like to test me?"

"Maybe I will."

He waited, his muscles tense.

She didn't move.

Without giving either of them a chance to do anything that would be unseemly, he lowered himself to the edge of the bed, perching on the mattress as far from her as he could without sliding off. "Retire to your previous spot. I shall sleep on top of the covers."

She scooted away from him until a thumping told him she'd probably flattened herself against the wall, clearly trying to make as much room for him—or between them—as possible.

He waited, counting to fifteen before inching back until his whole body was on top of the bed, only a hair's breadth from hers. Even though he tried not to brush against her, his leg grazed hers, and he shifted so that he was partially off the bed.

An inner growl of frustration pushed for release, but he swallowed it. He'd believed the bed was big enough for two small children. He'd been wrong. It was only big enough for one tiny infant.

He held himself rigidly. If he relaxed and spread out, he would end up touching her, and he didn't want that. Yet, how could he go the whole night without relaxing and inadvertently brushing against her?

Perhaps if he forced himself to stay awake? The trouble was, he hadn't slept well the previous night on Salt Spring Island in the barn because he'd been preoccupied with Sage and the kiss. Now after the long day of traveling, sleeplessness and exhaustion were catching up to him.

He shifted, trying to get somewhat comfortable, which was difficult to do with half of his body about to fall off the bed. As he leaned his head back into a pillow, his arm skimmed against hers.

Her breathing turned shallow and quick, and tension seemed to radiate from her.

This wasn't going well. His presence on the bed was agitating her.

He started to push back up. "This isn't working—"

"Don't go." Her hand snagged onto his arm, holding him in place.

He halted at an awkward angle. "You're certain?"

"This is just one night," she whispered. "And we're both honorable."

He didn't exactly feel honorable at the moment, not after putting her into this awkward situation.

"We will go to sleep, and in the morning, we'll never mention this night again to each other or anyone else." From the resolve in her voice, he guessed she believed they could do that. Maybe she could. But he wouldn't be able to forget spending a night in the same bed with her any more than he could forget kissing her.

The kissing had been the highlight of the week. In fact, the more he'd thought about it, the more he'd realized that nothing else in his life quite compared to it. She'd been so warm and soft and welcoming . . .

He closed his eyes and bit back a groan. He couldn't let himself think about the kiss again. Especially while he was lying so close to her.

He had to get the focus off himself and think about her. Perhaps if he asked her questions? Maybe that would distract him? He scrambled to find something to talk about with her. But what? He couldn't get his mind to center on any other topic besides kissing and lying in bed.

"Your family. Your father." He fairly barked the words in his need to get the attention on something else. "Tell me more about him."

"If you'll do likewise."

He hesitated. He wasn't fond of thinking about his father, much less talking about him. But he couldn't ask her to share personally if he wasn't willing to do the same. "Very well. I shall tell you about mine if you tell me about yours."

After a moment, Sage began to share about her father, his work at the mill, his sweet relationship with her mother, the onset of his white lung disease, the danger of him continuing to breathe in the dust of the factory.

The longer she talked, the more the tension eased from his body. Not only did it help distract him from their predicament, but he liked hearing about her family and what her life had been like before she'd come to the colony.

When she finished, he answered her questions about his father. Although he didn't want to reveal too much, he found himself eventually telling her about his strained relationship starting when he'd attended Mount Radford School in Exeter from a very young age and then had been apprenticed to an engineering firm by the time he was fifteen.

Even then he'd felt the pressure to do more, and he'd tried to follow in his father's footsteps, had journeyed with his father from England to Rupert's Land to work with the Hudson's Bay Company in York Factory.

The company had given him the job of surveying for roads and bridges, and he'd liked what he did. He just hadn't been able to please his father. His father had criticized him for not venturing out far enough, for not being willing to take more risks, for getting distracted too easily, and for at least a dozen other things.

Finally, Jackson had taken the Hudson's Bay Company's offer to move to Vancouver Island. The gold rush had just started, and the governor of the new colony had wanted someone who could help with the development of the roads, primarily to make the transport of gold more accessible. Jackson had kept busy over the past years and had gained a reputation as an intelligent and industrious engineer. Then the accident had happened . . .

Thankfully by that point, his father had already moved back to England to be with his mother, who'd been ill. Otherwise, his father probably would have traveled to Victoria to interfere in Jackson's business.

As it was, Augusta had come to interfere, and Augusta was infinitely easier to endure than Father.

Jackson hadn't wanted the same life as his father, hadn't wanted to explore, hadn't wanted danger, hadn't wanted new adventures. He would have been content working as an engineer in a simple position for his whole life. But his father had claimed that the time in the far wilderness outpost of the colony would turn Jackson into a strong man—a man just like him.

"It didn't work," Jackson whispered, staring through the dark up at the ceiling. "I didn't turn out to be like him in any way, and he cannot understand or accept that I'm different."

"Even after all you've accomplished with your engineering feats?"

Jackson's mind returned to the last time he'd been with his father in the colony's government building. Jackson had just returned from a wilderness expedition, surveying routes for a new road to an important trading post. He'd failed to find a suitable and safe route, and his father had called him a coward for not exploring one of the more difficult areas. "He only sees all my mistakes."

"Then you must take after him." Her whisper was soft but firm. "Because you see only your mistakes too."

Jackson's thoughts came to a halt. Was she right? Did he only see his mistakes?

"God has gifted you with so many incredible designs that I've seen," she continued. "And you probably have dozens more that I haven't seen."

She wasn't wrong on that score. He did have more tucked away in cabinets and trunks that could benefit from her organizational skills.

"With so many excellent ideas and projects that you can give to the world, you're focused on the one that you've gotten wrong instead of all the ones you could do right."

Was that what had happened? Had he turned into a version of his father even though he'd never wanted to? Was he just as critical and self-focused? How had this happened?

He couldn't let go of the question, even as she moved on to ask him about other things. They talked more about his family and Augusta, as well as her family and siblings. He asked her again about loaning the money for their passage, and this time she didn't immediately object to the idea, probably because she'd learned that Willow hadn't been able to save much yet and was realizing how long it could take before they earned enough for the rest of the family.

They whispered in the dark for a while, probably a few hours, until at last Sage's yawns grew more frequent and her whispers softer, and she faded into silence. From her steady breathing, he knew she'd fallen asleep. Even though he regretted not having her companionship, he didn't begrudge her the sleep. After all, not everyone could survive on a few hours of sleep the way he did.

With his eyes closed and his arms crossed behind his head,

thoughts of her ran through his mind and filled every corner. He'd never had such long conversations with anyone, especially a woman. But he found that the equal sharing and listening had been pleasant, more than he could have anticipated, so much so he wanted to talk to her again.

Tomorrow. He tried to find satisfaction in that. He'd get to spend tomorrow talking with her again.

If only he didn't wish he could keep talking with her forever.

Eighteen

QUIET WAKEFULNESS FILTERED through Sage. She couldn't remember when she'd fallen asleep, only that eventually she had drifted off.

She'd plastered herself to the wall, and Jackson had lain as close to the edge of the bed as he could go, and they'd whispered in the dark for a long time. Sometimes the talking had turned serious, and other times they'd rambled about the silly things she and her sisters had done growing up or his voyages on Rupert's Land and Vancouver Island.

She breathed in her enjoyment from the previous night. The frigid air hit her lungs and brought her to full consciousness. Even though the temperature had obviously dropped in the unheated room, she was warm and comfortable and strangely content.

With her eyes still closed, she pushed past the haze and exhaled.

In response, a nose nuzzled gently against her neck just below her ear.

Sage's eyes flew open to the sight of bright daylight filling the room, revealing a plain white wall just inches away.

Before she could make sense of the state of the sleeping arrangements, warm lips grazed at the same spot below her ear.

At the connection, her eyes widened, and every part of her body zinged to life, suddenly aware of every part of Jackson's body touching hers. The blanket was now tucked around both of them equally, and there were no barriers between them except her nightgown and his clothing.

His long, lean form was pressed against her from behind, curved and molded into her. One arm circled her from underneath and the other wrapped around her with his hand splayed across her stomach.

Her senses could only take in the way each finger pressed against her, flat and hard and possessive, and a swirl of new but pleasurable desire tightened in her stomach. She couldn't deny how much she liked his possessiveness now and last night. She felt wanted, desired, even needed in a way she hadn't felt in a long time, if ever.

As if hearing her thoughts, his thumb grazed her ribs.

The movement was so sensual and so unexpected that a gasp slipped out, and heat trickled along each nerve ending. What was he doing? And why?

His mouth pressed in again as soft as silk, but the stubble on his cheek scraped her jaw. His touch was a contrast of gentle and hard, the same as his personality. He was such a complex person—deep and soulful and sensitive. At the same time, he was honest about who he was, never hiding from her, never holding back.

His lips against her neck didn't linger, almost as if he'd given her the kiss absently, maybe didn't even realize he'd done so. Was he still asleep?

She hitched her breath and listened.

His chest rose and fell in a slow and even rhythm against her back.

Yes, he had to be asleep. He wouldn't be crossing the boundaries of propriety if he were awake. He'd proven himself to be too much of a gentleman to do so. Most likely, he'd gotten cold, crawled under the covers, and had moved against her for warmth. Or maybe she'd been the one to move closer to him.

Either way, they'd ended up in the exact situation they'd tried to avoid. Even though they had to persist in the sham of a marriage, they didn't want to stir up inappropriate desire. They needed to keep boundaries in place so that when they returned to Victoria, neither of them would feel despoiled.

At the same time, if the pull between them was this strong, then why were they fighting so hard against it? No, she didn't want to become Jackson's mistress or be a mere dalliance. But was it too much to think that something more could ever develop between them? That they could ever love each other?

Willow had believed love was possible.

It was easy in the moment, with the way he was holding her, to conclude her sister was right. Maybe Jackson did care about her. And maybe she cared about him too.

Did she love him already?

A strange panic pulsed through her. No, she didn't love him, didn't want to love him. The usual protest began to swell inside her—the protest that she'd never be good enough. But Willow's words interrupted her runaway thoughts: *You may have failed at one relationship, but that doesn't mean* you *are a failure and that you should punish yourself for the imperfections.*

Sage breathed out slowly, trying to release the panic. She didn't have to be perfect, perhaps couldn't ever be perfect, not with her family, not in life, and not in love. She knew God didn't expect it either.

Was it time to finally let go of her perfectionistic tendencies and accept that life was sometimes messy and unorganized and untidy? And sometimes love was messy and unorganized and untidy too.

Love. She didn't know if that's what she was feeling for Jackson. Everything was so different than what she'd ever experienced with

David. But perhaps she had to allow herself to explore what those feelings were instead of running away from them.

A slamming door somewhere nearby rattled the wall. Behind her, Jackson startled. He pulled his head back as though waking up. For a second, he seemed to be taking stock of the situation, as if he was just now realizing how closely they were lying together in the bed. In the next instant, he jerked his hand off her and scrambled away.

At a thud against the floor, she guessed he'd fallen out of bed.

She held herself motionless. Should she pretend she'd been asleep and hadn't been aware of how he was touching her? A part of her wanted to spare them both the embarrassment. But at the same time, with all the other deception they were perpetuating, she had to be honest when she could.

Reluctantly, she rolled over. He was in the process of quietly rising, moving slowly as if that would keep him from waking her after all of the other commotion.

At the sight of her face, he halted, half kneeling and half crouched beside the bed. His dark brows formed an angry V, and his mouth pinched tightly. "How long have you been awake?" His whisper was too loud after the quiet between them.

But apparently the rest of the pub guests were awakening now too, because boisterous talking resounded from the room below as did the clatter of a pan.

"I've been awake for a few minutes," she admitted.

With a groan, he bent his head, resting it on his hand. "I apologize profusely, Sage. Please forgive me for my indecencies."

A part of her wanted to tell him not to apologize. On the other hand, she was relieved he wasn't the type of man who would willingly use her or the situation to push them into physical intimacy.

She offered him a small smile. "It's not your fault."

He didn't smile back. Instead, his frown deepened. "I knew something like this might happen if I lay down next to you."

"We had no choice—"

"I could have used better self-control." He finished rising, jabbing his fingers into his hair. "I should have stayed on top of the covers and kept my hands to myself."

"Jackson, please . . . " Their attraction was growing, and why couldn't they just admit it?

He paced to the door and stood facing it.

She opened her mouth to attempt a conversation about their relationship and the changing nature of it, but she couldn't make herself speak. After several seconds, she clamped her lips together.

He inhaled and seemed about to speak.

Was he ready to have the discussion now too? What would he have to say this time? More of what he'd said the last time about how he couldn't offer her anything and wouldn't make promises he couldn't keep?

Without a word, though, he opened the door, stepped into the hallway, and pulled it closed behind him.

She could only stare at the door, at first too surprised to react. As his footsteps in the hallway pounded away, her heart plummeted in her chest. He was still shutting her out of his life.

Her chest pinched painfully. But just as quickly as the pinch came, she pushed up and stretched, trying to ease the ache. She refused to let herself dwell on his rejection. Besides, it wasn't even rejection. How could it be, when they hadn't made any promises to each other?

All the while she dressed, she chastised herself to stay level-headed and to keep her perspective on Jackson. Just because he'd hugged her during the night didn't change anything. Did it?

She quickly finished her morning routine, packed their bags, then with their luggage in hand, she started down the stairway. As she neared the bottom, the chatter in the dining room came to a halt, and all the attention centered upon her.

Thankfully, not as many men were present at the early morning hour, a few clustered at two tables drinking coffee, the heavy scent of the fresh brew lingering in the air.

Jackson, standing near the door and talking to the proprietor, abruptly stopped his conversation and started across the room toward her, scowling at the bags in her hands. As he reached her, he took the bags from her, then helped her down the last step. "I was coming back up to get the luggage."

"It's all right."

"No, it's not all right. You should not be carrying such items."

She'd hauled around much heavier things during her life and during her voyage with Augusta. But she wasn't about to contradict Jackson at the moment.

Rawhide Ralph was at Jackson's side in the next instant still attired in his Native garb, wearing his hair in a long braid, and smiling widely. Clearly, his attitude toward Jackson had shifted, probably because Jackson had paid him handsomely already for the meal and room.

"Hope the wedding night was special." Ralph winked at her as he took the luggage from Jackson.

Oh my. Mortification swelled swiftly inside her.

Ralph raised a brow at Jackson. "It was awfully quiet."

Jackson scowled at Ralph. "It's none of your concern."

Ralph just shrugged his shoulders as much as he could under the weight of the luggage. "Some of the fellas are saying you ain't really together 'cauz you're not acting like newlyweds."

Jackson's angry gaze swept over the other men in the dining room. "Like I said, it's none of your business."

"Told the fellas one kiss would prove it one way or the other." The proprietor's voice held challenge.

The others had placed their mugs on the table and were now staring at her and Jackson with undisguised interest.

Jackson glared back.

It didn't matter what the men thought. She and Jackson were

leaving and would likely never see these people again. She opened her mouth to say as much to Jackson, but before she could get the words out, Jackson's hands landed on her hips, and he was dragging her toward him, his gaze hungrily focused on her lips.

Her stomach flipped over itself. She needed to protest, to make Jackson see reason, to not let him be goaded into kissing her.

But his fingers on her hips tightened, and he tugged her until she was flush against him. In the same instant with a growl, his mouth descended upon hers. His lips were hard and greedy and ravaged hers in one easy swoop.

She gave up any hope of resisting. She had no desire to. Instead, her own hard and greedy need swelled swiftly so that she responded with a ravaging of her own. She rose into the kiss, letting her desire free from the carefully restrained closet where she'd relegated it.

Kissing him was everything she'd remembered from the first experience . . . except that this time she had no reservations. She was ready—more than ready—to mesh her mouth and body with his. It was almost as if she'd been starved, and this was her one and only chance at gaining sustenance.

A few calls and whistles penetrated the kiss, drawing her back to the dining room and to the fact that people were watching her kissing Jackson.

At her brazenness, she broke the kiss and ducked her head.

Jackson tried chasing after her lips, but she buried her face against his chest.

He gave a huff of protest.

The proprietor was chortling. "Pay up, fellows! I told you, they're wild about each other! That he ain't pretending nothin.'"

A few of the others groaned or cursed softly.

Against her, Jackson's chest rose and fell heavily. His fingers upon her hips were taut. And he seemed immobilized, as if the kiss had turned him into a marble statue.

She decided she needed to put an end to the show or whatever was happening. She took a step back, reached for Jackson's hand, and slipped her fingers into his. She had half a mind to tell the fellows exactly what she thought of them and their uncivilized demands. But she'd never been as vocal as Willow, had always been controlled and polite.

Tipping her chin up, she started toward the door, tugging Jackson after her, and he came along without a word of protest. As they stepped outside into the bright sunshine, she breathed in the lingering smoke from nearby campfires along with the heavy scent of pine.

A cloudless blue sky greeted them as did a clear and calm river ahead. The morning was cold, but she was overheated from the kiss and needed something to bring her back to reality—the reality that she and Jackson weren't really a married couple who were *wild about each other.*

As they started across the grassy bank toward the wharf, he held on to her hand and kept his fingers interlaced with hers. Of course, he was only doing so to carry on their charade because the proprietor was following with their bags.

When they reached the *Widower* and the gangplank, he gave a curt nod to the captain already in the pilothouse. Then before she could decide what to do, whether to protest or not, his hand within hers tightened, and he bent down and captured her mouth with his.

The kiss was just as hard and intense as the one from moments ago, but it was short and over before she could arch into him and kiss him back. The quickness and intensity stole her breath and left her aching for more.

But he released her and stalked toward the pilothouse without a glance back.

She could only watch him in all his contrasting and rugged handsomeness, with strange desire pooling inside. She'd never imagined she'd ever feel so strongly about any man. But she couldn't deny the craving pulsing through her that made her want to chase after Jackson and pull him back into another kiss.

They were only supposed to be pretending. But with every passing moment, their relationship felt more and more real. The question was, did she want it to be real? Was she ready for something real?

Even if she was, it didn't matter. He'd been clear the other day that he wasn't interested in more, and a couple of kisses wouldn't change that.

Nineteen

J ACKSON'S WHOLE BODY KEENED WITH the need to kiss Sage again—a need that wouldn't be quelled no matter how hard he tried.

He blew out a tight breath as he walked along beside her toward the parsonage at the rear of Christ Church. He never should have kissed her again this morning—not once, but especially not twice, not after spending a night in bed beside her.

Was she thinking the same thing?

She was quieter than usual, had been for the steamboat voyage the rest of the distance up the Fraser River to Hope. They'd talked a little, mostly him explaining the different sandbars they passed, the gold that had been discovered in the area, and how the miners had moved farther up into the Cariboo region now that most of the easy gold had been discovered.

As usual, she'd asked him questions not only about the mining but about the wildlife and the Natives and how the smallpox had spread over the past year, wiping out whole tribes.

However, the air between them had been strained, and he'd

caught her looking at him a time or two, as if she was wondering about his initiating the second kiss with her before boarding the steamboat. It had been one thing to kiss in the pub when everyone had been looking and demanding it of them. But it had been another matter altogether to kiss her when no one had been pressuring them.

Why had he done it?

He still couldn't compute a plausible explanation.

With frustration pounding in his temple, he kicked at a loose stone in the gravel alley that led to the parsonage.

At least they'd arrived in Hope by the afternoon. The town was bigger than Centreville, having once been Fort Hope and an outpost for the Hudson's Bay Company. It sat at the conflux of the Fraser and Coquihalla Rivers and was surrounded on three sides by mountains. The colorful changing leaves blanketed the mountains around them. It was truly a glorious sight, even with the clouds hanging low and filled with moisture.

Although each mile upriver brought him closer to the site of the accident, somehow the nearness wasn't as hard to bear as he'd expected. Was it because he was distracted with his desires for Sage and his search for Augusta? Or maybe he was starting to finally accept all that had happened and heal from it?

If only once in a while his mind could function normally like other people's. But it didn't. It never had. And he couldn't stop himself from being consumed with Sage—both in his waking and sleeping.

In fact, his need for her was growing more and more pronounced, so much so that he felt like he was one of the cables on a suspension bridge that was about to snap under the pressure. Should he just admit to himself and to her how much he cared about her? Even if he did, what would he be able to do about it?

Moreover, he needed to expend his mental capacity on their search for Augusta. Since their arrival, they'd walked along the waterfront, and he'd queried some of the regular stevedores he'd met on previous trips. One of them had finally recognized the small photograph of Augusta, claimed she'd been with a fellow but that he hadn't taken the time to look closely at the man. The stevedore hadn't exactly known where the couple had gone, but at one point, he'd seen them come out of Christ Church. If Augusta had been upset or struggling, the stevedore hadn't noticed it.

Armed with that news, Jackson had led Sage over to the church. Unfortunately, the reverend, John Roberts, hadn't been there, and now they were seeking him out at his home, praying he had seen Augusta and would be able to give them information about her.

"She has to be here in Hope somewhere," Sage said, peering past the parsonage at the small homes that were on the outskirts of town. Most were new and made of clapboards since Hope boasted of a lumber mill. However, the residences were simple and small, not nearly as elaborate as his home in Victoria. Even so, this town in the wilderness of British Columbia was one of the mining towns that had lasted when others had dissolved as soon as the miners had moved on.

The parsonage ahead was painted a light yellow, and lacy curtains hung in each window. As they started up the flagstone path that led to the house, Sage slipped her gloved hand into the crook of his arm and held on tightly, as though she was afraid of the news that awaited them.

He laid his hand over hers and squeezed gently. "We shall find her, Sage. I vow it."

She tilted her head so that he glimpsed her sorrowful eyes past the brim of her fancy bonnet. "I pray you're right."

He lifted a hand to knock, but before he could, the door swung open to reveal a plain but kindly looking young woman wearing a fashionable gown, a brooch at her neck, and a pearl circlet in her hair.

"May I help you?" She regarded them almost as if she'd expected them.

"Yes, ma'am." Jackson gave a polite tip of his hat. "We would like to speak with Reverend Roberts, please."

"I'm his wife, Mrs. Roberts." She clasped her hands together in a ladylike movement that reminded Jackson of his mother's mannerisms. "Regretfully, Reverend Roberts's duties have taken him out of town today to visit several mining camps."

"I see." Against him, he could feel Sage droop in disappointment. "Do you know when he will return?"

"It may not be for a couple of days, perhaps longer." She glanced in the direction of the river. Although not visible from the house, it wasn't far, and the whistle of an arriving steamboat echoed in the valley.

Should they wait in Hope until the reverend returned? During the interval, they could search for other clues, perhaps locate additional people who'd seen Augusta and could give them information.

"Thank you for your time, ma'am." He gave a slight bow. "When your husband returns, would you be so kind as to let him know that . . . " How should he refer to Sage now that they were in Hope? He'd planned to drop the marriage pretense, especially because he'd anticipated finding Augusta who could chaperone them. But now if they had to stay at a local hotel for any length of time, the gossip would run rampant if he introduced Sage as anything other than his wife.

Sage shifted beside him, her arm still tucked in his.

He tried to catch her eye, but she was too busy studying Mrs. Roberts and wasn't paying him any heed. He stifled a sigh at their continued dilemma. Then he did what he needed to, even though he didn't like having to lie. "I'm Mr. Lennox. Would you be so kind as to let the reverend know that my wife and I would like to speak to him as soon as possible? It's a matter of some urgency."

"Mr. Lennox?" She spoke the word with a note of relief.

"Yes."

"My husband left something for you."

Sage's fingers tightened against his arm.

He pressed her hand back.

"Just one moment, please." Mrs. Roberts closed the door, leaving them on the stoop by themselves.

"Maybe Augusta left us a note." Sage leaned into him.

"Let us pray she gave us more than one word this time."

"Yes, let's hope so."

He loved the way Sage's shoulder felt pressed against him and the closeness of her arm wrapped through his. But even as he relished her touch, guilt prickled him that he was carrying on the duplicity regarding their marriage. "I apologize for having to deceive the reverend's wife," he whispered. "I had hoped we could find Augusta and not have to continue with our charade."

"I regret that we have to lie too."

"Maybe we should have gotten married before departing from Victoria." As soon as the words were out, he inwardly cursed himself for blurting out the thought. It was one thing for him to mull over the possibility as he had last night, but it was another thing altogether to say it aloud.

He could feel Sage studying his face, likely trying to understand what he meant.

What exactly did he mean? He had to offer a plausible explanation. "It would have prevented us from having to lie."

She was silent a heartbeat. "I don't think that's reason enough for entering into marriage, do you?"

It wasn't. She was right. He'd already decided he didn't want to coerce her. But . . . were there more reasons for them to be together? Or was he simply letting his desires for her get the best of him?

Before he could answer her question, the door opened again,

and Mrs. Roberts stood before them holding out a folded slip of paper.

"My husband asked me to pass this along to you, Mr. Lennox, if you came while he was gone."

Jackson took the paper, which was no bigger than the size of an envelope, and he unfolded it. There on the sheet was one of his drawings. A bridge. The Queen's Bridge, to be exact.

He recoiled from it and let the paper fall from his hands and flutter to the ground. Augusta must have taken it from his study. Had she given it to the reverend? Or had the reverend stumbled across it at the church and realized it belonged to him as the builder?

Sage was already bending down and retrieving the paper. No doubt she recognized it after helping him organize so many other drawings and diagrams in his study.

"I wasn't sure what good the drawing would do you." Mrs. Roberts was watching him quizzically. "But my husband informed me that you are the talented engineer of the Queen's Bridge and that this was likely important to the rebuilding efforts."

Jackson could feel the angst swirling faster inside him, and he was afraid to answer for fear that his frustration would come out. Did the kidnapping have to do with his bridge? What if a family member of one of the deceased was seeking retribution and intended to use Augusta to make him pay for his mistakes?

As if sensing his turmoil, Sage slid her hand down and laced her fingers together with his. Somehow that simple movement seemed to seep inside and settle the storm brewing in his body. "Mr. Lennox's sister was kidnapped several days ago."

Mrs. Roberts's hand fluttered up to her chest. "Oh dear. I'm so sorry. I didn't know."

"Perhaps she left the drawing as another clue to her whereabouts." Sage fished in her reticule and pulled out the photo of Augusta they'd brought along. "Did you happen to see this woman? Or perhaps she saw your husband and gave him the drawing?"

Mrs. Roberts examined the photo then shook her head. "I'm sorry. No, I didn't see her. But my husband said she came to the church."

Jackson dragged in a breath. "Did your husband indicate her state of mind or well-being?"

"No, I'm sorry. He only spoke of the need to return the drawing. Apparently Miss Lennox said it was of the utmost urgency to see that her brother got it. I was to send it in the mail if Mr. Lennox didn't claim it by tomorrow."

Utmost urgency didn't sound good. It had to mean she was in more trouble than she'd let on, probably all she could communicate if she was with her captor.

After thanking Mrs. Roberts and heading back down the flagstone path, Sage's expression had turned grave, her eyes solemn. She'd likely arrived at the same conclusion. "She needs us."

He nodded. He needed Sage. In fact, a part of him didn't know how he'd ever functioned without her steadiness.

Sage pursed her lips as if checking off items in one of her mental lists. "Before leaving Victoria, she had to have known where her kidnapper was taking her."

"To the bridge?"

"Perhaps. Or perhaps she'll find a way to leave us another clue there."

If his theory was correct about the kidnapper being related to one of the bridge workers who'd died, then maybe the fellow would be waiting at the bridge with a list of demands in exchange for Augusta.

If someone was waiting for him, he wouldn't blame them. He hadn't exactly apologized or made reparations for his role in the disaster. He'd had his accountant send the remaining earnings and a stipend to each family who had been affected. But other than that, he'd been more focused on himself than on the suffering of the families. Even if his mind had a tendency to turn inward and fixate on things, that was no excuse for being so selfish and only thinking about his own pain instead of others'.

"How far is Hope from the bridge?" Sage's question cut through his thoughts.

He had to drag himself back to the moment. He was trying to find Augusta. He couldn't let himself get distracted with another mission, at least not until this one was completed.

"The bridge is at least thirty miles north of Hope, up the river past Yale."

"Could we get there yet today?"

"It's too late." Moreover, he didn't know if the steamboat captain would be willing to take them the last part of the journey to Yale. The captain had indicated the need to return to Victoria tomorrow, which meant they would have to find someone else to transport them.

Once in Yale, the river became too dangerous for steamboats. From there, most of the miners set out by foot, which was why the roads—and bridges—up the rest of the river valley were so important, particularly for transporting supplies to the mining camps and for carrying the gold out of the mountains.

As they reached the street, Sage glanced to the sky overhead and then to the western range. "Are you sure we can't leave today?"

"I am certain of it." He was anxious for Augusta too, could only imagine her fear and the distress she was feeling at this point. Every passing day only put her into more danger in the hands of a lunatic kidnapper who most likely wanted revenge or a ransom or both.

As much as he wanted to help Augusta, he refused to risk Sage's well-being. With the hour getting late, she would be safer if they waited to leave in the morning. They would take a hotel room, and tonight he would make sure to find one big enough that he could bed down on the floor.

As much as he loved his sister, the truth was, he was beginning to love Sage more. Though that thought should have surprised him, it didn't. It felt completely logical and sane and natural to admit the truth—that he was in love with Sage.

Twenty

WEARILY, SAGE BROUGHT HER HORSE to a halt beside Jackson's on the high mountain road.

She drew in a sharp breath at the sight of the bridge ahead, half of it suspended above the river far below and the other half gone, the jagged edges the reminder of what had once been whole and complete and solid.

In the fading evening shadows, the skeleton was dark and eerie. The area was empty and deserted since most of the other travelers on the mountain road were already making camp in the river valley below. Hopefully Augusta and her captor were also camped someplace nearby, perhaps hidden or just tucked away for the night.

Sage's thighs were chafed from the saddle, and her backside felt permanently bruised. But she'd insisted on continuing to the bridge, even though Jackson had suggested stopping a couple of hours ago.

With each passing day, the urgency to find Augusta kept growing. The dear woman had been a captive for at least five full days— one while Sage and Jackson had been on Salt Spring Island, the day of their traveling to Centreville, the next day in Hope, then one making their way to Yale, and finally today—the fifth day journeying on the horses Jackson had paid to use.

Sage had only ever ridden a horse once when she'd visited the Lancashire countryside, where her mum had grown up. Otherwise, she'd never had need to ride, especially since arriving in Victoria, where she and Augusta had used hired carriage drivers for their transportation needs.

When their traveling party had started out from Yale shortly after dawn, Jackson had been a patient teacher with her, had even held her reins and directed her horse during the sections of the trail that had been narrow and more dangerous. She'd thankfully caught on quickly and had been able to manage her horse for most of the journey.

The October weather in the higher elevations had been steadily growing colder, and all day Sage had struggled to stay warm. Even now, as she shifted on her mount, the cool evening breeze slithered inside her cloak and down her backbone, making her shudder.

"We'd do best to head down before it gets any darker." Pastor Abe pointed toward the river bottoms below. The three businessmen who were also a part of their caravan had already started down the narrow switchbacks that led to the river.

The businessmen heading up to Williamsville weren't very friendly, especially because Jackson had acted like a beast to them all day, cutting off any attempts at dialogue and practically snarling at them if they even briefly spoke with her.

The gruffness had only gotten worse the longer they'd been on the trail and the closer they'd come to the bridge. She suspected revisiting the site of the accident was difficult for Jackson, possibly something he hadn't done since the accident.

But Pastor Abe hadn't been put off by the beast Jackson had unleashed for the day. The young pastor who ran an orphanage in Yale had joined the group, apparently on a mission to rescue an orphan in one of the mining camps. Tall with fair hair and blue eyes, the reverend had spoken fondly of his wife Zoe, who had been on the bride ship the *Robert Lowe* with Willow.

Sage had enjoyed hearing Pastor Abe's tale of how he and Zoe had formed a marriage of convenience to provide a home to an orphan baby. While the marriage had started as an arrangement to benefit them both, it was obvious from the love shining from Pastor Abe's eyes that he adored his wife.

Now, as Pastor Abe nudged his horse toward the trail that led down to the river, Jackson only frowned at the man's broad back, but he didn't protest, likely realizing the need to wait until morning to search more for Augusta.

Sage had appreciated Pastor Abe's kindness throughout the day. If only her guilt hadn't continued to surface every time she referred to Jackson as her husband. She and Jackson had kept up the pretense in both Hope and Yale, but at least their hotel rooms in both towns had been large enough that Jackson had made his bed on the floor each night, insisting she take the bed.

She wasn't sure how she would have handled another night together in the same bed as him. One night had been brazen enough, and she still dreamt about having his arms around her. She still dreamt about his kisses too. But they hadn't kissed again. She'd been determined not to let it happen, and he'd seemed that way too.

Even with a strange, sizzling tension between them, she'd loved spending every minute of every day with him. The time getting to know him better had made her appreciate even more his brilliant mind, his deep thoughts, and his passion for things he cared about.

"Ready?" She reached across the distance between their horses and grazed Jackson's arm. She wasn't sure when she'd grown so familiar with him, but at some point over the past few days, she'd started touching him without really thinking about it.

He never seemed to mind the physical contact. There had even been a few times when he'd initiated brushing against her—at least, she'd assumed the touches hadn't been accidental.

Except for the muscles flexing in his jaw, he stared at the bridge, unmoving. After so many days of no shaving, he was reverting back to the rugged man she'd first met. He wasn't as unkempt and did take time to do some grooming, but having a clean-shaven face was obviously low on the priority list for most men out in the mountains.

If it was possible, that dark layer of stubble had only made him more handsome. Even now as he straddled his horse and peered into the distance, the sight of him made her stomach flutter, especially with the brim of his hat pulled low and lending him an even darker appeal.

It wasn't fair that he just kept getting more attractive the longer she knew him—both his outward and inward qualities. Perhaps the more she understood the complex but compassionate man he was inside, the more she was drawn to him.

He slid a sideways glance at her and arched one of his dark brows almost as if he'd heard all of her thoughts and knew the power he had over her.

She tore her attention from him and fixed it on Pastor Abe as he began to descend the switchbacks. Had the intuitive reverend sensed the marriage charade? While he hadn't questioned their claim to be married, he had watched them curiously a time or two, as if he didn't quite believe them.

Jackson didn't say anything, but he nudged his horse forward and waited politely until she trotted ahead of him before he took a protective position behind her. As she descended the steep mountainside, she wanted to ask Jackson more about the bridge—why he'd picked this particular spot for it, where they'd gotten supplies for building it, how he'd managed living in the wilderness.

Even though she sensed it would be healthy for him to discuss more of what had happened that fateful day, she also didn't want to push him to share if he wasn't ready.

She was learning for herself that healing took time and couldn't be rushed. She'd had to put months and an ocean between her and her hurts with David before they'd started to go away. Maybe meeting Jackson had helped to make her forget about David too.

Regardless, she couldn't expect Jackson to so easily put his past to rest and move on into a new future. Yes, he had mentioned that they should have gotten married before leaving Victoria. She suspected that he'd only been referencing an in-name-only marriage for the sake of the journey. But a tiny part of her wished he'd meant more by it.

As they reached the bottom of the switchbacks and arrived at a grassy area along the river, there were more groups camping than she'd realized. Some were still setting up tents. Others were cooking over campfires. A few were fishing along the river. At her arrival, their gazes locked in on her.

She didn't like drawing so much notice, but she was growing accustomed to it and learning to ignore the staring.

If only Jackson would ignore it too. But as he reached the level area where Pastor Abe and the businessmen had dismounted, his scowl was firmly in place and directed at the other campers.

He hopped down and was at the side of her horse before she could swing her leg over. He reached up and settled both hands on her waist. His eyes were dark and as fiercely intense as always, and his forehead was creased and his jaw taut.

"What's wrong?" she asked as he lifted her down.

An angry growl rumbled in his chest. "I don't like the way those men are staring at you."

"I don't mind—"

"I mind." Instead of setting her on her feet, he brought her flush against him.

Her body made firm contact with his, sending a cascade of sparks shooting along every nerve and skittering over her skin.

He angled his head, his gaze dropping to her lips. The desire there was stark and raw and unfiltered. He wanted to kiss her.

The soft fluttering in her stomach turned into a hard flapping. If he wanted to steal one from her in front of their onlookers, she would be helpless to stop him.

She lifted her face, offering her lips, offering herself. She could feel the hard thudding of his heart and knew that whatever this was happening between them was real and wasn't just a show for the men.

His focus was directly upon her mouth. But just as his lips brushed her cheek, he shifted and buried his face against her ear.

He held her tighter, nearly cutting off her air. But she didn't care. She savored the feeling of being so close and of having his strong body pressed to hers. His breathing against her ear was labored. And in the next instant, his mouth touched her ear.

The sensation of his lips and warmth grazing her ear was so sensual, she couldn't hold back a gasp.

He kissed her ear again, this time harder and longer, the desire achingly sweet so that she wrapped her fingers into his cloak to keep herself from buckling and sliding to the ground in a melted heap.

How was it possible that he could render her useless in just seconds?

"There." His voice was gravelly against her ear. "Now there's no question in anyone's mind that you are mine."

Without giving her a chance to respond, he released her as suddenly as he'd held her. He turned to his horse and began to unstrap a bundle of supplies.

Her knees were wobbly and her head dizzy and her body filled with a need she didn't understand. She had to grab on to the horse's halter in order to keep from collapsing.

She wanted to tug Jackson back toward her so that this time she could wrap her arms around him and kiss him right. But as she leaned closer, she glimpsed Pastor Abe casting glances their way as he knelt by a bundle of kindling and attempted to light a fire with a flint.

Her cheeks flushed, and she quickly backed away, putting sufficient distance from Jackson and grasping the bundle on the back of her horse.

Jackson had a powerful influence over her emotions and body—more so than she'd realized. How easy it was for her to fall into his arms, to fall against his body, and to fall in love with him.

Yes, it was the truth. She was falling in love with him.

Oh my. Her fingers trembled against the rope holding the bag in place.

She couldn't be in love yet, could she?

Even as her mind attempted to deny it, her heart thudded with the realization that she'd allowed herself to fall helplessly and hopelessly in love with Jackson Lennox.

She shouldn't have done it. She knew what it was like to be rejected by a man—how painful and devastating and life-changing it had been. She didn't want to suffer through that again.

A part of her wanted to believe Jackson was different, that their circumstances were different, that she was different. But Jackson had never given her a reason to believe he wanted a future with her, not even with his offhand comment about how they should have gotten married in Victoria.

Besides, even if maybe he thought he wanted more, he would learn she wasn't perfect enough for him. He could find someone so much better than her—a woman of his class who would be able to join his social circles and not be an embarrassment to him.

Even though he claimed she was more than just a lady's maid, the reality was that she was only a simple mill girl from Manchester. She had a family there who was counting on her help. She had Augusta who also still needed her.

Yes, she was living in a fantasy world to think that a man like Jackson could ever truly be interested in a woman like her. Of course he was attracted to her like the other men were. But that wasn't enough.

She simply wasn't enough. She hadn't been for David. What made her believe she ever would be for Jackson?

Twenty-One

I T WAS TIME FOR BED. AND SAGE WAS already in the tent. The very small tent.

Jackson gave his horse one last rub before tucking the brush away in the saddlebag. All the while he'd been grooming the horses and thinking about the coming night, his gut had cinched tighter until he felt like he couldn't draw in a full breath.

A part of him wanted to go into the tent, lie down beside Sage, and pull her into his arms. Yet another part of him objected to doing so because it would be wrong. Because sleeping with a woman—even innocently—was a privilege reserved for marriage.

The trouble was, with the hug they'd shared earlier still fresh on his mind, he wasn't sure he'd end up being *innocent* if he was in such close confines with her again.

He'd already proven he was too weak that night in Centreville above the pub when they'd shared a bed. The temptations had been too great and his desires too strong, and he'd ended up holding her.

With how much his feelings for her were continuing to grow,

he trusted himself even less around her. He didn't want to compromise Sage any more than he already had.

However, some of the other fellows camping in the river bottoms were still sitting around their campfires. They would notice if he didn't join his *wife* in the tent and instead threw his bedroll down in the grass. Not sleeping with her would raise too many questions he didn't want to answer, particularly from those in his traveling party. No, he'd have to go in and perhaps put their bags between them—if he could manage to fit them in the middle.

The reverend had bedded down near the fire, his arms crossed behind his head, his face pointed heavenward, his eyes still wide open. Two of the other traveling companions were sitting on a log by the fire and were sipping from whiskey flasks. The other was snoring loudly in his tent nearby.

Jackson drew in a breath of the cool night air and peered up at the cloudless sky and the dark firmament with the constellations on full display—Cassiopeia and Perseus shining the brightest. He'd spent many nights stargazing during his months camping in this area with his crew and had memorized most of the stars.

It was difficult being back. He couldn't deny that. His thoughts had been jumbled with memories and flashbacks during the past couple of days, and his heart had swelled with grief and pain that first moment he'd reached the bend in the road and saw the remains of the bridge as well as the debris on the riverbank below.

Nonetheless, he hadn't experienced the same level of despair that had plagued him since the accident. Maybe he'd been too distracted by Sage. Especially because a possessiveness had been compounding inside him, so that when any other man looked at her with even a hint of desire, he wanted to tackle them to the ground, punch them in the eyes, and then roar at them never to even glance at her again.

The beast he'd thought was tamed had reared up inside him. Would he always struggle with that beast?

He silently cursed himself for placing Sage into a situation like this where her honor was at stake ... because of him. But hopefully they would be able to put an end to their fake marriage tomorrow.

He hesitated only a second outside the tent flap before shoving it aside and crawling inside.

The triangular-shaped tent sloped low, and his head brushed against the canvas. The darkness prevented him from seeing her or the luggage, but he could feel a bag by his knees and could hear her shifting, probably trying to make more room for him.

He felt around for his bedroll only to find that she'd already laid it out with his blankets. Because the night would grow cold, he'd warned her earlier to sleep in her shoes and clothing, and he intended to do the same.

Crawling forward, he tried to move his bag to act as a barrier between their bedrolls, but he only managed to scoot it at an odd angle before he gave up, stretched out, and covered up.

When he finally lay motionless beside her, he allowed himself a breath. Maybe he could do this after all. Maybe the darkness and the cold would act as a natural barrier. Maybe she was asleep and wouldn't even notice he was there.

"Are you okay?" Her whisper skimmed across the darkness.

The kindness of her concern only made him all the more aware that she was mere inches away. But he couldn't think about that, couldn't start focusing on how close she was. Instead, he clenched his jaw and tried to put her from his mind. "I'm fine."

"You seem upset."

He was upset at himself. But he couldn't admit that because doing so would only force him to admit how obsessed he was over her.

She was quiet for several moments, so that the only sounds were the low murmur of voices from the campfire and the crackle of burning wood. "I'm sure being here is hard," she whispered.

Being back at the bridge *was* hard, but being so close to her was even harder. It was one thing to become immersed in his work projects and the engineering feats that he developed. But it was an entirely different matter to allow himself to be absorbed by a woman. What if he failed her? Made mistakes? Ruined things? Caused a disaster?

The truth was, he did often fail, make mistakes, ruin things, and cause disasters. The biggest one lay just up the river a hundred feet.

Was that why he'd called off his engagement with Meredith? Even though he'd never been consumed by her, maybe he'd been afraid he'd ruin their relationship and marriage with his propensity to make so many mistakes.

What made him think he could ever do better with Sage? In fact, with the strength of his feelings for her and just how much he thought about her, he had an even greater chance of causing a disaster.

"I just want you to know," she continued, "that I'm here to listen if you want to talk about anything."

"Thank you." Conversing more about his grief and guilt would take him another step forward in bringing about a resolution to the accident. However, he was in no frame of mind to discuss it, not with how turbulently his thoughts about her were roiling and not with how close she was beside him.

She drew in a shaky breath, as though trying to calm herself, but calm herself from what? Was she nervous to have him beside her?

His muscles tightened. He didn't want to make her uncomfortable with his presence here tonight any more than he had that night above the pub. He pushed up to his elbows. "If you would be more comfortable without me in here—"

"I'm comfortable."

"You're certain?"

"Yes." Her voice was almost shy.

The trouble was, he was the one uncomfortable, and he was

afraid he would end up reaching for her, even with his best efforts not to.

He exhaled a tight breath.

"Something is wrong," she persisted quietly.

Before he could think of how to respond, her fingers brushed against his arm.

He drew in a sharp breath this time.

She made a trail from his bicep down his forearm to his fingers. With each inch she moved, his muscles coiled tighter.

As her fingers grasped his and then began to intertwine, he was wound up enough that he felt as though all it would take was one more tiny touch from her and he would snap.

Swallowing hard, he tried to make his arm loosen and relax.

"Jackson?" His name from her lips was like a caress.

He managed a responding sound.

"I want you to know"—she hesitated—"that I care about you."

Her whisper was tender, but at the same time was like a seismic wave rolling into him and undoing all the control he'd willed himself to have.

A groan pushed for release. This was torture. For an eternal second, he closed his eyes and battled against the pressure crushing him so that he couldn't breathe, couldn't move, couldn't even think. All he knew was that he wanted her—and not just physically. He wanted all of her—body, soul, and spirit. And he wasn't sure how he could possibly go on another second without her.

A war—one he was afraid he'd lose—raged in every corner of his mind. He needed to crawl immediately out of the tent and stay away from her, even if that meant confessing to Pastor Abe that he wasn't really married to Sage.

"I think," she continued, "that . . . I'm falling in love with you." Falling in love?

He stiffened. Even though he'd already admitted to himself that his feelings for this woman defied all reasoning and that he was in love with her, her confession sent a burst of panic through him.

Hadn't he just told himself he wasn't ready for a serious relationship? That he'd only end up making a mess and hurting her?

She brushed her thumb over his, bringing all his attention to that spot, to the delicate touch, the warmth of her skin, the softness of her body, the beauty of every inch of her. For a second, he was lost in the sensations, and all he wanted was to lie beside her like this and feel her caress forever.

She shifted slightly.

She'd just told him that she loved him and was waiting for him to respond. But what could he say? He couldn't reiterate it, couldn't encourage her love, not when he was an utter mess of a man.

He sat up and tugged his hand from hers.

She grew motionless, didn't even seem to be breathing.

He had to say something, needed to explain why he was no good for her, but the words were trapped inside.

The air in the tent was suddenly stifling. His heart was pounding too hard, making his head throb. He had to go outside, get away from her, and try to make sense of everything. He swiped up his bedroll and the blankets and began to crawl toward the tent entrance. As he reached the flap, he paused.

In the darkness he could make out her stiff outline.

"I regret . . . " He wanted to assure her that she wasn't at fault, that the problems were all his. "I cannot—sleep in here—with you. It's a mistake . . . "

He blew out an exasperated breath then scrambled out of the tent, dragging his bedroll with him.

Across the low dancing flames, Pastor Abe pushed up to his elbows, as though he was ready to spring up and come to Jackson's aid. The other two fellows sipping whiskey paused to stare at him too. He supposed he looked like he was escaping from a burning building.

He stood to his feet and jabbed his fingers into his hair. The truth was, he was running away from fire before he played around with it and burned Sage and himself. He was doing what was best for them both. Wasn't he?

Why, then, did he feel as though he'd pushed her away and left her to suffer all on her own?

Despondency fell over him, and his shoulders drooped under the weight. He'd only wanted to keep from causing her pain, but what if in the process he'd hurt her even more?

He railed a silent curse at himself before lowering himself to the blankets and bedroll that sat in a heap outside the tent door. Yes, he'd done what he'd predicted. He'd made a greater mess of the matter.

That's what he was good at—messes and mistakes and never living up to expectations, especially his father's. Even though he knew he had to stop letting his father's voice define him, he couldn't seem to shake the echoes.

Twenty-Two

HER HEART HURT TOO MUCH TO SHED a single tear. In fact, she hadn't cried once during the long, sleepless night.

Now at dawn, as she knelt in front of the tent door and began to lift the flap, she hesitated.

She didn't want to see Jackson or talk to him this morning. All she wanted to do was search for Augusta, find her, and then ride back to Victoria together in the comfort of each other's presence.

That's why she'd come on this journey in the first place, so that she could locate Augusta, rescue her, and continue being her lady's maid. She hadn't come to draw closer to Jackson and practically throw herself at him and make declarations of love.

With a low groan, she buried her face in her hands, feeling the mortification once again, just as she had last night after she'd spoken the words. Oh why had she done it? Why had she told him how she felt?

She'd been foolish, too forthright, too naïve.

Apparently over the past days of traveling with Jackson, she'd lulled herself into believing he cared about her just as much as she did him. She'd felt his attraction, she'd basked under his attention, and she'd even felt a deep connection with him unlike any she'd had with past men.

But she'd obviously been wrong about him, just like she'd been wrong about David. Why had she been so mistaken? She'd spent the night making mental lists of all the possibilities, of all her flaws, of all the explanations why neither man had been right for her.

She'd come up with every plausible reason to add to each list. She would hang on to them tightly and remind herself of those lists every time she started to think about having more with Jackson and every time she contemplated changing her mind about becoming a spinster.

She'd been right about the need to remain single. That was the better path for her after all. She'd just allowed her head to get turned, to think more highly of herself than she ought, and to let hope for a future take up residence inside her.

She'd risked everything on loving Jackson, and she'd lost him anyway.

"I learned my lesson," she whispered. "I learned it well."

Even as the words settled over her, so did the pain—a pain so deep her heart felt as though it had been wrenched from her chest, which wasn't possible since it had already been ripped out the moment Jackson had left her alone in the tent last night.

The pain pulsed through her veins and to her limbs, and for a moment she couldn't move or breathe with the force of it.

It was worse than what she'd felt when David had left her. Then she'd cried and silently railed against him, mainly because she'd been feeling sorry for herself and all that she'd lost. And because she'd been embarrassed about having to tell everyone about her cancelled engagement and David finding someone else.

In the end, she hadn't really missed David. She'd missed the idea of the perfect life she'd planned for herself.

This time, she hadn't planned to have a happy life, she hadn't planned on falling in love, and she hadn't planned to even tell Jackson her feelings last night. But somehow it had all happened anyway.

She supposed it had slipped out because she'd sensed he was hurting and needed someone by his side as he faced his past. She'd wanted to be that person for him, had wanted him to know she cared.

But she'd said too much. She could have assured him she cared but then stopped there.

With a sigh, she lifted the tent flap. Even though his rejection hurt terribly, it was better that it had happened now before she allowed herself to care about him even more.

As she ducked outside into the early morning, the fire was low and smoky with the heavy scent of fried fish in the air. The sun hadn't yet risen over the eastern edge of the river valley, but the sky was light and cloudless, promising a beautiful autumn day ahead.

Pastor Abe was sitting on a log beside the fire, a plate balanced on his lap and a mug of coffee steaming in one hand.

At the sight of her, he offered a guarded smile, as if he didn't quite know what to make of the fact that Jackson had spent the night outside of the tent instead of inside with her. "Good morning, Mrs. Lennox. I hope you slept well."

Mrs. Lennox. Should she correct him and tell him the truth about her fake marriage with Jackson? She tried to smile back and prayed it didn't look like a grimace. "Good morning."

She glanced around for Jackson, hating that she wanted to see him even though she'd resolved to put him out of her mind. Thankfully, he wasn't present, which gave her a few more moments to compose herself before interacting with him today.

From the barrenness of the campsite, the others in their party had already packed up and left, as had most of the other groups.

Only a few men remained, and they were in the process of folding up their items and strapping them to their horses.

Soon, she and Jackson would be left alone. Yesterday she would have been thrilled at the prospect of countless hours with him—talking, hiking, and continuing to put their minds together to find Augusta. But today . . . she dreaded having to pretend she wasn't hurting when every part of her body ached.

"He's over there." Pastor Abe nodded upriver in the direction of the bridge debris.

She followed his gaze to find Jackson attired in his suit and hat and looking as gentlemanly and handsome as always even though he'd slept in his clothes and still hadn't shaved. He was standing in a rocky section of the riverbank in front of a heap of stone and wood. His hands were stuffed deep into his pockets, and his shoulders were slumped.

The ache in her heart radiated for him and all that he must be feeling this morning as he viewed the site of the accident after months away. Even though she hadn't known him long, she knew him well enough to realize he was torturing himself this morning with the memories and with all he could have done differently.

"Would you like some breakfast?" Pastor Abe set aside his plate and reached for the pan that was resting on a stone beside the fire pit.

"I don't want to impose—"

"You're not imposing." He began scooping a forkful of fish onto another plate. "I'm more than happy to share."

The morning air was cold, and a light frost coated the grass. As she took the plate from the reverend and began to eat, she huddled closer to the fire for warmth. He also offered her a mug of coffee, which she drank gratefully.

"I imagine you must be wanting to leave soon," she said after finishing her last bite.

"I'm not in a great hurry. I told your husband I can wait to leave until the two of you are ready."

Guilt once again prodded her. She couldn't lie to this man of God any longer about her relationship with Jackson. She glanced again at Jackson, who had started lifting away boards and stones, as though he was searching for answers to all his problems in the depths of the wreckage.

"Reverend?" she said hesitantly. "Jackson and I aren't really married."

The reverend, in the process of taking a swallow of coffee, spluttered.

"We've only been pretending so that we don't cause a scandal."

The reverend wiped his sleeve across his mouth and lowered his mug. "I admit I've been curious about the two of you, but you're both so in love with each other that I naturally had no reason to believe you weren't married."

"So in love?" She couldn't keep the scoffing from her voice. "Jackson doesn't love me. That's the trouble—"

"That man definitely loves you." Pastor Abe chuckled lightly, the corners of his eyes crinkling. "He's so in love with you, he could hardly keep his eyes off you."

This was a strange conversation to be having with a holy man, but she was already feeling better at having confessed the lying. "I won't deny he's—we're attracted to each other. But he doesn't reciprocate the love."

"He's not putting on an act. It's clear he deeply cares about you." Pastor Abe shifted his gaze to where Jackson was rummaging through the rubbish. "But it's also clear that he bears some burdens that might be holding him back."

"He blames the bridge collapse upon himself." Why was it so easy to share with this pastor? Was it his kind eyes? His gentle demeanor? Or perhaps after facing another rejection, she needed someone to confide in before she went crazy.

"It's easy to blame ourselves when things go wrong." Pastor Abe spoke quietly, as if he was remembering a time in his own life when things hadn't gone so well. "But much of what we face happens simply because we live in a broken world—a world like that bridge, one that's unsteady, incomplete, and unreliable."

She could attest to the brokenness. She'd seen it all around her in Manchester where poverty and disease and unemployment were the lot of life. The people born into that life—like her family—weren't to blame for the conditions.

"Even if he finds a way to repair the bridge," Pastor Abe continued, "eventually it will wear down and break again. That's just what happens."

"That sounds hopeless."

"We do what we can to fix the brokenness here in this life while we're alive, but ultimately we can never find complete wholeness here. Our real hope is found in the one place where we'll have a perfect life—in heaven with God."

She took a sip of coffee. That made sense. She'd already been learning that she had to stop striving after perfection, that it wasn't attainable. Maybe this was one more lesson in her journey, to remember that perfection could only happen in the next life, not in this one. And maybe Jackson needed to hear that too.

Pastor Abe nodded at the bridge remains. "Relationships are like bridges too."

"How so?"

"It takes a lot of work to build a bridge from both sides that eventually allows us to connect with one another." This reverend was proving not only to be a good listener, but he was also wise beyond his years. She didn't know his age, but if she had to guess, she would say he was in his mid to late twenties.

The bridge ahead jutted out over the river, the crumbling edges much more visible in the daylight than they had been the previous evening when they'd arrived. Would the bridge ever be able to span the distance and meet in the middle and become complete?

Pastor Abe poured himself another mug of coffee from a pot sitting among the embers. All the while, his expression was contemplative. "I guess what I'm trying to say is that with as much as you both care for each other, don't give up too soon in trying to build that bridge. You just never know when you might end up connecting."

Was she giving up too soon? Perhaps. But what could she do if he wasn't ready for a relationship yet?

She finished draining her coffee and then placed the coffee mug in the grass next to her plate. "Thank you, Reverend. I appreciate not only breakfast but your advice."

He smiled, his face taking on an almost boyish quality. "Good. Then you won't take offense when I tell you that until the two of you are officially married, you should refrain from traveling alone. I recommend that you have a chaperone with you at all times."

She ducked her head, unable to meet his gaze. Everything about their situation was embarrassing, including the reverend's foregone conclusion that she would eventually marry Jackson. "As soon as we find Jackson's sister, she'll be our chaperone."

"Perhaps you would allow me to accompany you until then?"

She met his gaze to find only kindness and not condemnation. "We don't know where Augusta's been taken by her kidnapper. We assumed we'd find her in Hope, and here we are miles north of Hope and we're still searching."

He gave a casual shrug. "The offer is available if you need it. I'm heading north to Lytton and from there to Dugan Lake. I can go that far with the two of you, and if you need to go farther, I know many people in the region and will help you find a new chaperone."

For the first time since leaving Victoria, she released a freeing breath. "That's very nice of you."

"Good." The reverend stood and stretched. "I think it's time to go build a bridge, or at the very least figure out why it's broken."

She didn't quite know what to say. Was he referring to the Queen's Bridge or the one that needed repairing between her and Jackson? She was fairly certain both would be difficult to fix, but should she at least try?

Twenty-Three

T HE NEED FOR SAGE PULSED THROUGH Jackson.

He'd been attempting to convince himself that the only reason he needed her was for her assistance in organizing his thoughts and writing down the mental list about the bridge that was running through his head.

Yet the convincing wasn't working. The need for her went deeper than that—much deeper. No matter how hard he'd tried to forget about her or ignore her, he couldn't. He was as aware of everything about her just like he always was.

From his position at one of the supporting piers up on the broken part of the bridge, he cast a glance at her sideways. She'd finished examining the rubble down by the river the way he had earlier, and she'd climbed up the switchback with Pastor Abe and was now searching the high mountain road, most likely for another clue from Augusta.

Sage's process was methodical as she'd scoured both sides of the trail, examining the rocky area that bordered the river valley and then also searching the grassy side that led to the forested hillside.

She was only a few dozen feet away, and yet she felt miles from his reach. She'd felt miles away since the moment he'd left her behind last night.

She hadn't looked at him for the past hour after she'd ducked out of the tent and joined the reverend at the fire. Jackson was grateful Pastor Abe had taken care of her sustenance, although he wished he'd been the one to offer her the plate of fish and mug of coffee.

He was surprised the reverend hadn't left with the other travelers earlier. But Jackson hadn't stopped to question Pastor Abe's plans and had instead become engrossed in the wreckage. Now that he was finally back at the bridge, his curiosity was overshadowing the shame and guilt from the accident.

Of course, the shame and guilt were still twisting through him, but they weren't clamoring as loudly anymore. He was growing in the conviction that it was past time to stop letting what had happened debilitate him. In fact, it was past time to institute a plan to rebuild—a plan that included a thorough study of the remaining pieces.

He paused at the rod that had been damaged, one that the ice had weakened. The expansion of the freezing moisture was the culprit in weakening the bridge. Was it possible he needed a different material for the rod? A larger diameter? An outer shell that repelled moisture?

What he really needed was her.

Expelling a long, exasperated sigh, he propped his knee on the nearest stone. He'd made a mess of things last night, which was no surprise. Instead of remaining calm while he was with her, instead of accepting her sweet declaration of love and responding to it with his own affection, he'd ignored her completely.

That's because he was an imbecile. Even if he wasn't ready for a relationship with her, he should have handled everything much differently.

"How is your search going?" Pastor Abe called to him as he meandered closer along the road.

Jackson straightened and homed in on Sage, who was poking around a trio of rocks off to the side of the road. She'd taken the time to fix her red-blond hair into a pretty chignon beneath her hat and to make sure she was put together. In a simple but stylish blue dress, she looked especially fresh and bright.

She was a lady every bit as much as Augusta. Maybe even more so. Not that her status mattered to him anymore. Not that it ever should have mattered.

The truth was, she was absolutely perfect for him.

The problem was that he wasn't right for her. He'd hurt her last night, was hurting her this morning, and would only hurt her again. As much as he wanted her, he had to resist a relationship.

Pastor Abe stopped at the end of the road and didn't venture out the way Jackson had onto the crumbling part of the bridge that remained suspended above the river.

"Sage said that your sister left two previous clues." Pastor Abe scanned a nearby beam. "A charm bracelet for the first and a picture of the bridge for the second."

"Yes, that is correct."

"Then we could be looking for just about anything."

"That is correct as well."

"So you'll know it's a treasure when you find it."

"Precisely."

Pastor Abe bent and peered underneath a board. As he straightened, he smiled at Jackson. "Sounds a little bit like what's happened in your relationship with Sage."

Jackson's swirling mind slowed to a crawl as he tried to make sense of Pastor Abe's line of reasoning.

Pastor Abe perched against a railing that was still intact. "I haven't been around Sage long, but it's easy to see you've found a treasure in her."

Sage was kneeling and running her fingers through the long grass. Her expression was filled with determination, her body radiated strength, and her back was stiff with purpose. She'd set out to find Augusta, and he had no doubt she'd do it, because she was an incredible woman. She *was* a treasure—a very rare and exquisite treasure.

"When God gives you a treasure like that," Pastor Abe continued, "you need to do everything you can to cherish and keep it."

Jackson studied the reverend's face. Had Sage told him they weren't really married? It sounded that way. He supposed it didn't really matter if the reverend knew or not. Maybe it was even better if the reverend was privy to the truth.

"Do everything," the reverend repeated.

"She deserves to be cherished." He agreed with Pastor Abe wholeheartedly. "But by a better man than me."

"If God gives the gift, then we can't give it back. All we can do is prove ourselves worthy of it."

Jackson's thoughts slowed once again. "I doubt God gave her to me, not when all I do is make mistakes."

Pastor Abe released a low chuckle. "Like the bridge?"

He nodded, shadows blowing into his mind. "It was my costliest. But I've made plenty of others."

"But you're here now trying to fix it?"

"I'd like to try."

"That's all we can do. When we fall down, we get back up and try again. Each time we do, we hope we don't fall as hard and that we get up more quickly the next time."

Jackson peered down at the cracked rod. He was learning from his mistakes on the bridge. It was taking him time and a great deal of effort—hours and hours of studying and calculating and examining diagrams—to make changes and fix the problems.

If he could put that much work into repairing a bridge, he could certainly do that with a relationship, couldn't he? After all, Sage was worth more than a hundred bridges. Could he spend his life putting in the effort with her to make up for his shortcomings? And when he fell and made mistakes, could he learn to do better the next time?

Hope surged inside him. He might not be worthy of Sage, but he could work on becoming better and fixing himself so that maybe one day his flaws wouldn't be so glaring.

The first thing he had to do was figure out a way to apologize for last night.

He shook his head at what a fool he'd been. "Reverend, I must admit—"

A scream rent the air. Sage's scream.

With his pulse picking up pace, Jackson's gaze darted in the direction where he'd last seen her.

The open cliff-side road spread out to the south and north. But she wasn't in sight.

His body tensed, and he glanced quickly around. Where had she gone? Had the same kidnapper who'd taken Augusta gotten his hands now upon Sage?

Twenty-Four

J ACKSON BOLTED OFF THE BRIDGE, HIS heart thudding with dread.

"Where is she?" He didn't care that he was yelling at the reverend. All that mattered was getting to Sage before she was lost to him.

"She was just here." Pastor Abe was scanning the mountain road.

Jackson careened down the path that led to where he'd last seen her. "Sage!"

"Help me, Jackson!" Her faint voice wobbled with fear.

"Where are you?" He surveyed the woodland that rose steeply on one side of the road. The route wouldn't be easy—would even be treacherous—but it was possible someone had hauled her up and into the woods.

"I'm here!" Her voice came again, this time closer.

He paused, examining the shadows of the woodland again, but he didn't spot her anywhere amongst the pine and fir trees.

"Hurry!" she called. "I don't know how much longer I can hang on."

Hang on?

His gaze shifted to the other side, the steep drop that fell to the river bottoms below. At the sight of a portion of earth that looked like it had given way into a cascade of rocks and dirt, his heart plummeted to the bottom of his chest.

Already Abe was veering toward the spot. Jackson shot out an arm to block him from going any closer. If they loosened any more of the earth it would fall onto Sage and whatever precarious hold she had.

Abe halted, and his expression turned solemn. "What should we do?"

Jackson's mind spun in a vortex of all the possibilities. Only one solution was viable. And if he didn't act immediately, even that wouldn't work.

"Grab on to my legs, Reverend." That was all the explanation Jackson had time to offer before he dropped to his knees, flattened himself on the ground, and then stretched out so that his head was peering over the ledge.

At the sight of Sage hanging on to a protruding tree root with both hands but dangling in the air, his body nearly froze with the horror of the moment. Thankfully she wasn't wearing her gloves, which would have made holding the limb much more difficult.

As it was, her knuckles were white and her veins prominent, the sure sign she was struggling to keep her hold. How long before she lost her grip?

For an instant, he was back at the bridge in the spring, staring at the unfolding disaster and in particular one of the workers who'd held on to a beam, suspended above the wreckage below. He'd called for help, and Jackson had nearly fallen off the broken bridge in his attempt to reach the fellow. But before he could snake his way down the remaining beam to grab on, the man had first lost one grip, then ten seconds later, he'd lost his other grip and had dropped. He'd yelled all the way down, and when he'd landed, silence had settled over the bridge, with only the river mocking them with its rushing life.

Jackson's throat went suddenly dry at the prospect of Sage losing her hold. "Don't let go." He tried to keep his voice calm, didn't want her to get more nervous than she already was.

"Help me, Jackson." Her voice was strained, as if she was already having trouble.

"I'm coming." He inched his way over the cliffside, and at the same time, he felt the reverend's strong arms wrap around his ankles, anchoring him in place.

Jackson knew he couldn't go straight down, not with the landslide that had already taken place. Instead, he had to angle his way toward her. It would take longer, but it was the safer route.

"Hold on, love." Jackson used his most soothing tone as he scooted down even more, stretching for her hand on the root. If he could just grasp her hand . . .

He had to get a little closer.

Roots and rocks and prickly plants scratched at his stomach and his face. Though the sun was barely above the eastern range and only beginning to chase away the chill from the night, perspiration formed on his brow.

"I'm almost there." He pushed himself over the ledge just a little farther. He could feel the strain on his legs and ankles where the reverend was clinging to him so tightly his knees felt like they might come out of their joints.

"Hurry," she said in an urgent whisper.

He lunged, trying to snag her wrist, but he missed. God above, help him. The reverend had been more than right. Sage was not only a treasure. She was the greatest treasure he'd ever known. Hopefully she could accept his obsessive tendencies, because they would be mostly about her. Hopefully she could accept that he would hover and be jealous and need her too much at times. And hopefully she would be patient with him as he tried to change so that he wasn't so hovering and jealous and needy.

God, You gave her to me. Don't take her from me yet. Not until I have the chance to prove I can cherish her as she deserves.

The silent plea rose in desperation as he dove for her again. This time his fingers circled her wrist. "I've got you."

A half sob escaped from her lips.

He could feel his own body slipping down, as if his weight was simply too much for Pastor Abe to bear. Would he and Sage both tumble to their deaths below?

He managed to wrap his other hand around her second one so he was clasping on to both of her arms now. "Pull me up!" he shouted over his shoulder in the direction of the reverend. "Now!"

At the heave on his legs, Jackson tugged on Sage, attempting to drag her with him.

She'd turned her face up to his and was watching him with rounded eyes that were brimming with fear.

"I won't let you go," he said. "Not here at this moment, and not ever." Now wasn't the time or place to declare his love and intentions to her. But the words had slipped out anyway, almost inevitably.

She watched him with trusting eyes, her lashes wet with tears.

He hauled her again, pulling her up a few more inches. "Promise you won't let go of me either."

She managed a nod.

Behind him, Abe grunted. No doubt he was in agony with the strain of holding two people.

With another heave, Jackson dug deep inside to the last of the strength he had. "Pull now!" he shouted at Pastor Abe. The reverend seemed to put his whole body into the hauling, and at the same time Jackson poured out everything, roaring with the pain of the effort, tugging her the rest of the distance.

In the next instant, she was crawling forward on solid ground, using her feet to propel her upward even more. He didn't stop pulling until she was well away from the edge of the cliff. Even then, he dragged her backward.

Pastor Abe released him and fell on his knees, breathing hard.

Suddenly weak and nearly sick to his stomach, Jackson sat back. He lifted Sage onto his lap then wrapped his arms around her and buried his face into her neck.

He'd come so close to losing her. Too close.

His heart was pounding hard, and he wheezed in a breath past his constricted airways.

Her arms slid around him, and she sidled closer so that he could feel her whole body shaking. She obviously understood, too, that she'd had a brush with death and had barely survived it.

His senses filled with the light fragrance of her soap, the softness of her skin, the silk of her hair, and the warmth of her body.

She was safe. She was with him. She was his. The three thoughts rolled through his mind over and over.

As his heartbeat slowed and his breathing evened out, one thought rose above all the others. He loved her. It began to repeat in his mind until it was a mantra that was echoing loudly.

Although he still didn't deserve her, he loved her, and he wanted to do whatever he could to make himself strong enough and worthy of her. Even if that took a lifetime, he'd do it so she would always know just how much he adored her.

First, though, he had to apologize for last night.

He loosened his hold just a little.

As if sensing his need to say something, she tugged back, forcing him to release her more. "Thank you for saving me," she whispered, her forehead now near his lips.

He didn't restrain himself. He couldn't. His lips brushed her brow gently, then harder as his passion swelled like it usually did.

She didn't move, probably didn't know what his kiss meant, not after last night.

He tilted away enough that he could see into her eyes—eyes full of questions and doubt and even pain.

"I love you, Sage." The whispered words were out before he could stop them. "I should have said it last night because I knew it then. I've known it for a while."

Her gaze softened. She opened her mouth to say something, but he lifted two fingers to her lips to silence her. He had to finish his speech before he lost his train of thought or got distracted or kissed her or all of those things.

"I don't feel worthy of having you," he said. "Not when I'm still a beast at times."

"It's okay," she mumbled against him. "I understand."

"No, I need to grow and change and become better." Her lips were so soft against his fingers, so full, so beautiful. Maybe it had been a mistake to touch them. Already his mind was veering away from the much-needed apology and filling with the longing to rub his thumb across her bottom lip.

"I need to grow too," she whispered.

"I love you just the way you are." His thumb disobeyed his head and caressed her bottom lip. It was every bit as perfect as he remembered.

"I don't know, Jackson." A wrinkle formed in her brow. "What if you regret choosing me?"

"You might regret choosing me." He shifted his fingers and drew a line along her elegant cheekbone. "You've seen how my mind works, and you know that it's different than other men. I get focused on something like my bridge and become obsessed with it and then I can't let it go."

"I love that about you."

"You do?"

"It just shows how passionate you are about the things you care about."

He dropped his gaze, suddenly embarrassed by what he needed

her to know next. "The truth is, that's happened with you the same way, Sage. I'm so focused on you that you're in my mind all the time. You're all I think about, all I want, and all I need."

She didn't respond.

He waited another second before peeking up at her face.

She was smiling. And her smile was beautiful and happy, filling her eyes with light and turning them a vibrant blue. Did that mean she wasn't put off by his obsession with her?

"Do you think you can tolerate the kind of man who might smother you at times with his attention and ardor?"

She slid her arms around his neck. "I'd much rather have you showing me too much affection than too little." Her gaze dropped to his lips.

Sudden heat cascaded through him. "Would you now?"

"I would," she whispered, tightening her hold around his neck and at the same time pulling his head down.

She didn't have to work too hard because he was more than ready to kiss her. In fact, in some ways he felt as though he'd been born to spend his life with this woman, holding her and kissing her.

He let her initiate the kiss, softly touching her lips to his, gently caressing him, sweetly tugging and tangling with his lips. She was everything he needed to survive in life. As long as he had her, he'd be able to do anything else.

As her fingers slid into his hair at the back of his neck, the pressure of her lips seemed to change, growing more needy and letting him know that she wanted to show him affection too.

Her need and desire seemed to give him permission to unleash his. His fingers on her back tightened, and he pressed her closer. He started to angle in, hungry for her mouth more fully. But before he could capture her, Pastor Abe cleared his throat loudly right behind them.

She jumped, nearly breaking free, except Jackson didn't want her to go anywhere, needed her close, couldn't release her yet, not after what had happened.

"So lovely to see you two together," Pastor Abe was saying through his cough. "But I do suggest that you be careful not to stir up too much desire until after you're married."

Sage had definitely told him about their fake marriage.

It was probably for the best. And Pastor Abe was right. They didn't want to instigate more desires than they already had. Not until after they were married.

And they were getting married. At least he wanted to. Why shouldn't they?

As if hearing his unspoken question, she hesitated. "We're from two different worlds, Jackson—"

"You're the only woman I'll ever want or need."

Her beautiful eyes rounded hopefully. "Are you sure?"

He caressed her jawline—couldn't help himself. "Are *you* sure about me? You know about my tendency to make messes—"

She was the one to cut him off this time as she gently dragged a finger across his bottom lip. "That's why we fit so well together, because I love to organize your messes."

He peered into her eyes, love radiating there. "Then will you do me the honor of becoming my wife?"

Twenty-Five

WAS THIS REALLY HAPPENING TO her? Was Jackson proposing marriage?

His ruggedly handsome face was only inches from hers, and his gray-blue eyes held hers with his usual intensity.

She let her fingers drift from his lip to his chin, relishing the thick coarse hair and the hardness of his jaw.

"Have you considered when you might like to get married?" Pastor Abe spoke again, his tone hinting at humor.

"Soon." Jackson spoke the word bluntly. "If Sage is agreeable ... to marriage, that is."

"I'm agreeable." Her voice had a breathless quality, and she focused on his shirt. "And soon is fine with me."

"Soon it is," Pastor Abe said.

"Very soon," Jackson added.

"How about now?" As the question tumbled out, she began to scramble backward. "No, that's absurd. I shouldn't have said it. It's just that we have a reverend, and it would solve the problem of needing a chaperone, and—"

"I concur." Jackson tugged her back, giving her no choice but to sit down on his lap again. "Now is perfect."

She pressed her hands to her cheeks to cool them. "Perhaps we're being hasty and need time to think more about it."

"I shan't need more time to think on it."

She released a short breath of relief. "Then neither do I."

"I love you." His words were low and rumbly. "I know I just said it, but I cannot stop myself from saying it again."

She couldn't contain a smile. "I'll never tire of hearing it."

"Good. Because you'll likely hear it a great deal." His lips curved up into a rare smile.

At the sight of it, her breath hitched. The smile transformed his face, taking him from handsome to devastatingly gorgeous. It revealed his nice teeth, defined the curves of his mouth, and made the sharpness of his chin more prominent.

She had her new mission in life—make Jackson smile more often.

"I don't have my prayer book," Pastor Abe said as he reached a hand toward her to assist her to her feet. "But I do mostly have the ceremony memorized and can lead you through it."

She took the reverend's help. As she stood, she remained as far away from the road's ledge as possible. Her legs were still trembling, but she managed to brush her hand over her skirt and release the dirt and gravel sticking to the material.

Those last seconds before her fall came rushing back. She'd been methodically assessing each inch of both sides of the road. Somehow she must have stepped too close to the edge. She'd felt her feet slipping and the ground giving way beneath her. She'd frantically turned around and grasped at the road, the earth, anything she could get her hands on. She still didn't know how she'd been able to grasp the tree root, but it had saved her life.

No, Jackson had saved her life.

He was standing beside her and brushing the dust and dirt off his suit. He'd lost his hat, and the morning sunshine bathed his head, turning the strands to a silky black.

Feeling her gaze upon him, he halted, and his eyes seemed to ask her if she was okay.

She was now. "I love you."

His eyes lit.

"I know I just said it," she said as she repeated his words back to him, "but I can't stop myself from saying it again."

His smile made another appearance, and it sent her heart into a dizzying spin. He started to reach for her, his gaze falling to her lips.

"Whoa, now." With a chuckle, Pastor Abe patted Jackson's chest firmly and positioned him beside her. "We'll never get the two of you married at this rate."

Jackson nodded. "Forgive me, Reverend."

Pastor Abe closed his eyes. "Let's pray."

Jackson's hand slipped into hers, and he laced their fingers together.

She loved the strength of his hand, the ripple of tension in his fingers, even the possessiveness of his hold. She loved him. She wanted to blurt it again, but she bit back the words, knowing she would have plenty of time later—the rest of her life—to tell him and show him how much she loved him.

As she stood beside Jackson on the high mountain road, the morning sun warmed her back. It was high enough in the sky now that it turned the mountainside into a golden cathedral. The tall evergreens standing on one side acted as their witnesses. The bridge ahead became their altar and the rushing river below their music.

Pastor Abe led them through the order of the marriage service with a reverence that seemed only fitting under the widest and bluest sky she'd ever seen. Jackson must have sensed the reverence too, because his voice was low and filled with awe as he spoke his vows. Hers were hardly above a whisper as she said hers in return.

As they finished, Pastor Abe smiled. "Now may God the Father, God the Son, God the Holy Ghost, bless, preserve, and keep you. May the Lord mercifully with his favor look upon you and so fill you with all spiritual benediction and grace, that you may live together in this life and that in the world to come, you may have life everlasting. Amen."

"Amen," she whispered, half expecting to wake up and discover she was just dreaming.

But Jackson's fingers still laced with hers were too solid. His arm pressing into hers was too real. The intensity radiating from his body was all-encompassing.

"If only I had a ring." He lifted her hand to his lips and kissed her ring finger.

His lips were gentle but sent a shudder of desire through her that was anything but gentle. She had the sudden need to press against him and feel the length of his body. It was a wanton thought, and it warmed her cheeks.

Thankfully, he wasn't aware of the power of just a kiss on her fingers. He was too busy scanning the landscape. "There has to be something we can use as a temporary ring."

Abe was patting his pockets, as though he was looking for a stray object they could use.

"It's all right—" she started.

Before she could finish assuring Jackson that she didn't need a ring for the marriage to be official, he stiffened, then broke away from her. With his eyes on something ahead, he stalked down the trail toward the bridge.

She tried to locate what he'd noticed in the morning sunshine. But she didn't see anything new or different. Of course, she hadn't gotten as far as the bridge when she'd been looking for clues from Augusta.

After the conversation with Pastor Abe earlier, she'd still been working up the courage to approach Jackson. She hadn't been willing to give up on their relationship yet, had decided to be patient and do what she could to continue building connections. But at that point, she'd been content to search along the trail and let Pastor Abe explore closer to the bridge.

Jackson didn't stop until he reached the part of the road that led onto the bridge—or what remained of the bridge. He stooped and pushed aside a tuft of grass. The sunlight glinted off what appeared to be a piece of metal.

Had he found something to use as a ring after all?

She wouldn't be surprised. He was ingenious and would probably be able to fashion a ring out of anything.

As he rose, he twisted the object, examining it before he shifted and lifted it so that she could see what he'd found. "It's a fork."

She started toward him, still wary of getting too close to the edge of the road.

Jackson was staring at the silver object again. "It was stuck into the ground with the prongs facing upward."

Pastor Abe was at Jackson's side already and looking at the item. "Do you think it's the clue from your sister that you've been searching for?"

As Sage joined the two at the edge of the bridge, she scanned the wreckage that stretched out a short way over the river. The stones and beams hung in disarray.

"I'm flabbergasted why she would leave us a fork as a clue." Jackson held the fork out to her. "Do you have any ideas?"

She took it and studied it. "It's one from your home."

"Is it?" He sounded surprised.

For such a smart man, he didn't always see the details, probably got too caught up in his mind and his projects to pay attention to things that didn't really matter. However, in this case, it did matter. But how?

"Clearly Augusta brought it with her." Sage dusted the dirt off the end that had been stuck in the ground.

Something about the clues and the methodical nature of Augusta's placement of them didn't make sense. It seemed too planned and too thought-out for someone who'd been kidnapped and whisked out of the house against her will.

Jackson's features creased with a scowl. "The big question at the moment is what is Augusta trying to tell us with a fork?"

The charm bracelet with the word *hope* and the picture of the bridge had both been fairly easy to decipher. But a fork?

Sage rubbed off more of the dirt. "Is there an eating establishment—a dining room, pub, or hotel that she might be leading us to?"

The three of them fell silent as they stared at the fork. A loud *cak-cak-cak* echoed above them as a hawk with gray wings and a light pink chest circled overhead.

"A fork." Jackson spoke the word slowly, as if in doing so he could unravel Augusta's clue.

She started a list. "Silverware. Eating utensils. Spoons. Knives. Forks."

Pastor Abe snapped his fingers and met Jackson's gaze. "Forks."

"Forks?" Jackson's voice still held confusion.

"The Forks." Pastor Abe nodded up the river. "The Great Forks."

"Yes." Jackson's face took on an animated light. "That is it."

"What is it?" she asked.

"The town of Lytton to the north of here used to be known as Forks or Great Forks, because that's where the Thompson and Fraser Rivers meet."

So Augusta had placed a fork near the bridge to let them know that their next destination was the Forks, also known as Lytton. "How far away are we?"

Jackson seemed to be calculating the distance in his head. But Pastor Abe spoke before Jackson could. "It's a full day's ride."

"Can we make it by tonight?" she asked.

Pastor Abe looked at the position of the sun. "Maybe. If we leave now and ride hard."

"Then let's go." Excitement shimmered through Sage. If—when—they finally located Augusta, what would she say when she learned about the wedding?

Sage pressed a hand to her chest to still the sudden rapid beat of her heart. Should she have waited and gained permission first? Obviously, she couldn't change what she'd done now. But maybe she would have to explain to Jackson that they needed to wait to make their marriage real until after they found Augusta and had her approval.

She'd seemed open to Sage liking Jackson, and she hadn't been opposed to them spending time together. But that didn't mean she'd welcome Sage into her family as a sister. What if Augusta didn't give them her blessing? Would they get an annulment?

Protest rose inside Sage at the prospect. But she had come to the colonies first and foremost to be a lady's maid. She couldn't abandon Augusta. At the same time, she doubted Jackson would support her continuing in that role now that she was his wife.

Regardless of the dilemma, they had to leave right away and continue the search. Augusta's life might depend on them. And they couldn't waste another moment.

Twenty-Six

S AGE AWOKE WITH A START.

They'd finally stopped moving. Thank the Lord.

A gentle kiss against her neck brought her back to the realization that she was riding with Jackson on his horse.

After leaving the bridge earlier in the day, she'd started off on her own mount. The traveling, though, had been difficult, and for most of it, they'd ridden single file because of the narrow trail. When they hadn't reached Lytton by the time darkness had fallen, she'd asked to keep going, hadn't wanted another night to pass for poor Augusta in captivity.

Both Pastor Abe and Jackson had reminded her that there wouldn't be much they could do for Augusta so late at night anyway. But Sage had pleaded with them to continue, and they'd agreed only if Sage was willing to share a horse with Jackson. She hadn't needed much convincing to join him while Pastor Abe guided her horse behind his.

She'd been exhausted by that point from the stress of staying away from the edge of the road and the trauma from her fall earlier.

Her sleeplessness of the previous night had probably also caught up to her.

So even though she'd wanted to stay awake during the last leg of their journey and enjoy her time in the saddle with Jackson, she'd fallen asleep only minutes into their ride and had slept the whole way—had it been one hour, maybe two?

Whatever the case, she was sore from the long journey but couldn't think of anyplace else she'd rather be than in the saddle with Jackson. His strong arms surrounded her and were cradling her against his chest. His legs boxed her in too, and one hand rested flat against her stomach.

As her mind roused to the fuller awareness of just how close she was sitting to him and the intimacy of his hold, a warm thrill spread through her abdomen. She was his wife, and they could kiss and hold each other as much as they wanted, couldn't they?

"We have arrived in Lytton," he whispered against her ear.

Just his whisper and the brush of his lips sent more warmth spilling through her. She tilted her head to an angle that would allow him more access. As she did so, his lips touched her neck again, as though he was taking full advantage of her offering.

This time his kiss wasn't so gentle. It was hot and demanding and hard. She wanted to shift in the saddle, wrap her arms around him, and mesh her mouth with his.

But he ended the kiss before they could get carried away, which was a good thing since the sounds of town life filtered through her senses: fiddle music and laughter, the rattling of a passing wagon, the thudding of horse hooves, a woman's distant voice in a heated argument.

Her eyes opened now to find the darkness of night surrounding them, but not as encompassing as it had been on the trail. Not with the light radiating from windows from the structures all along the main street and especially from the lights in the windows of a large and elaborate building in front of their horses. The sign hanging from the post at the base of wooden steps read: The Globe.

"It's a new hotel, the best in town." Jackson straightened as he surveyed the rest of the main thoroughfare. Except for a couple other buildings made of clapboard like the Globe, most were constructed of logs. "I know the owner, and I'll ask him for the best room."

A flush bloomed inside Sage. She knew exactly what Jackson wanted with the best room, and she wanted it too. But she couldn't . . . not tonight.

"Jackson," she started, her whisper containing a hint of her embarrassment at having to bring up the topic at all.

"Am I moving too fast?" His voice held genuine concern.

She appreciated his consideration, that he'd even ask that.

"We can wait," he said softly.

His words proved all over again what a kind man he really was and just how much he loved her. In addition, his words only fanned her own love for him . . . and her desire. But she also didn't want to have any regrets, especially about Augusta.

Sage brushed her hand over Jackson's, loving the tautness of each finger splayed over her stomach. "I am worried about what Augusta will think of my marriage to you."

"She will rejoice in it."

"Do you think so?"

Jackson hesitated.

It was a moment too long. "You're worried about her reaction too?"

Jackson was silent, staring straight ahead at the hotel.

At the livery next to the hotel, Pastor Abe had already dismounted and was in the process of speaking with a young man, probably making arrangements to board their horses. No doubt the reverend would be on his way tomorrow to his next destination while she and Jackson continued the search in Lytton for Augusta or for another clue.

"Be honest with me, Jackson." She brushed a hand over his cheek, loving the fact that she could do so whenever she wanted now. "Should we get Augusta's blessing first?"

He was silent for a few more seconds, then he spoke gruffly as he began to dismount. "I have your love. That is all the blessing I need."

"I know Willow will give us her blessing."

"We shall visit her again just as soon as we return."

"I would love that."

"And I shall pay the passage for the rest of your family to immigrate. No arguing with me about it. I shan't be swayed."

Without waiting for her response, he lifted her out of the saddle but didn't set her down and instead cradled her against his chest. As he did so, he bent in and let his lips touch hers in a short but passionate kiss. "I love you."

She wrapped her arms around his neck. "I love you too."

"I'll get two rooms for tonight." He started toward the front door of the hotel.

"No." Her protest came out quickly and emphatically. "I want to stay with you."

His muscles tensed.

"You can hold me like you did that night at Centreville."

"I had the strength of a saint that night," he growled. "Don't expect another miracle."

Her lips curved into a smile.

He swung open the hotel door.

"My dear husband"—she loved the way the word *husband* rolled off her tongue—"are you telling me that you can't resist me?"

"That's exactly what I'm saying, my dear wife." He smiled down at her, and the sight of the smile, like always, took her breath away.

She couldn't help herself. She tugged his head down and at the same time rose into a kiss. She barely had time to brush his lips, when he jerked back and stared straight ahead, his mouth falling open.

"What is it . . . ?" She followed his gaze only to let her mouth drop open too.

There, wrapped in the arms of a large man, was Augusta. The proud bearing, dark hair, tall, thin body belonged to none other. Not only was she pressed against the man, but she was kissing him with an enthusiastic fervor.

She didn't appear to be harmed or disadvantaged or even co-erced. In fact, from the way her arms were roaming over the man's chest, she'd moved in and taken up residence there.

Jackson released a low growl and lowered Sage to her feet. "Just one moment." He stalked across the hallway toward Augusta. His footsteps were loud and ominous.

A gentleman stepped out of a side room with a smile and a greeting on his lips, but Jackson passed by him without a glance. Jackson didn't stop until he reached Augusta. Then without a word, he ripped the fellow away from his sister and shoved him against the wall. With a roar, he lifted a fist and swung it.

"Stop!" Augusta yelled. But she was too late. Jackson's punch connected with the big man's gut.

The fellow's eyes rounded, and he emitted an *oof.* With mature facial features, a trim beard, and a few strands of silver in his brown hair, he appeared to be a middle-aged man. Attired in a simple blue suit, he had a gentlemanly look, although without the same suave aura that Jackson had.

Jackson's features were gathered with fury, and he raised his fist for another punch. But this time, Augusta grasped his arm. "Don't hit him again, Jackson."

"Hitting is the least I plan to do to him for kidnapping you." Jackson threw another fist into the man's stomach.

"No!" Augusta practically screamed the word, the panic in her voice and on her face finally halting Jackson.

A strange premonition sifted through Sage as she took in Augusta's flushed face, swollen lips ... and the beautiful sapphire ring on her left hand.

Augusta yanked Jackson back. "He's my husband!"

Jackson stared at Augusta for a long moment. Then he dropped his arm. "You're married?" His voice held a note of shock.

Augusta's eyes filled with censure. "Is it so hard to believe that a spinster like me could find love?"

"Yes ... no ... " Jackson rubbed at his knuckles, likely now bruised. "I do not begrudge you the love of a man, Augusta. Not in the least. I wish you much marital happiness. But ... "

"But what?"

"We thought you were kidnapped."

For the first time, Augusta glanced at Sage, her eyes warm and welcoming but without the least amount of surprise that Sage was present.

"This is my husband, Nelson Roundtable." Augusta reached for the big fellow's hand and positioned herself by his side. Although he was watching Jackson warily, he tenderly tucked Augusta's hand into his.

"The cook said he heard you scream," Jackson said, "and saw a man carrying you from the house."

"I didn't mean to scream when we were leaving, but when Nelson swept me off my feet to carry me outside, I was taken by surprise."

"We thought you were in trouble." Jackson's glare was still foreboding.

"I have never been happier in my life." She smiled up at Nelson, and her eyes truly did radiate with a happiness that Sage had never seen there before. Her husband peered at her with just as much happiness.

"How? When?" Sage fumbled over her questions since there were too many, and she didn't even know where to start.

"I met Nelson in India when he was working there for the East India Company." Augusta leaned in and pressed a kiss to his cheek. "But since he was in the process of moving, we couldn't make any plans, not until we knew where he would be sent next. When he wrote that he'd taken a position here in British Columbia in Lytton, that's when I decided to come."

"I had no idea," Sage said. How had she spent months with Augusta and never once had a discussion about Mr. Roundtable and the possibility that Augusta would reunite with him in the colony?

"Why didn't you tell us you were getting married?" Jackson asked, some of the tension gone from his tone. "Why run off like this?"

Augusta had the grace to look chagrined. "I apologize to you both. But I sent a message to Nelson the first day I arrived in Victoria. Yet I did not want to tell anyone about my love interest until I knew for certain he still felt the same."

Sage nodded in understanding. Augusta probably didn't want to face anyone's pity if the relationship with Nelson didn't work out.

"I most assuredly did feel the same." Nelson spoke so tenderly that Sage already liked him.

Augusta exchanged another smile with the man. "I'd been checking the post every day for a letter in return and had even begun to inquire about traveling up here to Lytton by myself."

That accounted for all of Augusta's secretive errands, the many times when she hadn't wanted Sage to accompany her.

"Of course, the moment I received her missive," Nelson said, "I dropped everything and came to Victoria as quickly as I could. I sent Augusta a message the night I arrived."

"The night of the dinner party," Augusta added. "I decided to send you both to Salt Spring Island together so that I could leave without you knowing what I was doing. We left for Hope not long after the two of you departed and were married the same day by Reverend Roberts."

If Augusta was in a hurry to pack and leave, was that why she'd left her room in such a state of disarray?

"You could have told us," Sage offered. "I would have understood."

"Then you would have insisted on coming."

"You're right." Sage had almost stayed home that morning because she hadn't wanted to leave Augusta behind even for the short trip to see Willow.

"And if Nelson had rejected me," Augusta said more quietly, "I didn't want anyone to know."

"I wouldn't have." Nelson patted her hand affectionately.

"That doesn't answer my question, though," Jackson persisted. "Once you learned Nelson still cared about you, why didn't you stay and introduce him to us? Why did you run away with him?"

This time Augusta shrugged sheepishly. "I also knew that the only way to make you face your feelings for Sage was to force you to spend lots of time together."

Jackson arched a brow. "So the clues were nothing more than a matchmaking mechanism?"

Augusta arched a brow back. "Did it work?"

"We were worried about you, Augusta." His voice turned sober.

"I regret any distress I may have caused." She gave both of them an apologetic smile. "But I was hoping you would forgive me once you realized the brilliance of my plan."

Jackson crossed his arms and glared at his sister.

Sage ducked her head to hide a smile.

Before they could say more, the hotel door behind her swung open. Pastor Abe stepped inside, bringing with him a gust of the chilly October night.

He smiled broadly at Sage. "And where is that husband of yours? Once he had you in his arms, I didn't think I'd ever see him let go."

Sage's smile only widened, and she cocked her head in Jackson's direction.

"What?" Augusta's eyes rounded. "Husband?"

Jackson coughed.

"You and Sage are married?" Augusta's voice took on a screech as she pinned Jackson with a look of wonder.

Pastor Abe continued to smile. "I married them this morning. Never have I seen a couple so much in love—except for myself and my wife, of course."

Sage didn't realize she was holding her breath until Augusta screeched again, this time with an enormous smile. She released Nelson and flung herself upon Jackson, hugging him tightly.

In the next instant, Augusta crossed to Sage with outstretched arms. "You're married!"

Sage captured the woman in an embrace, releasing all the worry that had been building. When Augusta took a step back, tears lingered in her eyelashes. "I'm so happy for you both."

"Thank you, Augusta. We wanted your blessing."

Jackson reached for Sage, slipping one arm behind her and tucking her into the crook of his arm. "She's the best thing that ever happened to me."

"Let's hear you say it." Augusta grinned slyly at Jackson.

"Hear what?"

"That you're not the only brilliant one in the family. That I am too."

Jackson scrubbed a hand over his mouth and chin, unsuccessfully trying to hide a smile. "Fine. You're brilliant."

Augusta laughed lightly. "Thank you."

"No, thank *you*." Jackson pressed a kiss to Sage's head. "I couldn't ask for anything or anyone better."

"If I had to search the whole world over for a woman for you, I couldn't have picked a more perfect bride."

"I agree."

Sage leaned into Jackson, the love for him swelling into her chest and bringing tears to her eyes. She wasn't perfect, and neither was he. But they would be perfect together, and that was all that really mattered.

READ ON FOR MORE FROM THE

Bride Ships

NEW VOYAGES

SERIES

Don't miss the next romantic
Bride Ships: New Voyages novel
by Jody Hedlund and Patti Stockdale.

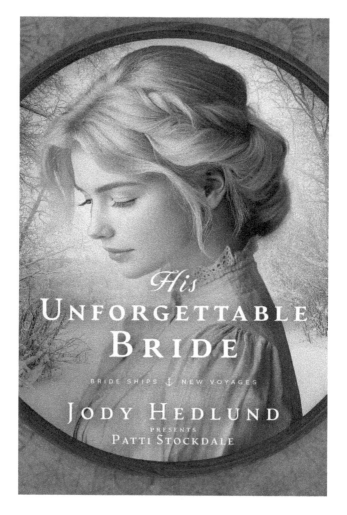

A pickpocket turned lady and a prince
with a forgotten past find love in the
most unexpected place...

Orphan and former pickpocket Juliet Dash yearns to leave her troubled past behind. When she arrives in British Columbia and takes a respectable job working for society sisters, she's closer to her dream. But an unexpected encounter with an unconscious man turns her world upside down, forcing Juliet to choose between her heart and aspirations.

Weary of royal life, Prince Henry Graighton seeks solace and anonymity. When Henry is suddenly thrust into the role of heir apparent, he doesn't even have time to grieve before he's kidnapped...and loses his memories when he finally escapes.

When he's discovered unconscious in the woods of an unknown land, Henry finds hope in Juliet, his savior and the key to his forgotten past. But their romance is threatened by secrets, blackmail, and thefts plaguing Juliet's workplace. With danger lurking and royal duties looming, can their love survive?

One

To be truly polite, remember you must be
polite at all times and under all circumstances.

Victoria, Vancouver Island
Monday, November 1863

J ULIET DASH KNEW HOW TO SPOT A THIEF.
Once upon a time, she'd been one.

Standing in the doorway of her attic bedroom and staring at her roommate, Juliet's heart thumped in a wild clip. "You stole from the Firths?"

The cold November wind rattled the rafters as Ruby O'Reilly crouched to scoop up what sparkled like an emerald ring from the chilly floor. Juliet's roommate stood, hiding the gem inside the folds of her dingy navy cape. "I don't know what you're yammering about."

And yet Juliet had spied the ring with her own two eyes—the ring that Mrs. Firth hadn't been able to find today. "I disagree."

"Says you."

Wasn't that obvious?

A flickering tallow candle cast shadows on the unpainted walls and meager furnishings—a wooden bed, a two-drawer bureau, and a wash basin. She'd grown accustomed to the musty scent and had no quarrel with her living arrangement for the last ten months.

Other than the person who shared the space.

She and Ruby had little in common except for their employment and perhaps a thievery tie. But Juliet hadn't swiped as much as an apple since she was ten.

They certainly looked nothing alike. She was average height and had fair hair, pale skin, and blue eyes. Ruby, small-boned and red-headed, had dark, knowing eyes that appeared older than the mighty ocean on the edge of Victoria. The purplish-green bruising around her left eye had nearly faded.

Juliet undid the cuff buttons on her black chambermaid dress and glared at Ruby, who stared back. The missing emerald wasn't the first disappearing jewel in the house. A pearl-trimmed hatpin and an expensive brooch that had once belonged to the Queen's daughter and awarded to the Firth family had also gone missing over recent weeks.

There had been unannounced inspections of the servants' rooms ever since. Would another happen before bed tonight? "If you took the ring, give it back."

"Don't tell me what to do, Miss High and Mighty. You walk around with your nose tipped toward the sky day after day."

"Huh?" The opposite was true, and for good reason. The only thing Juliet had done with her nose was shove it against the grindstone. Never had she deemed herself better than anyone else because she knew deep in her heart she wasn't.

"If you must know, I dropped a trinket from my beau. That's what you seen on the floor." Ruby tossed her cape's hood over her head and stomped out of the room. A moment later, the servants' back staircase creaked as she descended.

Juliet raised her eyes to the ceiling. The slanted walls peaked like the letter A. Where was Ruby sneaking off to on the brink of bedtime? To meet her man or for another reason? A troubling reason?

What could Juliet do about it? The easiest option was to crawl into bed and pray for a better day tomorrow. This wasn't her business. She didn't need to get involved. She wasn't at fault.

After all, what if she'd been mistaken about what she'd seen Ruby drop? What if it was just a trinket? Yet Juliet's experience and gut told her no. The stone on the bedroom floor had glinted like a priceless emerald, something she'd held and seen firsthand long ago.

The truth was that thievery was wrong. Juliet had learned that lesson the hard way. If Ruby had stolen the jewels from the Firths, especially the priceless heirloom from the Queen, she needed to return them. Now.

Besides, Juliet couldn't sit back and do nothing, not when the Firths had been so kind to her over the past months of working for them. The least she could do was investigate where Ruby had wandered.

Juliet grabbed her black shawl from her drawer, tossed it over her shoulders, and tied her headscarf under her chin. Then she quietly crept down two narrow staircases to reach the bottom level and cracked open the door to a small back entrance hall without making a sound. Good or bad, she had a knack for sneaking around and doubted anyone would see her tonight.

Light shone underneath Mrs. Quinborow's office door down the hallway, and Juliet hesitated. What if the strict housekeeper was about to do one of her surprise searches? There would be countless questions if she found Juliet and Ruby missing.

One more reason to return to the attic and not get involved.

Yet, if she didn't do something now, Ruby might keep stealing. And Juliet would be just as guilty for allowing the crimes to continue.

Straightening her shoulders with resolve, she slipped from the servants' entrance and into the starry night. The moon offered a heavenly glow—perfect for catching a thief. An owl hooted a greeting. Or perhaps a warning.

With no time to lose, she dashed across the loose-stone lane used for deliveries, then hid behind an evergreen tree in case anyone else stepped outside.

If she were Ruby, what would she do next? Hide the ring to get it out of the house, but conceal it where?

Juliet narrowed her eyes to study her surroundings. The sprawling manicured gardens spread out in a maze behind the mansion. She'd seen Ruby disappear into the gardens on other occasions and had assumed the maid met her man there. But what if she'd gone out to hide the jewels instead?

Juliet crept along the pathway. At times, she had to feel her way forward in the darkness of the tall shrubs. Ahead in the moonlight, she glimpsed the fancy wrought iron fence separating the Firths' property from the neighbors'—the Lennox family—which meant she neared the back gate.

She halted at the clink of metal against rock and strained to listen. Was someone digging?

Was Ruby hiding the jewels? What if Juliet caught her in the act? Then she couldn't deny the stealing any longer, and Juliet would have the upper hand. Maybe she'd threaten to report her to the police if Ruby refused to return the jewels to the Firths.

She stepped out into the open without giving herself a chance to second-guess her plan.

Ruby was kneeling, gripping a garden trowel, and stabbing the earth.

"What are you doing?" Juliet asked, even though it was apparent.

Ruby gasped and raised her head, her face hidden in the folds of her hood. "Why did you follow me?"

"To see if you would bury the goods. Looks like you are."

"It's not your business."

Well, that wasn't true. "If you put Mrs. Firth's jewelry back where it belongs tonight and promise not to steal again, this ends here and now. No one needs to know anything more."

Ruby leaned back on her haunches. "You can't prove nothing. Where's your evidence?"

In her roommate's pocket, or maybe already in the ground?

After shooting Juliet a glare, Ruby continued to spear the earth with the garden tool. "Go ahead and tell them what I'm doing. I'll be long gone before you get back."

Juliet had seldom snitched in all her nineteen years, but if Ruby refused to cooperate, what choice did she have? None, other than to tell Mrs. Quinborow before Ruby got away.

What if someone linked her to the thievery? Shivers streaked over her skin at the mere thought.

Juliet turned and began returning to the house, winding through the shrubs, past raised beds and elegant fountains. It was impossible to know how the next few minutes would unfold. But one thing was certain. She had no intention of losing her position because of an upstart named Ruby O'Reilly. Or anyone else. No, ma'am.

Besides, she couldn't allow Ruby to hurt the Firths any longer.

Juliet loved the stability of working for the family and the routine of domestic service—the schedule of rising at dawn and cleaning the same rooms day after day. She ate every meal in the same chair and table in the servants' common room. After supper, she often completed mending or polishing and chatted with some of the other staff.

The rhythm had grown familiar and close to perfect, and Juliet wanted life to stay the same. Every day, she silently thanked Mrs. Morseby from the Immigration Committee for finding her this position when the bride ship arrived at Vancouver Island last January. Such an opportunity wouldn't have been available to a nobody orphan like her back in Manchester. Now she lived in a house with lacy white curtains, embossed velvet wallpaper, and lush carpets.

"No!" Ruby's distressed cry in the distance broke through the night. Had Ruby changed her mind? Was she telling Juliet to stop?

Juliet slowed her pace and waited once she reached the servants' entrance.

Ruby caught up with her a moment later, panting and carrying a small cigar box. "Tell the truth, did you follow me out to the back fence once before?"

"No, why would I have done that?" And why was Ruby back at the house? Hadn't she been planning to run away with the jewels?

The contents rattled as Ruby reached for the door latch. "You did so tonight, so it's not much of a stretch."

"Well, I didn't."

Ruby huffed and stepped inside, with Juliet trailing behind her. Instead of moving toward the staircase, Ruby veered down the hallway toward the housekeeper's office. Was she seeking out Mrs. Quinborow? If so, why?

They passed by the kitchen, and the dark, empty room cast shadows. Beyond the kitchen, they reached Mrs. Quinborow's door, which was tightly shut, with the light still glowing from the gap underneath.

Ruby lowered her hood and knocked.

"Enter," Mrs. Quinborow called. The woman disliked drama, particularly with her staff, but tonight she'd receive a handful, whether she wanted it or not.

Ruby opened the squeaky door, and they both stepped inside the cramped little room and were greeted by the scent of honey. Only a framed needlepoint of the Lord's Prayer adorned the walls, and a small table held a silver tea service and the honey pot. Two empty, straight-backed chairs rounded out the furniture.

Even on a good day, the housekeeper's lined face appeared strained. Now it had scrunched like a leftover winter apple. She'd piled her gray hair in a tight bun atop her head, and not a single wisp had escaped.

"Whyever are you two out of your room?" She rose behind her wooden desk, wearing her everyday blue uniform with white cuffs and collar. A thick collection of keys dangled from her generous waist.

Ruby lifted her chin. "I have something to say." A wall hook held a lit lantern, the flame matching Ruby's locks—a blend of red, yellow, and orange. Even though her roommate looked like an innocent angel, she wasn't.

"I need to tell you something too," Juliet said. "Something important."

The housekeeper crossed her arms. "Can't this wait until morning?"

"No, ma'am," Juliet said simultaneously with Ruby.

"Then proceed, and don't dawdle."

Ruby glanced at Juliet before releasing a rapid-fire spew of words. "She dropped a fancy ring on the floor in our room. I wager it's the missing jewel that belongs to the mistress."

Juliet's breath caught in her chest. "That's a dad-blamed lie."

Mrs. Quinborow's brow wrinkled. "What's this?"

"What Ruby described is what she did, ma'am. Afterward, she went outside. I followed and found her digging in the yard, but I didn't stay to learn if she was collecting something or hiding the ring."

"Juliet unburied a box, then I grabbed it to show you." Ruby opened the front of her cape and withdrew the cigar box, which she set on the desk next to a stack of papers. Then she raised the lid to display a handful of stones. "Don't know the reason for the rocks, but thinking Juliet planned to hide the ring inside here."

She tapped the container. "She probably snatched the mistress's other jewels too."

Juliet thumped a hand on her waist as anger shot through her. "Another lie. I followed you outside, and . . . you retrieved the box, not me. When I said I was leaving to tell Mrs. Quinborow, you charged after me, cooking up this . . . twisted version of what happened."

Ruby burst into tears.

What? Not only was Ruby a good thief but also a top-notch actress.

The housekeeper withdrew a neatly folded white handkerchief from her desk drawer and passed the cloth to the weeping woman. "Do either of you have physical proof that the other stole the jewels?"

"Ruby has the ring on her person, I believe."

Mrs. Quinborow's expression grew more severe—if that were possible. "Remove your cape and empty your pockets, Miss O'Reilly. You do the same, Miss Dash."

Juliet followed the instructions, and Ruby also heeded the order. Mrs. Quinborow thoroughly examined them from head to foot and found nothing suspicious.

Where had Ruby stashed the ring?

Juliet's mind raced, trying to piece together a solution to her predicament. All she'd hoped to do was the right thing and protect the Firths. But nothing was going according to her plans.

"I've been employed here for ten months and have a clean record." What else could she say to convince the housekeeper she'd done nothing wrong? "The stealing didn't start until after Ruby arrived months back."

"Maybe you was waiting to get comfortable." Ruby sniffled. "Then you figured you could pin the blame on me since I'm newer."

When Mrs. Quinborow pursed her thin lips, they nearly disappeared. "If clear-cut evidence existed, I'd immediately send for the constable. Instead, I only have a box of rocks and two differing tales."

The housekeeper sighed deeply as if she'd stored the breath in her chest all day. "These insinuations now cast doubts on your characters. Therefore, pack your things, both of you. You're fired, and I shall not give you letters of recommendation."

Juliet huffed out a breath of exasperation. How was this happening? "But I'm innocent."

"I can't take the chance." Mrs. Quinborow stepped around her and Ruby before opening the door. "I'll escort you upstairs to gather your personal things. Naturally, I'll report this incident to Mrs. Firth in the morning."

The world was tipping out of control, and Juliet placed her hand against the wall to steady herself. Where would she go? Her two friends from the bride ship, Willow and Daisy, had married and lived a boat ride away. Willow's sister Sage lived next door but had left town with her employers, the Lennox family. And Juliet didn't know why.

Would Mrs. Moresby help her find a new job despite the accusation? All the other women who had arrived on the bride ship from Manchester had either wed or resided with their employers. Nobody lived at the marine barracks, their first home on the island, anymore.

The housekeeper left the room as her charges filed behind her, silently parading to the attic. In the bedroom, Juliet quickly crossed to the dresser, opened one drawer, and retrieved her empty flour sack before stuffing her belongings inside—tattered shoes, scant clothing, Grandfather's precious journal, and other small items. The uniform on her back belonged to her, the cost removed from her wages.

Ruby packed as well, grumbling as she did.

Afterward, they retraced their steps to the back service door before the housekeeper dismissed the women outside. The wind cried in the trees, and Juliet swallowed her tears of frustration. The stars shone dimmer than before. Or did she only imagine the lack of luster?

Ruby slung her bag over her shoulder and glared at Juliet.

Emotions whirled inside her, with anger and desperation near the top of the heap. "This isn't my fault. You stole the jewelry."

Ruby's shoulders sank. "You can't imagine how much trouble I'll be in for this."

"Losing your job?"

"Losing everything."

"Trouble with who?"

When Ruby failed to reply, Juliet turned and strode down the service lane, her feet as heavy as her heart. She had better things to do than worry about Ruby, starting with where she might lay her head tonight. The wind gusted, and she tightened her shawl over her shoulders. Several paces later, she rounded the brick house and a rosebush hedge, moving toward the main road and cutting through the grass.

Losing her job wasn't fair. But dwelling on what was just and what wasn't had never done her a speck of good.

Ruby caught up with her in a few steps, and they walked side by side in the house's shadows. "My man, that's who. He wanted the Queen's brooch."

The rare heirloom was probably worth thousands of pounds, if not more. Losing it was undoubtedly a giant failure.

Would Ruby pay the price? Another black eye? Or worse?

Juliet's chest tightened. As mad as she was at her former roommate, Ruby didn't deserve someone hurting her or pressuring her to commit crimes.

"You still shouldn't have stolen it or any of the jewelry, Ruby." Undoubtedly, she sounded self-righteous, but maybe she had earned the right tonight.

"And you shouldn't have interfered."

"I didn't."

"Then how did the rocks get in the box?" Ruby's voice turned threatening.

Juliet sidled sideways a pace, her heart clamoring. "I have no idea."

"I think you know more than you're letting on." Ruby started to lunge at Juliet's neck, her empty hand like a claw. "Maybe you've stowed the brooch somewhere and plan to keep it yourself."

Juliet blocked Ruby's arm and quickly unsheathed the small knife tied to her calf. She'd carried it with her since her orphan days of living on Manchester's streets. "You keep to yourself." She pointed the knife at Ruby and let menace fill her voice. "And I'll do the same."

Ruby backed up several steps. "Tell anybody about what happened tonight, and you'll regret it."

A bluff? Probably not.

She watched as Ruby disappeared into the night's shadows. With the weapon still in her fist, Juliet moved west toward downtown. A woman never knew what to expect on the streets alone at night, but Juliet was accustomed to caring for herself. She'd had lots of practice.

It was too late to bother Mrs. Moresby. She'd have to wait until morning to explain tonight's disaster and ask for help finding a new position.

Fortunately, Mrs. Moresby was a good woman, and Juliet could use one of those now. She hadn't known many in her lifetime. There was Willow, Daisy, and Sage. And Molly, her friend from the orphanage.

She shifted her gaze toward the starry night sky and pictured God somewhat like her grandfather who'd raised her for a while— trustworthy, wise, kind, and loving. But after his death, God had disappeared too. Still, she paused and squeezed her eyes shut.

"Dear God . . . " A minute passed, then two. "I'm still sorry for all the mistakes I've made."

Quick as a pickpocket, a heaviness pressed against her chest, almost stealing her breath. "What will become of me?" she whispered to the night.

Although Juliet no longer believed in fairy tales, she wished she did.

Instead, a hard reality stared back at her. She was homeless again.

No one writes Western historical romance like Lacy Williams! Journey to Wyoming and discover five mail-order brides and the men who love them in our Wind River Mail-Order Brides series.

AVAILABLE NOW!

NOTE TO READER

Thank you for joining me for another trip to the Pacific Northwest! Although this journey wasn't quite the same as for the other women who voyaged to Victoria on one of the bride ships, I hope you still enjoyed getting to set sail with Sage Rhodes and her adventure to find true love.

When I first crafted Willow Rhodes's story in Finally His Bride (if you haven't read it yet, what are you waiting for?!), I just knew that I needed to pen Sage's story too. I could tell she would experience heartache and loss so that by the time she reached Victoria, she would be ready for a new and fresh start at life and love. Obviously, it took a little convincing (and scheming on Augusta's part) for Sage to finally open herself back up to having a relationship again. But in the end, Beauty and the Beast are truly perfect for each other, wouldn't you agree?

You might be wondering what ever happened to those stolen jewels that Sage discovered in the Firths' backyard. Well, never fear, you will get to find out what happens to both the jewels and to Juliet in the next book in the Bride Ships: New Voyages series. In His Unforgettable Bride, Juliet gets to have her chance at finding love in a very Cinderella-like story. Make sure you look for the book soon!

Thank you for reading my stories. As always, your love and support mean the world to me!

Until next time... Jody

CONNECT WITH SUNRISE

Thank you again for reading *His Perfect Bride*. We hope you enjoyed the story. If you did, would you be willing to do us a favor and leave a review? It doesn't have to be long—just a few words to help other readers know what they're getting. (But no spoilers! We don't want to wreck the fun!) Thank you again for reading!

We'd love to hear from you—not only about this story, but about any characters or stories you'd like to read in the future. Contact us at www.sunrisepublishing.com/contact.

We also have a monthly update that contains sneak peeks, reviews, upcoming releases, and fun stuff for our reader friends. Sign up at www.sunrisepublishing.com or scan our QR code.

About the Author

Jody Hedlund is the best-selling author of over fifty sweet historical romances and is the winner of numerous awards. She lives in central Michigan with her husband and is the mother of five wonderful children and five spoiled cats. When she's not penning another of her page-turning stories, she loves to spend her time reading, especially when it also involves consuming coffee and chocolate.